YOU

ARE

FREE

TO

GO

YOU ARE FREE TO GO

A NOVEL

SARAH YAW

Engine Books
Indianapolis

Engine Books
PO Box 44167
Indianapolis, IN 46244
enginebooks.org

Also available in Hardcover and eBook formats from Engine Books.

Printed in the United States of America

ISBN: 978-1-938126-21-5

Library of Congress Control Number: 2014935319

For Doug

Why do you stay in prison when the door is so wide open?
—Jalal al-Din Rumi

*Easy is the descent to the Lower World; but to retrace your steps and to
escape to the upper air—this is the task, this is the toil.*
—The Sibyl to Aeneas, *The Aeneid*

PART I

You, friend, will miss the most of me.

MOSES

MOSES DOESN'T HAVE THE opportunity to count blessings very often, so when he walks into the mail room, the seasoned wood of the counters and the boxes used for sorting that have been here since the prison's beginning a century and a half ago, the old, oiled smell of the room, and the light tickle of her citrusy perfume move him. She stands on the other side of the low wall. She wears her uniform. Institutional slacks, a conservative white shirt tucked in, comfortable rubber shoes that let her stand for hours. A fuzzy lavender fleece cardigan keeps her warm. Her hair, shoulder-length, blond, soft and curled, is lightened by whispers of white. She lights him up the way a mother does her child. Lila is an island Moses claimed for himself when he was lucky enough to get transferred from laundry fourteen years ago.

"I'm glad you're here, Moses," she says, "We're all backed up."

She smiles. He grins. She pulls a brown paper package off the sorting table where she works, opening letters, removing contraband. "Surprise for you," she says.

It's no surprise. Moses has been waiting weeks. She brings him the box and, breaking protocol, hands him the letter opener only she uses. Like a kid who won't rip the wrapping, he slices along the edges of the box and makes clean cuts. When he's done he hands the opener back to her, and before he opens the box, she walks back to her sorting table and locks the letter opener in a drawer.

Moses waits for her to get back to his side before he flips up the top and looks in. He removes the bubble wrap and takes out his new glasses. They are in a brown faux leather slipcase. Attached to them is an envelope. It says, *Please Read Carefully*. He places the envelope on the table next to the box.

He's not up on fashion since he's been inside for thirty years, but he's sure these glasses are ugly. Medium brown, solid plastic. The lenses are trapezoids with rounded edges; the nosepiece has an opening that shows the space between the eyebrows.

"Let's see them on," she says.

He's embarrassed. Moses has always taken care of himself. Keeps fit and has always known he has a good look. His dark hair is slicked off his face. He could always get a girl with a sideways glance—he has that kind of eyes. He keeps his fresh mouth open in an irreverent smirk, which makes him look young and up to no good, and it used to drive the girls crazy. On the inside he maintains himself. Spends his eighteen cents an hour on the right things: Soap. Toothpaste. Shampoo. Hair gel. Cigarettes, his only luxury. Unlike some of these lowlifes who trade their commissary credits for drugs and think it's OK to smell like they're rotting from the gut out. Like Collin, Georgy, and Don. They hang around in the gallery of B block all day watching television, getting stoned. Georgy, that cross-eyed, pimple-faced illiterate, spends his whole day with a Hardenberg phone book trying to get people to read him numbers so he can call girls collect and hope someday someone will care he's in here and pay him a visit. Moses doesn't do that anymore. He used to, but he's reformed. Accepts his punishment, tries not to cheat God.

"Put 'em on," she says. "Here, I'll get you a mirror so you can see how you look." She crosses the room to the locked door that leads to a small office where she keeps her essentials. Moses can't be alone in the mailroom. He knows this. She looks back at him. He nods and she unlocks the door and disappears.

Moses puts the glasses on and opens the envelope. Inside is a piece of official stationery from the optometrist, Dr. Thomas J. Rothschild, and the state Department of Corrections. It reads:

The Rules and Responsibilities of Glasses Ownership

Congratulations. Your good behavior has earned you the right to own a pair of Rothschild glasses. Glasses are a privilege granted only to those who earn it. They can be taken away at any moment. Please note the following:

Glasses may not be used as a weapon in any way.

Glasses must remain in one piece. If there is a missing piece, they will be confiscated immediately and a full search and seizure of all inmate belongings will be conducted until the missing piece is recovered and accounted for. If the missing piece is not recovered, it will be assumed that it has been stashed as a weapon, and the prisoner will be punished according to section 11.214 of the Prisoner Code of Conduct, thus resulting in loss of the right to own future eyeglasses, and /or keeplock or isolation.

All repairs must be made by Dr. Thomas J. Rothschild as surrogate of the State of New York Department of Corrections and will be made at the expense of the owner. Commissary credits can be used to cover the cost of repairs and/or replacement.

Sincerely,

Dr. Thomas J. Rothschild, O.D.

LILA RETURNS WITH A fancy compact in her palm. "Oh, they look very nice," she says. "How do they feel?"

Moses looks around the room and adjusts them on his face. "They're ugly, aren't they? I don't think I need them." He's lying. Everything looks clearer. He can see the cobwebs on the ceiling, the dirt on the floor. (Corn, the porter who cleans in the mailroom, could use a pair, but his popcorn habit keeps him flat broke.) Moses looks back at Lila. He can see the fine lines around her eyes, the parentheses around her smile. She looks pleased for him, so he's not going to let on that this is humiliating. He feels old.

"Take a look." She holds up the compact for him.

The compact is white and gold and has an embossed emblem on the outside like a royal seal that reminds him of the ones he stole as a child in Buffalo. He used to sneak into the elegant homes on Elmwood Avenue, find the lady of the house's dressing table, and steal the vanity sets, the brushes, the long-handled mirrors, the compacts filled with silky powders and puffs. These were his mother's favorites, the ultimate symbol of wealth and luxury. He'd kneel next to wherever she laid—her bed, the rough and lumpy couch—and give them to her the way a subject presents an offering to a queen. But first, he'd clean the hair from the brushes and roll it between his fingers into a silky ball, hold it to his nose and smell, rub it along his cheek, then add it to his collection. He kept boxes of women's hair, sorted by color, under his bed. In his cell, he has a Styrofoam cooler of Lila's hair under his cot. He keeps a small ball of it in his pocket and fingers it when he needs to calm himself. There's one in his pocket now.

He tries to find himself in the compact she is holding up for him and all he can see is a gigantic nostril.

"Other side," he says.

"Oh, right," she says, and flips it so he can see his whole face.

He wants to hold the compact. Wants to feel something luxurious, the weight of it like gold, heavy in his palm. He hasn't touched money or anything that feels like wealth in years. He takes it from her, and his hand covers hers. Moses sees a blush rise to her cheek, and it thrills him. He loves that he can still do this to a woman. He loves that he can do this to Lila.

"It was my grandmother's," she says, looking off to the side.

"My mother had one of these," he says.

Moses expects to see how good he looks. The glasses are horrible. But that's not the worst of it. The hair at his temples is almost completely white. His teeth are yellow; his skin is gray and old, the color of clouds. Deep cutting lines map out years on his face. What the fuck, he thinks. He doesn't say this aloud. He'd never swear in front of a lady.

He snaps the compact shut and hands it to her. "I like what I've read so far," he says, turning away. "I think that Aschenbach has a good perspective on the world." Aschenbach is the main character, or the protagonist, as Lila instructed him, of Thomas Mann's story, "Death in Venice." He's reading it because she's reading it for her college World Literature class. He's always trying to impress Lila, so Moses doesn't tell her that Mann should think about writing a story that doesn't require a dictionary because Moses can't use one—until now the small print was torture—so he keeps getting caught up on unfamiliar vocabulary and hasn't gotten very far in the story. Nevertheless, he likes what he knows about Aschenbach so far. Like Aschenbach, Moses has come to believe in the redemptive power of work. His job in the mailroom has given him significant position in the prison among the guards (except Miller, of course) of which he is very proud, and this, combined with the pleasant routine of his friendship with Jorge, and the settling in of time, has given Moses some contentment and unlikely faith that he's already paid his dues for what he did, and he's come to believe that from here on out it's just the simple decomposition of the body and then all this crap will be over with and he'll be free of this life and on to the next and the next will be a whole lot better.

In the meantime, having important work in the world and the ability to bring a blush to the cheek of a good, chaste woman like Lila (a rarity) and having a good friend like Jorge who is well-liked and has Moses' back when the B block lowlifes act up, these are the good things. He's been inside since he was a young man and life on the outside wasn't ever so good, so life now is the best it's ever been. He's learned to feign weakness around the young, violent gangbangers to prove his irrelevance. He farts whenever he's around them so they think he's old and weak and they tell him *go die* and call him *motherfucker*. His pride doesn't suffer from this. Moses is a survivor. And he, like Aschenbach, believes that the position he's earned through his hard work proves he's above the lowlifes.

He tells Lila he feels connected to Aschenbach in this very way. Then she says, "I find it strange, frankly, that you think Aschenbach is the sort of character you'd want to identify with, given your feelings about homosexuals and pedophiles."

Humiliation aches in his teeth, and anger tightens his tendons. Why did he speak before he knew the story? Lila has promised to ask her professor if he would read and grade a critical literary paper on "Death in Venice" if Moses were to write one. She knows his greatest desire is to go to college. The paper was her idea. She probably regrets it now.

He puts his hand in his pocket and fingers her hair. He's not angry at Lila. Lila is pure as snow with that flossy, bouncy hair and that smooth, motherly skin and her practical pants and her practical rubber shoes that protect her feet from all the standing. Lila is the perfect, pure woman. He's angry with Jorge for waking in fits of fury and laughter last night while Moses tried to read. He's angry at Miller for forcing them all to go to chow early this morning, cutting into his reading time, for holding him in the gallery for an extra long time before he was cleared to report to work. He's angry with himself. For getting old. For not being able to see.

He stays quiet for a while and focuses on the job at hand, sorting the letters by block and by cell, pulling all the letters for inmates who can't receive mail for one reason or another.

Lila returns to her post on the other side of the low wall that divides the mailroom and is silent, too. (Moses must always stay on his side of the wall. Always.) Lila focuses on opening the mail and removing contraband: joints sent by lovers, baggies of heroin sent by brazen friends, razor blades sent by sworn enemies. She dumps them into a bin where all the contraband goes, then she reads the letters with a big black pen in her hand, blocking out anything she deems dangerous or incendiary.

Moses has seen some wild things working in the mailroom. Letters sent by women to that Berkowitz son of a bitch years after his incarceration, panties sent to the preppie Central Park strangler. Who were the women who asked for it like that? Who sent underwear and overtures to these disgusting men? He distracts himself thinking of this. Thinking how low all the people around him are. When his sorting is over, before he loads up his satchel, before he straps it over his shoulder for his daily delivery, Moses admits, "I haven't gotten very far in the story. I promise to finish it over the weekend."

"I look forward to talking to you about it Monday then, Moses. I'll see you when you return," she says.

THE PRISON IS A walled city. It runs east-west and was built along a river by the very prisoners it was to house. The river, which Moses has only seen twice, is the reason for the location of the prison. It provided power for Industry, which was at the heart of the philosophy that built this place: inmates would find redemption through labor. The goods manufactured here would offset the costs of the prisoners' incarceration.

During a period of budget crisis a decade and a half ago, the state attempted to defray the costs of a growing prison population by hiring fewer corrections officers. There was a decision at the highest levels to evaluate the responsibilities of the prison guards and identify tasks that could be assumed by prison labor. By law, prisoners are allowed to send and receive mail. Each of the five stacked rows in each of the four cell blocks that run the length of the complex houses an official U.S. mailbox. It was the daily job of the COs to empty this box, deliver the mail to the outgoing bins in the mailroom, and then retrieve the mail for their row and deliver it to each of the inmates. Over the years, there had been complaints from the officers. More than a few COs felt like servants and were gladly willing to offer up these tasks to a trustworthy inmate. The state agreed, and an inmate in each facility was identified to work in the mailroom and deliver the mail to those who could not retrieve their own for reasons of illness, age, or punishment. The matter of emptying the US mailboxes was reserved for the COs; it was considered distasteful by all to give an inmate a key to anything, let alone the property of the United States government. So a job was created, and Moses chosen by the Warden himself.

His rounds, therefore, are the proudest part of his day. And he is endowed, as he leaves the administration building at the most easterly end and ventures from the clean and respectable offices out into the shaded alley between the hospital and administration and then out into the sun that shines on the yard—a large concrete court flanked by five-story blocks, built block on block of stone, and striped like old-school uniforms with lines of barred windows—with a sense of importance that grows each day. As he carries his bag he feels the weight of his office, a position that dwells in the in-between, and his confidence grows. He is, according to the historical intentions of the place, a success. He walks along the cavernous walls of block housing that stack men on men with the stride of a man who has earned a place, his glasses hidden in his breast pocket.

Moses decides on a few things to talk about when he sees Lila after his rounds so her lasting impression of him for the weekend won't be that he has subconscious sexual desires for little boys. He plans to ask about her garden, about the bulbs she planted last fall, to ask what the trees in the park by her house look like. Have they begun to bud out? Are there flowers? Are there leaves? There are no trees in the prison yard like there used to be, so Moses doesn't know spring anymore, except its upbeat warmth in the breezes; he doesn't know fall except its tugging chill that pulls at his bones. If it wasn't for Lila and the decorations she puts out with each upcoming holiday like a kindergarten teacher, Christmas-less years would pass unnoticed. At Easter, there are pastel egg cut-outs on the walls, for Halloween, a witch, at Christmas a crèche made from pictures cut out of magazines by the porters who clean the mailroom: The three wise men, Fidel Castro, Omar Sharif, and Yasser Arafat; Mother Mary, Benazir Bhutto; the baby Jesus, Brad Pitt.

Moses passes a line of porters and he nods at them. "Moses," they say, acknowledging him respectfully because of his job. He enters A block at the center of the yard. He climbs the steps and opens the door with purpose, walks through standing tall so his number can be seen on the breast of his green shirt, and the guards open doors for him. As he makes his way through the gates into the lower gallery of A block and starts down row one giving out letters to keeplocks, he acts like he's as free as a CO. When he is finished with his row, he strides haughtily along the cells so as to inspire a little envy in those not allowed to move about as he is, and makes his way to the stairs at the front entrance of the gallery. A CO unlocks the gate for him and he ascends into the birdcage. Rows two through five have long pathways that run along the cells, and there is a cage of bars that runs from the second story floor to the ceiling to keep men from falling to their deaths. Moses doesn't like the upper rows. He doesn't live on one. He lives on the ground floor because of his age and because of his good behavior. Nowhere else in the prison does Moses feel more confined than in the birdcage, so he keeps to the outside of the pathway to distance himself from the men in their cells and he stays out of trouble. Until he doesn't. One of the letters he's palming slips out of his hand and glides gently to the floor. Just the corner of it slides under the cell bars. Moses glances at the cell's inhabitant. There's one quiet, angry-looking Latino lying on his cot reading a porno with Spanish all over the front of it. And that burns Moses' ass, all the Spanish in America. He bends down to grab the letter and says, "Learn some English, *muchacho*." Before he knows it, the guy's at the bars, and as Moses stands, a fist meets him in the temple. The punch sends him across the pathway. The bars keep him from going over the edge to the gallery floor below. He sees stars. The guy yells something at him in Spanish and jumps around like an ape. Moses, just for fun, turns his back to him and farts audibly, flips him the bird and takes off down the path, his satchel hitting his hip in time with his heavy breath.

The block is mostly empty. It's three p.m., rec time for A block, a quiet time. But all the keeplocks are at the bars reaching out trying to get Moses as he flies past feeling giddy despite the stars he's seeing and the ringing that's settled into his ears from the blow.

He looks up and sees the officer in charge look out from his office, blurry-eyed and bored. The officer yells down for number forty-three to settle down, and Moses knows that the keeplock just got another two weeks in his cell without rec time or meals with the general population and that makes Moses' day. He thinks people like that need to be shown their place. He thinks it's his job to do it.

THE MAILROOM IS EMPTY. He looks around for her. Goes to the low wall and looks to the left into the intake room, as if she's hiding in there. "Hello?" he calls, but she doesn't answer. He looks at her station, packed up and tidy. Her grandmother's compact is pushed off in a corner, set neatly on a stack of sticky notes. It is strange that she is not here. He quietly opens the door in the low wall and walks to her station. He's never been there before. He's never broken the rules. He picks up the compact. Turns it over in his hand like a nugget. He smells it. It's sweet from the fake smells that cover up the real meaty smell of a woman. He pulls on the drawer where she keeps her letter opener, but it's locked.

He hears the lock on the door to her office and he quickly moves across the room and slips through the low door. He hovers over his sorting table, pretending to look for something. She walks in from the other room and looks a little caught off guard, though he always comes back at the end of his rounds. She smells like sweet smelling soap and there's a red mark on her face where she was messing with a pimple. He imagines her hands damp and cold from running under the faucet after sitting on the toilet, wiping herself.

There's something different about today. It's quiet. Lila is alone; there are no visitors here to gossip.

"I'm done for the day," he says and puts his satchel away under his sorting table.

"OK," she says in a quiet voice, as if she's just discovered that they were alone for the first time without the company of tasks. "Where are your glasses?" she asks and Moses feels silly that he didn't want to wear them on his rounds. He puts his hand on his breast pocket to put them on, but they're gone.

"They fell out," he says innocently, but inside he boils, imagining the keeplock who nailed him stomping and crushing his spectacles with glee.

"Where did you lose them? A block? I'll call down there," she says. She turns to use the phone. Moses likes watching her do this. Loves the concern he hears in her voice when she says, "Hi, Jack. Moses thinks he lost his glasses. Would you take a look and let me know if they're there? He spent a year saving up for them and they've just arrived." She turns to Moses who's been staring at her back. "He's going to look. Did you hear them fall? Wait…" She holds a finger up. "You do. Thank you." Then she listens to the CO on the other end of the line, thanks him again and hangs up.

"He said you were hurt today."

Moses sticks his hand in his pocket and touches her hair. "Just some angry keeplock. It was nothing."

"Is that where he got you?" she asks. "There's a mark."

Moses puts his hand on his face and suddenly feels for himself, though he gets leveled running into someone or something just about every week. Seeing Lila's reaction to the truth of this place makes him pity himself. He hangs his head. This is better than asking about her garden.

She comes over to take a closer look and stands nearer to him than she normally does. She inspects the mark on his face and puts her cool fingers to it. He can smell the sweet smell of her hand soap. He can see the red blotch on her face where she was squeezing the pimple. He thinks he can detect the raw smell of her blood. He wants to touch her. "Do you want me to call the infirmary?" she asks.

"No." Moses pulls away.

There are factors that determine whether or not he gets to go to work, like fights and assaults on the guards, and decisions among the guards to keep everyone on their toes by disrupting mail delivery for a few days so the men are reminded that they are no longer citizens, not in here. On these days, Moses isn't called to work. A trip to the infirmary is a sure way to blow this out of proportion. Sometimes the biggest assaults go ignored and the smallest, like this, can cause disastrous interruptions. The decisions of the guards are random; it's best to keep a low profile.

"If you say so. It's going to get blue."

"Did he say he has the glasses?"

"Yes. He has them in the OIC office. You can go get them when you're done here. Jenkin is the officer in charge. But I forgot the good news! Wilthauser will read your paper. The catch is you must have it ready for me to bring to him next Wednesday; it's the last day of class. He's going to read it when he grades the rest of the papers, and he'll grade it based on the same criteria he uses for the rest of us. No special treatment."

Moses claps his hands together. "Hot dog!" he says. "That's good news. Hot dog!"

"I knew you'd be happy. Go get your glasses and get to work. Remember, you can't just summarize. You have to prove why or how something happens in the story through analysis of literary devices or character development, so remember this while you're reading. I'm doing a Freudian reading of the work," she says proudly. "I'm glad for you, Moses. You're a smart man. You deserve to feel like one."

Lila turns away and Moses sees a beautiful ringlet, a single strand of sun, clinging to the back of her fleece. He reaches forward and hooks his finger through it. As she walks, it unravels itself from the fleece and wraps itself tightly around his finger.

"**What the hell do** you think you're doing?" Jenkin asks when Moses forgets who he is and barges into the office. Jenkin is sitting with his feet up on the desk, looking at the porno keeplock forty-three was reading before he clocked Moses. At first Moses thinks it was confiscated, but then he sees his glasses on the table dangerously close to the CO's feet. "These yours?" Jenkin asks.

He knows they're his.

The CO uncrosses his feet and uses one to gently slip the glasses to the floor. They land lens down under the tilted-up leg of Jenkin's chair. "Go ahead. Get 'em," Jenkin says, pretending not to pay attention to Moses. Pretending to look at the porno. Moses bends down on one knee and reaches for them. "*Mucha caliente puta, cuarenta y tres!*" Jenkin yells to the keeplock. The keeplock yells something back fast and cackles. Moses reaches his hand to the glasses, but Jenkin lets the chair drop and Moses pulls his hand out of the way. Jenkin stops just shy of the glasses and leans back again, casually. Moses wants to take the leg of that chair and flip Jenkin over. But he doesn't. He can do this. He can suffer the humiliation of this ignorant bastard for the thrill of proving himself to Lila, to a professor. He's imagined the praise the professor will shower on his work. He's imagined the lecture he'll give to his students about the best paper in the class being written not by them, despite all their advantages, but by an unexpected talent discovered by Lila Hathaway. He thinks of this as he reaches for the glasses and Jenkin lets the leg drop. Moses gets his hand over the glasses in time and the leg grinds into the top of it. Jenkin bends over, "Don't cause any trouble around here again," and lets the chair up.

Moses takes the glasses and puts them on. They are bent and loose. His knee is stiff from kneeling and he has to put his good hand on the floor to steady himself because the other hand feels like it might be dead.

"Get the hell out of here," Jenkin says, opening the magazine. Moses makes his way to the stairs outside of the OIC office where he waits for Jenkin to come and unlock the gate for him. Jenkin stays where he is. He sexy whistles real loud; forty-three yells something in Spanish and all the keeplocks come to the bars. The one closest to Moses spits on Moses over and over again. A loogie lands on his prominent left cheekbone.

FROM ADMINISTRATION THERE ARE exactly seven locked doors Moses must approach and await a guard to let him through. If there are other guards, employees or civilians passing through, he must stop exactly where he is, step aside, back against the wall, eyes averted, and wait until the passageway is cleared. Once cleared, the guard can let him pass and lock the door behind him. Upon entering B block there are several doors in a row. He must wait for the first to be unlocked, then step through, wait for the guard to lock the door behind him, step aside while he unlocks the next door, step through only a few feet, and, once again, await the guard as he locks the door behind him. It is a laborious commute replete with a lot of waiting around, and when he's had a long day, like today, he feels the burden of his incarceration.

To finally enter the open gallery of the ground floor of B block is like pulling off a stop-and-go highway into neighborhoods of suburban residential quiet. But instead of green everywhere, it is a concrete landscape. The calm is not typical. He lives in special quarters where the inmates are mostly older, mostly quiet, mostly peaceful. This is where they bring tours of college criminal justice students, local dignitaries, state DOC officials, and others the prison administration wants to impress. The only thugs are Collin, Georgy, and Don, but they are here because it is a privilege to live here and they are afforded ill-begotten amenities all the time. Moses ignores the loud television and the men milling around. He is exhausted from delivering letters, sore on the temple from forty-three, covered in spit and desperately in need of a piss. But before he reaches his cell, he hears the distinctly lazy voice of Sergeant Ed Cavanaugh coming from within.

"I'm quite sure Gina is still alive and nothing has happened to her, Jorge. She's living in New York City and working for the *Evening News* with Arthur Fairchild. Jorge, you know this. You watch the show in the evenings just like Sid and me. We watch him almost every evening and we always look for Gina's name at the end of the program. Besides, I'm sure Shell would have told me if something had happened to Gina." Moses watches Ed bob and duck as he talks to avoid the flutter of wings.

Sergeant Ed Cavanaugh is either mean or weak, depending on his mood. He's never kept his pecker in his pants and whenever he cheats on his wife everybody knows it because he blows up like a balloon and has to get bigger pants. This is widely known because he has a confessionary streak a mile wide and he talks to the wrong people about the wrong things a lot, including prisoners. Cavanaugh thinks he's father of the year because of all the good he's done for Jorge—and Moses doesn't fault him that. He has done that. But Moses believes that the faith Jorge shows in him is his one miscalculation in life.

Cavanaugh is sitting on Moses' cot, his knees off to the side because the space between the cots, which is less than a foot, does not fit his giant legs. Cavanaugh holds a letter in his hand. It is not one of Gina's letters, the ones Jorge rereads all through the day and into the night, remembering his daughter first as a little girl who wrote only in crayon, then as a whiz kid in science and math, then as a lanky, ivy-bound teenager who broke his heart by abandoning their mutual love of science, ornithology specifically, to study broadcasting, and who, today, is a fancy Upper East Side resident and producer of serious TV news. This is a different letter. From the door of the cell, Moses can see that Jorge wrote it himself. This agitates Moses. Jorge never writes a letter without having Moses read it for errors of spelling or subject-verb agreement, even the letters he writes to his daughter, because Moses learned his grammar from nuns and Jorge, a perfectionist, is afflicted by his mother tongue.

Cavanaugh leans forward with a dramatically knitted brow. He worries his fingers along the edge of the letter and ignores Moses. The cell is already crowded and simply can't fit three men, two cots, the locker that doubles as a desk, the comby, a seatless john and sink in one, and at least ten sparrows. Birds fill the room and fly playfully just over their heads; the cell is just seven by seven by seven. Jorge sits slumped by the weight of a great and recurring worry for his daughter. A small sparrow with a red thread tied to one leg sits on his shoulder, preening and chirping a sweet chirp that is returned by another sparrow sitting on the locker. There are spots of dried white droppings on the floor, on the edge of the sink, on Moses' clear plastic typewriter, on the concrete walls and the edge of the john, even on Gina's diploma from Brown. Jorge has not cleaned today.

"Well, I can't remember who is dead and who is alive anymore of these days," Jorge says in a moment of honesty about the slips and jumps his mind's been making. But the confession isn't anything Moses wants to hear. Lately, a lifetime of poorly treated epilepsy is catching up with Jorge. He's forgetful. He's confused. And at his very worst, he's questioned his deepest beliefs.

Everybody likes Jorge. He's kind and he lives his faith and everyone believes in his goodness. The guards. Even Georgy, Collin, and Don. Without him, Moses would get his ass kicked daily. Of this Moses is only too aware. When Jorge's family was still a family and they used to come inside for respite weekends in the trailers in the yard and Moses was left alone to fend for himself, he would get pummeled. Jorge would return with the pink glow of love and Moses would have a purpled eye ready to pop like a ripe plum. Without Jorge, he'd be ashes by now. Without him he would surely run into the fist that would kill him, but that's not the half of it. In Moses' weakest moments, when he needs something to believe in, Jorge is his faith.

Moses steps further into the cell and walks into Cavanaugh's knees. The birds respond with a group ascent out of the cell. Moses swats at them; they know to scatter when he arrives. Cavanaugh is not so well-trained. Instead, he looks at Moses but doesn't see him. He looks worried. Jorge is scaring Cavanaugh into believing that he is near the end with his dementia, and Cavanaugh, that pussy, is buying it. Of course Moses knows this is stupidity. Jorge's been slipping for years.

Cavanaugh finally stands. He towers over Moses, looks down at him, and they resume their roles. Moses lowers his head, backs out of the cell and waits for Cavanaugh to notice that he's waiting to go in. As an afterthought, Cavanaugh waves his huge hand, and Moses scurries directly to the john. He pisses and drains some of the life from his aggravation.

Jorge says to Ed, "If Gina is still alive, as you tell me, then it must be Gina, not Marie—do you hear me, Ed? Not Marie!—that comes for claiming me. I am afraid for what she would do. Gina will bury me; I will have the last rights. Marie will throw my ashes into the trash or forget me behind in the back of the closet when she moves to Miami and I will be stuck in purgatory."

"Do you mind?" Moses says looking at Jorge. "I'd like to have some peace and quiet. I have reading to do." He sits on his cot and pulls the *World Literature Anthology* onto his lap. He opens to "Death in Venice," and as he begins to read, he thinks of Lila and is disgusted with himself. He fears what he is about to learn about Aschenbach.

Cavanaugh fills the cell door and blocks the light. "Jorge, I assure you. You have a long life to live yet. You're healthier than most men I know. But in the event…" Ed stops. "I will make sure Gina gets this letter. You'll be in good hands." Ed steps forward and leans down awkwardly and shakes Jorge's hand. Jorge grabs on. "I wasn't a real father. Not like you are," he says. "But without you, Gina would have had a death in my heart long ago."

"Oh, come on with all the faggotry," Moses says. "We'll cry when you're dead, Jorge. In the meantime, peace."

Jorge waves his hand at Moses and laughs at him. "You, friend, will miss the most of me."

"I won't miss all this noise."

Ed looks at Jorge with concern. "Good night, men."

When he's sure Ed is gone, Moses swings his feet to the side of his bed, squeezes down on his knees between the cots, his back to Jorge, and pulls the cooler of Lila's hair out from under it. He takes out the ball in his pocket and inspects it to see if he can find the new strand. He can't. He smells the ball of hair and caresses his cheek with it, then puts it in the box. He looks over his shoulder to make sure Jorge isn't paying attention, and he reaches his right hand, the one with the bruise forming from Jenkin's chair, into his pocket and pulls out the compact. He holds it greedily in his palms. It's heavy and warm. He holds it up and smells it, then stashes it quickly away under the bed of hair.

JORGE

A-ONE-AND-A-TWO-AND-A-THREE. Moses pushes up in the military style of the old school: one-armed! Like the black-and-white picture that hung on his childhood bedroom wall of the Air Force man, sinewy and powerful. The man in flat-front slacks, hair slicked back off his face, a cigarette hanging from his lip, Air Force jacket on the back of a chair in the background. Moses never saw his father in person, but he'd been an airman before he became a radioman, so Moses clipped the picture from *Life* magazine and hung it on the wall. At night he'd look at it while he listened to his father's voice ringing across the airwaves. A man without a face, just a clear, strong voice, his father forever young. A cigarette hangs from Moses' bottom lip now. He's reassured as he pushes up against the humid air that he's as strong as he's ever been. Swipes the hair back from his eyes. Four-and-a-five-and-a-six.

"*Permiso*, Moses," Jorge asks from his cot inside the cell. "Is this the letter?"

Moses ignores him. A-seven-and-a-eight.

Jorge asks again, his Ecuadorian accent still thick after all these years, "Is this letter written in the hand of *mi hija* after her death?"

Moses switches to his right arm, "What do I look like? An expert in fucking penmanship? Anyway, you know what it is. Stop acting like this."

Jorge holds the letter out to Moses and shakes it; birds flutter off the locker, and off the shelf above the john. They fly up and out of the cell. "If it is a letter written by Gina after her death, then she is alive. *Claro?*"

"English!" Moses demands.

"Look at it, Moses. Tell me the date. Tell me, is it signed *Te quiero, Gina?*"

Moses ignores Jorge and enjoys the blood coursing through his veins. A-ten-and-eleven-and-a-twelve. He's taking a break from "Death in Venice." With the revelation of each of the story's menacing, teeth-baring men, there's been a tightening in his gut. What a fool he'd been, identifying with Aschenbach the way he had. "Reading this Thomas Mann is like wiping my ass with sandpaper," he says to no one in particular, then he works faster, harder, pushing up and up and up. Sweating. He can smell himself. Vitality surges through him. He is not old.

Jorge, on the other hand, is really showing his stripes. His goggley old eyes, his slipping mind. He's only sixty-seven, ten years Moses' elder, but in here you age fast, like a dog. That combined with the piss-poor medical treatment and a lifetime of phenobarbital has Jorge acting like an old bat. Moses isn't having any of it.

He's just begun his second read of "Death in Venice." He's only now seeing how Aschenbach became a puff and how he should have seen it coming. What Moses wants to know is why Mann would write such a story. Aschenbach seemed like an upstanding man in the beginning. Moses is waiting for Miller to call him to report to work. He plans on asking Lila this very question when he gets there. In any case, his preliminary thesis: Aschenbach got what he deserved.

Just then, Jorge throws the blanket off his lap, looks at Moses with the veined eyes of a madman and asks, "Moses, is Gina *mi hija* or is she the girl that I strangled?"

Moses drops to his knees. He takes the cigarette out of his mouth and sits back on his heels. "Oh, Jesus. Let me see the letters." He walks into the cell and takes his eyeglasses from the locker where they lay next to his typewriter and a few false starts of a paper's beginning. He puts them on. They're already missing an arm.

Friday night, Miller called them and as they made their way to chow, Collin caught sight of Moses' glasses and he punched Moses in the back of his head with as much strength as he could gather, which was a lot because Collin is young and covered in tattoos. He is almost always high and either sleepy or violent because of it. Moses' glasses soared through the air and he could hear them skid across the floor somewhere near everyone's feet. The only guard who saw it was Miller, which meant nothing was going to be done about it. Moses had a horrible ringing in his ears and an ache in his temple from that Latino keeplock and one screaming pain radiating up from his shoulders through the base of his skull. When he stood up again, he looked Collin right in the eye and spat at him there. Collin decided to kill Moses; Moses could tell by the look that came over him. But Jorge held up his hand. Just held it up. Like Jesus or some saint. And Collin lowered his fist and instead of killing Moses, he pushed his chest into him so Moses fell against the wall. Collin slapped his face a few times to let him know what he was. "You're nothing. You realize that?" Collin looked around and someone handed him Moses' glasses. He took a look at them and smirked, put them on, pulled his pants up to his ribs, and pretended to be a geezer.

Georgy, hopping like a flea in a flea circus, was still screaming *Fight! Fight!* But Jorge turned to him and said, "Georgy, my boy, no fights tonight, or they might take away your book of numbers." Georgy stopped his hopping; the crew of them fell back in line and made their way into the chaos of the mess hall for their nightly poisoning. At the long table, Collin looked at Moses. He was pretending to try to see him, pretending to be old. Moses stared back, took a bite of his food and nearly threw it up from pain. He stopped eating for fear he would end up in the infirmary and miss a day with Lila. Instead he focused on the silky texture of the blood red sauce the bits of chipped meat floated in and prayed the day would end soon.

He wouldn't indulge Jorge like this normally, but truth is he got a late start on the reading and the paper because Collin held Moses' glasses hostage for the weekend until Jorge finally went and negotiated for them last night. Moses only had to give Collin ten bucks in commissary, and even though this nearly wiped him out, it was nothing compared to what Collin might have asked for. He owes Jorge some mind.

"Moses, look at this letter and compare it to this other letter. Are you sure it is the same hand that wrote both of these?"

Moses looks up at Jorge and he can't believe the weak old man who looks at him desperately is his longtime friend and protector. Jorge has diminished. Always of a medium build, he's the size of a woman now. That big, rectangular head of his, his powerful Indian nose, that shock of black hair, the deep wealth of color in his skin, the strong teeth, these have all withered and begun to disappear. Moses is disgusted by him. Repulsed by his age. His smell. He sits next to Jorge, who is holding one letter from Gina written when she was fifteen, just before his wife, Marie, told Jorge she was dead, and another letter from a few months later, after Ed Cavanaugh told Jorge that Gina was still living and began arranging weekly meetings.

Poor Jorge, Moses thinks as he compares the letters. He endured Marie's lies for so long that, even though he saw Gina with his own eyes at Christmas five months ago, he has started to worry again that maybe Gina really was murdered by those boys. Maybe all that he's enjoyed of her success, her acceptance to Brown, his fatherly struggle to accept her disinterest in science, her big job in television, the news that she bought herself an apartment on New York's Upper East Side with all the rich, white people, even the postcards and letters she sends, have been nothing more than mirage. Moses blames it mostly on this place. The lack of a horizon line, or maybe it's the constant color of cement, or it could be the half-rotten beef they've been eating for what seems like months that must have been rejected by the retard institutions. Whatever the cause, Jorge has convinced himself Gina is dead.

There is a change in the handwriting. Moses looks closely and can see the difference. The first is written in a big swooping hand. The second is different. The letters are small and constricted, it appears, by lines that aren't even on the page.

"It's the same, Jorge. Just more adult. It's the same. I assure you."

Jorge looks at Moses with the look of a child searching for

reassurance and truth. "I don't believe you, Moses. Thank you, my friend, *mi amigo*, for trying to make me feel better. Thank you. But I deserve her to be dead."

Moses pushes the letters back into Jorge's hands, waves his hand at him and returns to his post at his typewriter. He swats a sparrow off the top of it. But he can't work.

He wedges himself onto the floor between the cots, pulls out his cooler, draws the hair to the side, and pulls out Lila's compact. He looks over his shoulder to see if Jorge is looking. He's not. He's shuffling the letters, turning them over, looking for clues. Moses sneers and turns back to the compact, puts on his glasses and looks at himself. He looks better and stronger than he did the day before. The bruise from last week's keeplock has blued and veined, giving him a tough-guy look. His gray skin is now pink with blood. The silver at his temples not as prominent in the cell's dim light. He places the compact under the bed of hair and selects a soft ball of it, rolls it between his fingers, rubs it along his cheek, stashes it in his pocket.

LILA GATHERS LETTERS AND strides efficiently through the swinging door in the low wall. "Here," she says. "The keeplock letters for D block, and here are the forward lists." She hands Moses the stack and list of inmates who have been transferred to other facilities or moved to a different block. He smiles at her. She winces. "Are you OK?" She brings her right hand to her face, "Do you want to go to the infirmary?"

"I'm fine. Hey, why do you think Mann would write a story like that? Aschenbach seems like a good enough guy at the beginning. Why does he make him suffer like that?"

"That's interesting," she says, turning to him and putting her hand on her hip. "Wilthauser says you have to resist the desire to bring the author into it. You should look at how the story functions instead. There *is* a striking connection, though, between the character and Mann himself, you can tell by just reading the footnotes. So I don't know why he does it. Maybe he does it to punish himself and his own urges."

Moses hasn't thought of that. He read the footnotes and now that she mentions it he remembers the connection between Aschenbach and Mann. "I have a preliminary thesis. Would you like to hear it?" he asks.

"Preliminary? Moses, the paper's due in two days!"

"There was a delay," he says. He would tell her Collin commandeered his glasses and he couldn't get started until yesterday, but he's embarrassed that he was pushed around like a weak old man.

She seals her lips shut and closes her teeth, setting her face in professorial judgement. "OK. Let's hear it."

"OK," Moses turns to her and sets himself up for a little drama. "My thesis is…" He lifts his hand as if to scroll it in the damp air of the mailroom, "Aschenbach Got What He Deserved!"

"Hmm," Lila says as she flips through the stack of letters.

This worries him terribly. Is that all she's going to say?

"Why?" she asks.

"What do you mean *why*?" he grunts. He can feel his face tightening up; his stomach hurts. He shoves his left hand in his pocket and mashes the ball of her hair.

"Why does he deserve what he gets?"

Moses hates admitting it, but it's a damned good question. "I hadn't thought of that," he says.

"Well, you should. Wilthauser always says, 'Tell me something I don't already know. And then prove it to me.' So you need to say *why* he deserves to die in Venice."

"Well, because he's a puff and he can't leave that kid. He stays around too long. Look, let's face it the guy doesn't know when it's time to leave. You'd never want to invite him to a party."

"Do you think his desire for Tadzio was merely sexual?" Lila asks. She quickly blushes at the word. It stops Moses, too. A word like *sexual* has never had an opportunity to bare itself in all their discussions about literature. The words have always been sandpaper dry, purposely chaste. "I mean, it's not just Tadzio that he doesn't want to leave. He doesn't want to leave Venice. He can't stand that this will be the last time he sees the place. I think…Well, Professor Wilthauser pointed out to us that isn't it possible that maybe he's afraid of death? And he's holding desperately onto youth through his affection for Tadzio?"

Moses looks at her in awe. This is it! This is what he loves about Lila. About the stories they read. That he gets to have this conversation. "So you're saying he is afraid of death?" Moses asks.

"Yes. And by holding on too long, he does get what he deserves. You're right about that, I think."

Right at this moment Cavanaugh comes in. Interrupting. Ruining. Fat Cavanaugh sidles up to Lila's worktable and she quickly leaves Moses. Cavanaugh's pants are busting. He's fatter than ever. Moses wonders what kind of a woman would have an affair with him. Cavanaugh doesn't look over at him. He looks concerned with Lila. She hands him a letter and he opens it, reads it and shakes his head. He smiles at her and laughs. He leans down, elbows on the counter, big ass to Moses, and speaks in a voice not at all audible on the other side of the low wall. Lila looks soft and happy. She whispers something back to him. Her body close to his.

Moses doesn't believe what he's seeing. Not Lila. He laughs to himself out loud. If Cavanaugh thinks he has a chance with a woman like Lila, he's got another thing coming. But then he hears Lila giggling. Responding. Giving in to him. "I have a question," Moses says.

They both turn without letting on that they have been close to one another.

Moses knows this job, even the parts that are hers, but he holds up a letter anyway, waves it and waits for her to walk to him. She looks like she doesn't trust him, suddenly. She comes swiftly. She is cautious and guarded and stands farther from him than she usually does. "What's the problem?" she asks courteously.

"Maybe Aschenbach betrayed his true nature and that's why he got what he deserved."

"Maybe," she says. "Do you have a problem with a letter?" she asks tight and full of formality.

"Can't read if this is a D or a B. Is it Darman or Barman," he says politely smiling at her.

"Where are your glasses, Moses?" She points to them in his breast pocket. "Put them on."

"That's not a good idea. Can you just read it for me?"

"Moses, if you can't read, put on your glasses."

"Listen to the lady, Moses," Cavanaugh says picking food from his teeth as Lila's workstation holds him up.

"That's a B, I think," he says.

"Hey, put 'em on," Cavanaugh commands.

"He must be a new inmate," Moses says, resisting. But he looks at the ground and shamefully takes out his glasses. An arm is missing. She read the *Rules and Responsibilities of Glasses Ownership*, too, and knows that there are consequences if it can't be recovered.

"Give it to me," Lila says. "I'll check in the system."

He takes his glasses off quickly and puts them back in his pocket. He hands her the letter. Without looking at him, she takes it and walks back through the swinging door over to her counter. She pulls up a stool and sits in front of her computer and begins to type quickly, the keys popping loudly. She leans over to Ed and whispers. He turns toward Moses and smiles and looks arrogant.

"It's a B," Lila calls to Moses.

"Thank you," Moses says, humbly.

"What happened to you? Walk into a door?" Ed smirks. "You better watch out. These doors have a way of giving you a good pounding every once in a while."

Moses returns to his letters. To the menial. To the mundane. To the miserable tasks of the mail. Where he once found pleasure and pride, he now only finds insult. Writing that paper, reading "Death in Venice," talking about it with Lila as if he too were a student, the little nibble of a student's nourishment, have ruined him for the simple pleasures of his life. What he's always wanted was to prove his smarts. He has a good mind.

He sorts his letters, prepares his satchel for his route, and he can hardly understand how he ever found any of this satisfying. He wants to think about ideas. He wants Ed Cavanaugh to disappear. For Lila to take back her coy gestures. Her batting lashes. Her sweet hip-bend. Her come-closer whispers.

Moses swings his satchel over his shoulder. "That was a beautiful compact of your grandmother's. Was it quite old?" he asks.

Lila turns. "It was. I'm very sad about it, though. I've lost it, Moses. Last I remember I had it here. I don't know what happened to it, but it makes me sick just to think about it. You didn't see it by any chance?"

"No," he says. "Too bad you lost it."

On his route he's burdened by the mail. The bag is heavy. His limbs feel weak and leaden. The halls, always a dank and dungeonous journey, are particularly foul this late afternoon. It's dark as night, despite the lights. There is a smell that sometimes erupts on wet days when the hundred-year-old sewer backs up, reminding them that they are little more than rats. The problem with his conversations with Lila is that they make him sensitive. They expose him to everything. Every detail of his day is infused with the meaning of his life, so this smell of shit, this occupies too much of his thinking about himself, as he wanders aimlessly into the deep of D block.

He passes Corn with his bucket and his mop on his way to push dirt around the mailroom floor. Corn says, *Howyadoin, Moses?* Moses ignores him. He is consumed with the angst of art. What Corn passes without comment or even notice takes on huge meaning for Moses. A spider. A web. The sound of the big metal doors opening, some by machine, others by crank. The sound of those doors shutting. The sound of his demise. He's being dramatic, but why, he wonders, would she give a rat's ass about Cavanaugh? Why would she turn away from him in the moment of revelation of the true meaning of the story? Why at that crucial high note would she pull the arm of the phonograph, screeching the conversation to a halt?

Each keeplock he passes looks more menacing, more violent, more disturbed until he gets to the very last cell in row five. In it sits a man Moses tries to avoid at all costs. It would figure that today he'd have a letter to deliver to him. The man sits at a desk. He is neatly dressed. He is reading from a book. Moses thinks it's always the same book, but he doesn't know which one it is. He's sure it's not the Bible because this man is as much a devil as any he's ever known. The man is fairer than fair. His skin sees no sun. He's lived most of his life in the hole. He is freckled and the sharp contrast of the melanin creates a pocked, rough, rocky look that is deceiving; his skin is really rather smooth. He wears a fedora. And this reminds Moses of Aschenbach, the men in brimmed hats who lead him deeper into the story, closer and closer to death.

"Caruso?" Moses asks.

The devilish man turns slowly and mechanically. There is a certain movement acquired by some of the longtime residents. It is slow, robotic, as if they are acutely aware of each muscle and the work it performs to move the parts of the body, as if the simple experience of living in a body becomes the landscape one explores over a lifetime of forced monastic introversion. This man, this Caruso, he moves like this. Men like him make Moses feel like a mosquito. Like he has a monkey brain. Can't sit still. The simple task of waiting for the man to push out his chair, remove his glasses, adjust his pants, smooth his hands over the front of his shirt, over his low, protruding belly, adjust his brimmed cap, step his foot out from in front of the chair, then the other foot, then slowly journey across the tiny cell, makes Moses vulnerable to his preoccupations and fears. He didn't ask Lila what the hell an in-text citation is. He forgot to have her explain a Works Cited page. He's forgotten how he was going to proceed with his thesis. What do "Aschenbach got what he deserves" and "he feared death" have to do with one another? He is tired. He can't remember things the way he once could. Why does it feel, he wonders as the man moves slow as a mountain, like the tectonic plates of his life are shifting and he's about to fall into the pit?

"Moses," Caruso says quietly.

They know each other. They don't know each other as men. They haven't spent long hours in conversation, but they lived in the hole side by side at the beginning of their tenures as prisoners so they know each other's patterns. What the other sounds like when he uses the john. What the other sounds like when he cries out in his sleep. They know each other like that.

"Le-le-le-etter for you." Moses gasps. The stutter shocks him nearly dead. It's been too many years to count since it reared its ugly head.

"Is that a stutter, Moses? I never knew. Are you nervous? Things have worked out nicely for you, haven't they?" Caruso asks, slowly scratching his low-slung belly with long, yellowed nails. "You've made a life for yourself inside, such as it is. You and I are not meant for civilized society. We must be separated at least by walls. But you are a man of strong character, Moses." When he says this he smiles. Long, horrible teeth hang wide and yellow as popcorn.

"T-take it," Moses struggles.

"Oh, good. A letter from one of my young admirers," he says, his voice slow and silky, intended to chill Moses to the bone. And it does. Caruso has an unspeakable history with children. When he sees Moses cringe, he laughs, and his low hanging stomach jumps and bounces.

Moses tries to dart away, but it's a hobble. He struggles to carry his satchel, to move quickly along the path as men hiss at him. Caruso laughs and Moses' body aches. I'm losing my hold, he thinks, as the stutter pursues him. Ho-o-o-l-l-ly Mary Mo-o-other of Go-o-od. He tries to repeat the phrase. He's a young man again, sitting at a desk, mouth full of marbles, a nun standing over him making him repeat the phrase: Holy Mary Mother of God. The nun. His mother. His sister, who shall remain nameless; he's haunted by memories he hasn't thought of in years. They swarm up and out of him like a tempest. He is losing his hold! "Since human development is human destiny..." the story read...Stop! Stop thinking like this, he thinks. His hair falls into his face. He rushes clumsily along the narrow path and remembers how, as Aschenbach tried to leave Venice the first time, he saw the Bridge of Sighs, along which, the footnote read, the condemned prisoners would proceed when walking to life imprisonment from the Ducal Palace.

TUESDAY, THE NEXT DAY, is surprisingly glorious. Lila has called in sick (he assumes she needed the extra time to finish her paper), so while Moses misses seeing her, he has the entire day to write. And in the perfect spring light of day, which streams into the gallery, lavishly lighting the wings of the sparrows that dart and play and soar along the wall of bars, and after the sacred clarification of sleep, Moses decides he overreacted to Lila's acceptance of Cavanaugh's overtures. And this, only this, was the root of the unexpected rearing of that ugly stutter. He reminds himself that she is, above all, kind, and not one to reject another human being. Unlike Moses, she wouldn't judge Cavanaugh harshly. She would go out of her way to make anyone feel good.

Not only does Moses wake cleansed (no hint of apprehension in his speech, thank God), when Jorge wakes, he is his old self. Lucid and fun. Kind and fatherly. He takes a walk out into the gallery and lets Moses work, even joins the others for rec and goes out into the yard so Moses can write. When he comes back in, his cheeks are flushed from the warm spring air. He is sweaty and smells like a young man. He doesn't look at Gina's letters maniacally. Instead he stretches out on his bed, folds his arms to support his head and starts to tell Moses stories.

Moses isn't entirely done with his paper. He has the bulk of it written. He just needs a conclusion, and he has a general idea how he is going to wrap things up. He is going to declare that "Death in Venice" is proof positive that you better not mess with your true nature. And if you start turning into Caruso and lusting after some young boy, you're sure as hell done for. Something to that effect only more academic. He intends, in any case, to call the lessons in the story cautionary.

Despite the loose ending, and his fear of proper documentation—the stylebook Lila loaned him is as clear as the penal code—he takes a break to enjoy Jorge's lucidity and decides to finish the paper in the morning.

"I came here from Ecuador an orphan, *entiendo*."

Moses knows, but that's OK. He settles in on his bed, lights a cigarette, and revels in the smoke curling slowly out from between his lips and the security of Jorge's storytelling lilt.

"I came on a boat full of café and landed in Brooklyn. Portencia," Jorge says, "Resented the beans it took to keep me alive." Moses knows the story: Jorge's mother's cancer, his evil aunt Portencia, her plot to break him by sending her son to steal Jorge's beloved's heart, starving Jorge until he was driven to murder; but he loves hearing it because at the end he hears how Jorge and Moses became friends and this story, like the story of one's birth, is endlessly captivating. It fills him with peace each time he hears it.

"When I was convicted of killing the girl that I loved, I didn't even know what happened to me! I didn't speak *Ingles*. I had no education. I knew nothing of birds. I couldn't even read Spanish! At the end of the trial, my lawyer turned to me and he say, *Descuple, Jorge*. It was the only word I understood him say to me. It wasn't until I was at Sing Sing that someone told my fate to me: I was in for life!

"You know what happens to a man's heart in that moment, Moses. I broke every rule. I spit in every face, I hit, I yelled. They moved me up here to Hardenberg, and put me in the hole. That, Moses, is where I first knew Cavanaugh."

"Stop!" Moses puts up his hand. "Stick to the script, Jorge. I don't want to know anything about Cavanaugh. Not today."

"Moses, I need to tell you something I have never told no one. You need to know why I trust him. Why I give him the letter for Gina. I want to tell you because you are my dearest friend."

Moses flicks his cigarette into the toilet and lights another. "I'm not happy about this. This is not the story I want to hear."

"Please, Moses, *permiso*. It is the root of it all."

"Get on with it, then. And cut the E-Spanish, will ya?"

"Ha! You understand all that I say. Why should I?"

"Because this is America. And in America, Jorge, we speak E-English."

Jorge waves a hand, laughs, comes to the edge of his cot and leans forward, "This story is to show you that it is through kindness, even the most unexpected and undeserving kindness, that we are saved. You cannot use this story against Ed Cavanaugh. And you can never tell another what I am about to tell you. Agreed?"

"Why would I agree to that? I don't even want to hear it."

"Do you agree?"

"Who the hell else am I going to tell? You're all I talk to anyway. Agreed."

"OK. Ed was at Sing Sing when I was there and he had a reputation as a crier."

"A crier? Ha!" Moses cackles.

"Shh. Moses, listen. So when he put in for a transfer up here, he got it right away. I was transferred around the same time. You see our lives have been like this. They are parallel. He was assigned to the hole and I was there soon enough. For three years we spent nearly every day together. What you must know is that he was put there as punishment for what the others thought was his weakness: He was too nice. They put him there for the same reason they put me there, to break our spirits. They wanted to make a killer out of him, and I saw in Ed's eyes a young man like me, *scared* like me. We were both locked in a box with no light and no hope, for what seemed back in those long away days an endless sentence.

"When he was by himself he never did nothing mean. He never spoke bad to no one. He just did his *trabajo*. Maybe he was a little quiet, intimidated. Some of the men down there they sensed this, so did the guards. The guards would force him to beat us just to toughen him up. He used to do this to me. And Moses, I tell you, I saw myself in him. Those men, they were like Portencia. Horrible and cruel. Working to make us bad, you know? When he beat me, I felt for him. It was just my body that was hurt and my body would heal, but I knew that each time he hit me it was his spirit that was destroyed. I saw it in his eyes.

"Don't be angry, Moses," Jorge says. "Ahh, Papito! Finally! Where have you been?" he says to the little brown bird with the thread tied to one leg that lands on his shoulder and chirps and turns his head as if in response. Jorge takes a cracker from the top of the locker, breaks off small pieces, and feeds them to the bird.

"He was just doing his job," Jorge continues. "You know the kind of COs around here who are so brutal. He was saving himself. But he hurt himself bad. When Ed toughened up, they transferred him to D block. I too had been released out of the hole. Marie found me then and saved me by giving me Gina. And that same year, Ed and his wife, they gave birth to their *hija*, Shell. So we were young fathers together. Oh, I was so jealous of Ed each day when he come to work with those red eyes of his. He got no sleep her first year. He got no rest from the demands of his tough little wife. He started messing up on the job.

"One day, he was the OIC on my row and he had the keys. He

was trying to let guards in and out of the gate at the stairs and trying to get the keeplocks back from the showers, and at the same time letting a crew of mess hall porters through the gate from the gallery upstairs so they could report to work and there was a group of *hombres* who had just come back from Industry and they were crowding around him asking him all kinds of questions. Where is the paper I requested? Can I go to the infirmary? You know how it can get, and he lost the keys. He left them in the gate. I saw them and grabbed them myself. When I saw Ed reach for his keys and realize they were not there, I said something horrible—I don't even remember what—something to make him come after me. And he did. You've seen the temper they built in him. He took me down to the floor and punched me and I slipped the keys back on his belt. It was a kindness from one new *padre* to another, *entiendo*? No one noticed that Ed had committed the cardinal sin and let the keys fall in the hands of an inmate.

"I tell you this so you can know the power of such a kindness, Moses. You see I had been jealous of Ed. Jealous that he could hold his *hija* whenever he pleased. That he could sleep in the same bed with his *esposa* every night. But something changed for me after that day. I began to see myself differently. I knew that I had returned to the same person I was when I lived with *mi mama* in Ecuador. When I did the kindness for Ed, I felt like I had been reborn.

"After that, Ed come to me to talk. He told me terrible things that were in his heart. He told me that one night he heard his *hija* crying and he got up and went to her room and saw her behind the bars of her crib and he flipped. He hit her hard because he couldn't tell the difference between his *hija* and one of us, you know? He said he forgot where he was and who she was. He cried. That's how hard his heart was from this place. He told me this in return for helping him.

"When you arrived, I did not like you," Jorge laughs and Papito jumps from side to side.

"I remember. You don't need to remind me of all that," Moses says, the bashful burn of a teen on his cheeks.

"When I found you," Jorge laughs. "You were mean. Like a mongoose. You had a quick bite and you'd take anything you could get from someone. Moses, be careful. I know you took that mirror from Lila. You must return it to her, *entiendo?*"

Moses looks away. "Get on with it," he says.

"I had a dream, you see. *Jesús Cristo* come to me and he showed me the blood on my hands. He told me that blood is the blood of passion. My crime was hunger, hurt, and fear. I recognized this in you. Your crimes were like mine. You killed that woman you loved because she beat you.

"I know why I'm here," Moses interrupts.

"Moses, you must be honest about your crime or it will not go away. It will stay with you in death. You killed her because you wanted to save yourself. When she heard your stutter and laughed, when she beat you, you felt it in your body. The blood is on your hands, Moses, not your soul. You will be saved, but you must be honest. This is why you don't make the phone calls no more. You must never give in to the temptation to avoid your punishment and the truth about the crime you have committed. You must promise me, even after I die, you will live an honest punishment. If you have served your time well, you will be saved. No calls and no more stealing, *claro?*"

Moses sneers. He doesn't understand why he's getting a lecture, suddenly, or how Jorge knew about the compact. "Claro," he grunts.

"Good. Let's thank *Díos* that we are going to be saved, and get a good sleep. You have much to prove tomorrow, *mi amigo*. I remember when I did my studies how worthy I felt. I'm proud of you, Moses. Now turn and give me some *privacidad.*"

Moses lies on his side, facing the wall and he hears Jorge sit on the can right next to his head. He shits. Thankfully it is not the unhealthy shit of an old, worried man, as it's been. Jorge finishes his business, washes his hands and face in the small sink, and gets into bed.

On nights like tonight, Moses believes Jorge. He believes that goodness, even here in this rotten place, is possible, and that there will be peace on the other side. The pain of the procedures of his days, the humiliations that weigh him so heavily each night will all dissolve when he relinquishes his hold on this life. And he believes his passing will be peaceful because he will have lived out his sentence, paid for his crimes. He imagines that when he leaves he'll be so pure, leaving his body will be the feeling he has when he looks at Lila and his breath suspends because she is innocence. He doesn't need breath in that moment, looking at her. He rides on some other fuel. He has decided that the moment he leaves his body will feel like this; only it will be sweeter for every night he's spent here. He promises himself he's going to return Lila's compact tomorrow.

Moses turns his head and looks over at Jorge, already a lump under the thin blanket in the bed beside him. He thanks God for his friend, and he prays someday there will be a peaceful end to it all.

MOSES WAKES CLEAN AND calmed from a death-like sleep. He rolls over onto his back and looks to the ceiling. There are eight black spiders running to the far right corner. He looks around to see if it is his cell he's in or maybe heaven, and when he does he sees Jorge twisted and stiff. His torso hanging between their beds, arms over his head, Gina's letters crumpled in his gnarled old hands, his knees bent up tenting the sheet, bruises on his skyward face.

MOSES SITS ON THE edge of his bed rereading his paper, making small edits with a pencil. Ed Cavanaugh comes in and sits down across from him on Jorge's cot. It's already stripped and vacant, exposing its cheap and lumpy impressions. He only died that morning, yet all his belongings, the letters he'd thumbed to shreds and the pictures he worshiped of Gina, her diploma from Brown, are already gone. But the smell is still thick from his body's release. They mopped, but it just moved it around. The sparrows have been flying in and out in a frightened panic all morning. The chirping frenzied.

Cavanaugh looks tight and red-eyed.

Moses tries to ignore him and keeps rereading the same sentence, but he can't focus. "The doctor's already been here and filed his report," Moses says.

Moses knew Jorge's death would interrupt the regular schedule and the guards would tighten security in the block in case tempers flared, but Ed's visit concerns him. It isn't officially necessary. And despite Jorge's final directive to be kind to Cavanaugh, he just can't make himself.

Moses looks at Ed and he's instantly pissed off at Jorge. He doesn't like how he found him half on the floor like that. It agitated Moses. Death, like Lila, was supposed to be sweet. *La dolce vida*, Jorge said. But Jorge struggled. And Moses knows he wasn't nice to the doctor; word must have reached Cavanaugh.

The doctor asked him a lot of boring questions taken straight from the form he was filling out. *At approximately what time did you find Jorge Padilla?*

"How would I know? I don't own a watch," Moses said. "What time did Miller say I yelled for him? I yelled for him when I found Jorge, so you should ask him." The doctor didn't react to Moses' crankiness. He was civilian. An older Italian man who stood in the doorway of the cell with medical disinterest and recorded Moses' answers as coldly as if he had lifted the information from a toe tag.

And can you describe in detail what you saw?

"I saw a pathetic, old Ecuadorian," Moses said, "with blue lips, lying in a pool of his own piss, smelling like shit, clutching a bundle of letters from his daughter, who incidentally, he couldn't anymore distinguish from the girl he murdered forty-eight years ago."

The doctor scribbled some notes and asked, *And had he demonstrated any unusual behavior lately?*

"No," Moses answered, "Did you hear what I just said to you? He was fucking demented." The doctor didn't answer him. He wrote a few more quick notes and left without saying goodbye. Moses returned to his paper. He had found his conclusion in the night. Aschenbach, he wrote in pencil on the draft, had betrayed his true nature because he feared death. Because of this, he left behind what he believed in, making him vulnerable to evil and turning him into what he'd once despised.

Moses looks up from the paper. Ed is acting like he has something on him. Moses wonders what the doctor told him. "When they examined Jorge they discovered a large contusion on the right side of his head and a black eye. Do you know anything about that, Moses?"

"He had epilepsy. Have you ever seen a seizure?"

"So you didn't hear anything during the night?"

"I was asleep," Moses says.

"You don't seem upset. What's your problem?"

"Look, believe what you want. He was my friend. I didn't touch him."

"You didn't hear anything."

"I heard nothing. For once, I slept like I was dead."

Cavanaugh sits quietly for a moment. Ed's eyes are swollen and his face more flat than usual.

"Jorge was a good father. He was a good man," he says.

"A lot of good it did him," Moses says, but Ed doesn't act like he's heard him.

"When I first met Jorge, I'd just come on the job. I had a new baby and a wife who was on me all the time to work extra shifts and make more money and Jorge was also a new father. Gina was just a tiny little thing. God, I remember those girls when they were girls. It's all over. They're women now, which means I'll never understand them. And this," he says waving his hand toward Jorge's empty side of the cell.

"I promise you; I didn't hear or see anything." Moses doesn't want the boys thinking he's getting friendly with Ed Cavanaugh. He imagines Collin sending Georgy to spy so he can run back and tell him if Moses is in with Cavanaugh or not.

Ed taps his foot and looks up at the ceiling like it might fall on him. Moses can feel everything going horribly wrong. He imagines what they'll do once they know Ed's in here blabbing like a Goddamned girl. With Jorge gone, he has no protection. And he needs some peace so he can finish his paper. He needs to give it to Lila this afternoon.

"I'm sure you know all about Marie. She's one for the books."

"No. I don't know anything about her." Moses isn't lying. Jorge sheltered Moses from the emotion of his unexpected family life because it was unfair to bring it up.

"It's only a matter of time for any of us, I suppose," Ed says and then seems to understand for the first time that he's let himself go in front of Moses. He stands up quickly. "I'll be in touch once they find out the cause of death. I'm sure you'd like to know. In the meantime, I'm going to have to take those papers and the typewriter. And that book over there. It's standard procedure."

Cavanaugh takes his paper right from his hands, packs up all of Moses' scraps, his typewriter, his *World Literature Anthology*, the stylebook he needs to complete the documentation and walks out of the cell. Moses' rabbit heart beats. He watches Cavanaugh leave and can hardly breathe.

IT ISN'T UNTIL HE sees her that the tidal surge of his mourning hits him and lifts him up, suspending him in a state of acute and tender sorrow. He stands in the entrance of the mailroom, and it doesn't feel like his feet are even on the floor. Her back is to him. She doesn't yet know that he is there. He imagines walking up behind her and resting his cheek on her shoulder, nestling his nose in her hair and resting. Just resting. Taking a moment. It isn't until hours after a tragedy that people of Moses' nature realize that indeed they have endured an event that trumps all others, a calendar-clearing travesty that wipes away goals, expectations, hopes, desires, and, above all, familiarity.

Lila turns. "Oh, sweet Jesus, Moses. I didn't know you were there."

Moses doesn't feel like he is. He feels like there are two worlds. The world where Lila, Ed Cavanaugh, his paper, his typewriter, Wilthauser, the morgue where Jorge lays, the prison, its guts and functions, the other prisoners, the outside world, the town, the cars on the streets, the traffic lights, the cawing crows, the river, the dark sky, its clouds, the wetness of spring all exist, and then there is the world in which Moses finds himself. It is a different place entirely.

"Are you OK?" Lila asks.

He reaches out to her, as if he's going to be able to reenter her atmosphere. He waves her over with a meek flop of his hand. He wanders over to his workstation because he could use something to help hold him up against the weight of his disappointment and loss.

"You look rotten. Did you stay up late working on the paper?"

The paper! She doesn't know. "I d-do-on't ha-a-a-a-ave it," he suffers; his speech sounds like a typewriter.

Her eyes widen in shock. "Moses, have you had a stroke?"

He shakes his head and attempts to speak, but it's as though the words have become bullets and someone else is firing the gun.

"I'm calling the infirmary."

"N-n-n-o!" Moses yells and she turns around. He holds a finger up to her to tell her to wait. Wait just a fucking minute, he thinks. He puts his hand in his pocket and pulls out the ball of her hair.

"What is that?" Lila asks.

He shakes his head. Wrong pocket. He puts it away and puts his hand in the other pocket and his fingers find the compact. He pulls it out slowly and reaches it out to her.

She takes an unbalanced step backward into the swinging door in the low wall. It hits her in the calves.

Moses points to the compact with his chin. "He-e-ere."

She shakes her head. Refuses to come to him. She starts to back away, so he lifts his arm into the air and makes like he'll smash the thing on the floor. "No, don't!" she says. "I'll come." She steps cautiously forward and reaches into his hand. "I don't know what's wrong with you, Moses." She starts to cry. "What's wrong with you?"

"S-s-s-top crying!" he demands. "Just stop."

She swallows and looks down at the compact. "I'm going to have to report for you this. I don't have a choice, you know. You've left me no choice, Moses."

Moses looks down, ashamed. He watches her comfortable rubber shoes turn away from him. No, he thinks. Don't leave me, please. Just don't leave me, he murmurs. His ears fill with the wild sound of wind. It's the ether that fills the space between worlds that he's hearing. He is so terribly alone now. He is standing in the middle of the mailroom, but it feels as if he is a lone man on a lone planet. He lunges forward, ripping through the divide, crosses to where she is on the other side of the low wall, grabs her hair, knots his fingers in the back of it, and pulls her to his side of the room. He wrestles her close to him. Holds her tightly in place. Rests his cheek on her shoulder, noses her hair; hair caresses the tops of his closed eyelids.

GINA

It begins with Gina hidden. Behind the couch. Or under the bed. In the pantry. Or up against a shower wall. It is always dark, at first, until Arthur wants to catch her and wants an advantage, then he throws on the lights and there is really nowhere to hide. The apartment is enormous and mostly empty. A large loft with furniture that is organic in shape like mounds of earth, placed not in ordinary sitting circles but in random Easter Island or Stonehenge-type pop-up-out-of-nowhere patterns. The whole place is built for this. For them. They've been at this game for a long time. But it is only a matter of time now.

He's been inviting others. Girls from the show who want to make it big. He brings the girls boxes of lacy things, makes them try them on, invites the girls over. There will be one tonight, Gina's sure.

She uses her key. Follows their rules and installs herself under a table. It is a side table, not a large one. And being tall, it takes a lot of twisting and turning to get all of her in, leaving nothing jutting out for a streetlight to hit and make a shadow. Soon there will be a knock at the door. Some *she* will find it is already open. She'll come inside. Arthur? Are you home? Why are the lights off? She'll giggle because she is still a girl. Just out of college.

He's been getting a bit blunt lately. He is losing his finesse. It used to be that the iron or the whip were accents. Small, quick punishments administered for not making him work hard enough. And it used to take him a while until he got there. Not anymore. He is hurting the girls first, scaring them into the game. He has resorted to this because not one of them is a natural, like Gina.

It has always been the challenge of the search and the fact that Gina is not easy to catch that makes this work. And for most of nearly seven years now, this has been exhilarating, exciting, perfection. But lately, when he catches her, he ties her up and comes in with a sandwich. Takes out the gag and feeds her, talks about work. Sometimes he switches on the TV. Lately, he's been touching her wounds tenderly and she likes it all right, but she's been left asking what is the point?

There. Someone. Running. Is she wearing the same uniform? The lace black, the garters tight, the breasts left to hang open? Gina looks hard into the dark trying to see who it is. Is she from the show? Did he deliver the uniform with the same ritual? Gina isn't jealous, exactly.

There! The body again! Racing the floor. Frantic. Scared now.

Then silence.

Gina waits. To see if what comes next is the right kind of scream. It isn't.

This girl is terrified, not fortified. Gina exhales and goes a little limp under the table. Her foot kicks the leg and the table scrapes the floor just audibly.

"Not you, too!" Arthur yells from somewhere close by. "Won't anyone just play the fuck along?"

Gina puts her head in her hands. Like a married couple, they've hit a wall. To Arthur, the answer is obviously a network girl, and the girls agree because look at Gina Padilla! They want her life. She is in charge. She won her first Emmy as soon as she graduated Brown. She is cutthroat. That good. So these girls, they want to be somebody, they want Executive in their titles, too. They'll do "whatever it takes." Those words. Those are always the words they use, and it always ends badly because they are wired for ambition; they are not wired for this. They are invited, coaxed, encouraged, flirted, massaged, gifted, flattered, eased into agreeing to come to Arthur's place at ten p.m., and wear this, and just let yourself in, and then, he whispers in their diamond-studded, perfumed ears, hide and don't let me find you.

Because they always think it is just sexy and cute, they come.

Really it is much more. The iron. The whip. The gags and whatever else is found that day, and something intangible, too. It is the part in Gina that is not ruined by this, or scared or abused or let down; it is the part that is found, opened, needed this all along, couldn't live without it: reject, get caught, get punished. It scares the hell out of these women because they are not Gina.

Gina hears him jump out, imagines him lifting his whip to bring it down on the girl a second time, and she must have made eye contact—she must have thought it would make a difference—because she giggles. "Arthur!" she says, all coy. "Come *on!*" And of course he brings it down on her too hard and she falls to the floor, crawls off alarmed and gets quiet, finally.

Arthur is pleased. The rules finally established and understood. The game is now on.

Arthur knows she is under the table. He is pretending to look for the other girl, but he knows where she is, too—she's lost her nerve and has fallen completely to pieces on the floor of the laundry. Before Arthur just gets flat out mad at the spoil-sport, Gina makes a break. She bolts out from under the table, and runs fast as she can right past him.

"You bitch," Arthur mutters and takes off after her. She knows how to do this. To make him run her down. To make him work for her. For tonight she can satisfy his urges and hers. She'll run until he conquers her. She'll hang on the rack, crucified, while he makes a sandwich. She'll act grateful when he takes out the gag and feeds her a little something. She'll pretend, again, that this is still working. For the girl's sake, sure. But more for her own.

"YOUR FATHER WAS THE only good one," her mother sniffles on the line. It is the next morning and Gina, who is not hearing her, stands on the corner of Fifty-Seventh and Park in a slew of nine o'clock men with briefcases, a slew of men in suits. She looks at all their faces and knows them from O'Malley's. They are lawyers. They are newspapermen. They are bondsmen and traders. They are in advertising or film. They all fuck like she isn't in the room. This is the way she likes it. She is not her mother.

"Your father was the only one who would never leave me. 'Til now, the rotten *bastard*," Marie screams and Gina hears her throw her shoe at the wall. She knows it is her shoe because that's what she does when her men leave, sits at the table and takes off her shoe and throws it. She could have done more damage with the ashtray, heavy ceramic, but then she'd have to give up her cigarette and would have nothing to hold onto. Gina thinks of this, not of what is being said.

"He couldn't leave you, mom. He was locked up." The light changes. She moves into the black cloud of light spring overcoats and aftershaves, mostly of a high quality, and she breathes them in, these men, exhales them out. Obstacles swarm her—carriages, ten dogs on linked leashes, cars that try to find the weak spot and push in—but Gina feels the men around her. There are women, naturally, but it is the men she feels, and even here on the phone with her mother—what is her mother trying to say to her?—she's caught the eye of the man whose shoulder she shouldered up to and he, ever so lightly, leans in to her as they wait for a car to pull through. She pulls back. *Asshole*, she whispers.

Her mother locks her legs around anyone who turns his gaze, even if for a moment, to her, and tightens like a noose when anyone looks, even at the newspaper, away. Or goes to work. Or moves out screaming, *You crazy bitch*. Her mother would unzip a man's pants right at the breakfast table with Gina eating corn flakes just to keep him, any him, from going to work. Don't go to work, she'd say. Stay, she'd say, and get on her knees to beg. Do it for us, she'd say and smile at Gina and wink.

"He was my best man," her mother sobs, softer now, her voice drifting just from the mere suggestion of her other men.

"You saw him once a week," Gina says. "The others didn't have a chance. They saw you every day. Odds of making you happy were against them."

And the once-a-week visits do it. She finally feels her mother's news. *He's dead*, she'd said. *He finally left me, the fuck.*

New York, the men, the ten-to-a-leash dogs, the carriages, the cars, the car horns echoing up the sides of buildings that reach to the sky and lock them all in, the yelling of drivers at pedestrians, the yelling of medallioned cabbies at gypsy drivers, the rumble of the subway beneath their feet, the hot, dry gusts blowing up their pant legs from underground, the deep hum of fans, the suck of HVAC systems, the click and buzz of street lights, the whipping and whirr of helicopters throwing air over their heads, the low horns of ships coming to port, she wants all this to fall to stillness. She wants to tell the whole stupid story to stop. The only person she ever loved is dead.

And just like when she was a kid balancing on his knee while he tapped his foot up and down and sang a song that sounded like galloping across the desert, and the guards yelled TIME!, and he told her, Go *angelita mia*, you be good, I'll be good, we'll do this again next week, and Gina said, *no, Papa!*, wrapped her skinny arms around his neck refusing to let go—guards calling her animal because of how hard she loved him—just like then, she stands stock still in the street like she can make it all stop. But the cars come at her; the men mix around her; the dogs bark at her; carriages clank her ankles; a driver screams at her.

She knows better. Long ago she learned the world doesn't stop for criminals. "There's not a soul that doesn't leave, Gina."

"I've got to get to work, Mom."

"See?"

"WHAT'S EATING YOU?" VERONICA follows Gina into her office and shuts the door behind them. She places a giant cup of coffee on Gina's desk and flops into a chair. Gina stands at the windows and doesn't turn around.

"How'd she do?" Veronica asks.

"Who?"

"Last night's girl. Lauren, I think. She's too new to have a name."

"Box up her things. Arthur won't want to see her today," Gina says.

"That bad, huh?"

"Mind your own business." Gina looks fifty stories down to the streets below and places her hand on the glass. The city's vibration pulses up through the building into her, giving her something tangible, bringing her back into the room. She can do this. She can shut down what is coming up into her over and over: Her father, stony dead on a concrete slab in the basement morgue of Hardenberg Correctional Facility. Suddenly, she wants to teach Lauren a lesson.

"I changed my mind," she says. "When she comes in, I want you to send her in to see me."

"Aye, aye, sir." Veronica pulls herself from her chair. "Everyone is waiting to see you. When can I start sending them in?"

"After Lauren," Gina says.

"After Lauren it is," Veronica sings cheerfully. She returns to her desk and seductively crosses her long legs, pulls out a nail file and begins filing her nails to the great consternation of five salivating writers who are at once wanting to pounce on her and wanting to get to Gina because there is, of course, breaking news and the whole show, as always, needs to be reworked.

Gina sits at her desk. She doesn't bother to appear busy. She wants people to suffer today. She wants to start with Lauren. The writers are a bonus. They pace. They pound her door. They yell in, *Gina, Are you fucking trying to take us all down? What's the deal?* Some peel away and decide to go rogue and produce the spot themselves because then at least they'll have something, some interviews lined up, a reporter on scene. They can get their Capitol correspondent on the line, at the very least. Somehow she thought because he was in prison he was safe from death. She knows that doesn't make any sense, but she always found some comfort in the interminable nature of *in for life*. Until now, until this very moment, this was something she understood as permanent. She fingers the red viewfinder hanging from her keys, picks it up and looks through it. Gina, Ellen, and Shell at Coney Island, the Cyclone rising and falling behind them. Shell knows by now, of course, and Gina wonders if she'll bother to call her. Two years have passed since both Shell and Ellen got married. Since Gina never sees them anymore, marriage seems like a sentence a lot like her father's.

An argument erupts outside her door. "There is no way you are getting in there until I talk to her. Who are you, even? How can this intern get in to see her before I can? I'm a senior writer. For fuck's sake!"

Gina goes to the door and opens it, grabs Lauren by the arm and pulls her in.

"Sit down," Gina says without looking at her.

"This is a once in a lifetime opportunity. I'm not going to screw this up," Lauren says.

"What opportunity are you talking about?" Gina says, finally getting a good look at the intern.

"I can learn how to play the game. I'm as tough as you are," Lauren continues, but Gina isn't listening. She sees someone else sitting there.

"Leave," Gina says to Lauren.

"Leave your office, or leave the studio?"

"I don't care," Gina says. She combs through her bag looking for her cell phone, but Lauren is still there waiting. "Now," Gina demands.

Gina scrolls through her contacts and finds Ellen's number. Calling her feels like climbing an old familiar mountain and she wonders why she's doing it. Was it just Lauren's striking resemblance? She dials and her silk shirt catches on a slender fish-shaped blister on the pale underside of her arm. Even the cool silk of the shirt makes it smart and she remembers Ellen reaching across a table in the tea house they'd found in the snowstorm, placing her cool fingers on a blister on her neck, her touch soft, the urgent rush of pain dissipating.

The phone rings. A woman with a Spanish accent answers, "Hello? Collins residence."

Kevin, the angry head writer, busts into the room and yells, "Gina. If I can't get five minutes with my executive producer when there's a major news event breaking, we need to talk about my future here."

Gina ignores him. "Yes, may I speak with Ellen, please? This is Gina."

"Yes, please. Hold one minute, please," the woman says.

"Gina, I demand you hang up the phone right now and talk to me. I have offers. But I care about this show. About what we're trying to do here."

Gina presses the phone to her ear and hears the woman calling for Ellen. Ellen asks if it is the caterer, and the woman says no. Someone named Gina. And Gina can hear Ellen's tone change, and for a moment she worries it will be like after Ellen's brother Ronnie D. died, when Ellen looked through Gina like she was a piece of glass. But she comes to the phone and is very kind. "What a surprise. It's good to hear from you. What makes you interrupt your busy day to call me?"

"Gina, for the good of the show, hang up the fucking phone," Kevin demands. Gina is relieved to hear Ellen's voice. Why had she worried? She opens her hand and looks at a delicate scar between her thumb and forefinger. "Ellen," Gina says, and she pauses a minute to get up her nerve. "My father died."

"You have a father?" Kevin asks. "Shit," he says and finally leaves.

Gina waits for Ellen to speak. She thinks of Ellen's small room filled mostly with a bed, an old faded red armchair with rips in the upholstery shoved in a corner, books pitched tentatively on its broken springs, the small rickety table and chairs pulled in from off the street, fresh orange gerbera daisies lurching from a jelly jar on the table amidst piles of books and clothes, jars of gray liquid, paintbrushes extending precariously out of them, art covering the walls from floor to ceiling—oil paintings, some charcoal sketches and watercolors here and there—newspapers, art sections mostly, in scattered piles around the edge of the room, black soot covering the windowsills, dust bunnies on the floor, a smell, yes, garbage, soft, smart talking coming from a small radio in the kitchen, Ellen in her dumpy art clothes, an easel set up in front of the stove, her gestures discerning and precise, a sip of coffee, then the mindless placing of the cup on the counter behind her, all the while considering the canvas Gina couldn't see. The studio was a rat's nest, but Ellen was the most beautiful sight Gina had ever laid eyes on. To someone who didn't know her, Ellen might have appeared peaceful. But Gina saw it, the sag of sadness in her shoulders. Loneliness.

This is where Gina imagines Ellen to be. The old room. New York then, the New York in the viewfinder, when they all found each other again after college, Hardenberg far, far away. She hears Ellen whisper something to the housekeeper. Something like, *hold on* or *not now*, and remembers that Ellen's life looks nothing like that now and Gina has an impulse to hang up the phone.

"Goodness, Gina. That's awful," Ellen says.

"Can you meet me tonight? Just for a drink after the show," Gina asks. "I'd like to see you and Shell."

"I think I can. Where? O'Malley's?"

"Yes, at seven."

"OK. I'll see you there. Gina, I'm sorry."

"Thank you."

When Gina calls Shell, Shell says, "I already know. I was just about to call." Gina says, "Sure you were," and they laugh the way you can laugh when things are going terribly wrong with people who really know you.

"O'Malley's at seven," Gina tells her.

"I have someplace I *have* to be, but I'll make it work. Don't try to be strong and alone," Shell tells her. Gina rolls her eyes.

THAT NIGHT A WHOLE crew of salesmen in from St. Louis, Detroit, Saratoga, and who-really-cares-where holds down the east end of O'Malley's. Patrick works them before she even kicks in off the street. She can see him. She can read his lips. *Watch out*, he says. *Black curls with the legs to there will eat you alive.*

O'Malley's is hers. It is dark and smoke from the past still hangs. It is dim enough to hide what you don't want seen. Nothing trendy there. No cool vellum light. No sleek metal surfaces. Just old brass taps. Kelly green glass. Patrick works the boys for her, but she doesn't care.

When Gina was a little girl she'd tell Jorge, "This week I made a new friend," and she would make up a girl's name and tell him how they played with dolls and she invented elaborate games like the ones she imagined girls played when they visited one another's houses. She eavesdropped on girls at school, collected their stories, and often got caught and admonished for having cooties or wearing second-hand clothes. She wove these stolen stories into weekends spent with fake friends, and told them to her father. Her mother never blew her in; Marie was more concerned with the attention Jorge showed her. "Jorge, do you like the way my breasts look in this dress?"

At the end of fifth grade Gina came running to him, past the reaching hands of guards. "Papa!" she shouted. "This week I really did find friends. Two friends! They are beautiful and they are kind and they live in the nicest houses. Ellen's house! It's a mansion! There are beautiful things all around. And Shell is a little fat, but very funny." Jorge looked at Marie. "It's true," she said. "They're a couple of snobby brats." And Jorge put his hand on Gina's cheek: This was no way for a child to grow up.

Gina cranes her neck and looks inside O'Malley's. Shell is there. She is looking around to see if anyone is looking at her. Ellen isn't there yet. Gina pulls her sleeve down and holds the cuff with her fingers— the cool of her silk shirt calms the fire of the burn and Gina comes into O'Malley's tough side out. She slides onto a bar stool, throws her bag and keys on the bar, and pretends not to care about the boys in the back watching her. (She doesn't see the stranger. The stranger is part of the shamrock wallpaper, for all she knows.)

"Ellen's just late," Shell assures her, as they kiss each other's cheeks. She picks up Gina's keys and looks through the viewfinder. "I can't wait to see Ellen, too. I'm sorry, Gina." Shell takes Gina's hand, opens it and looks for the scar they share. "Your father loved you."

"Don't be dramatic, Shelly. These things happen to people," Gina says and gently pulls her hand away to reach for the drink Patrick has placed in front of her. "How are you?"

Shell looks as though she is going to put on her regular show, but she lets out a defeated breath. "Awful," she says. "The movie is done, but we're broke. If we don't get this deal tonight, we'll be out on the streets. Literally."

Gina listens. She nods. But there is a movement. A certain gentle flicker out of the corner of her eye. Gina thinks she sees her, thinks she senses her coming in. She looks toward the door. "Huh," she says.

"What?" Shell asks.

"Nothing. I thought I saw Ellen, is all." Gina is confused. She so

YOU ARE FREE TO GO

completely felt Ellen coming toward the bar she can't understand how she was mistaken. Shell is speaking to her about *Panoptic,* the film she and her husband just completed. "We've just come too far to fail. This is why I can't stay," Shell is saying, but Gina doesn't hear. Worry washes all over her. Her father rushes in, too. There he is again: gray and bloodied from the injuries of a seizure, perhaps (how could no one have told her how he died?), laid out on a slab in the prison's dripping-with-cold morgue. She tries to pull the thoughts back in, but she sees Shell's eyes fall on the blister on her arm and she feels worse. Shell is not Ellen. Shell judges. And in every judgment is the old indictment: We were at your house. It was your idea.

"Did your father tell you anything?" Gina asks; her voice cracks. "Patrick, two Grey Goose," she barks; she is drinking too fast.

"Right away," he says.

"No," Shell says. "He said there would be an investigation, but that didn't mean anything. He thought it was natural. He's sending you a letter. Look out for it. Jorge gave it to him. He must have known…" Shell has said too much. They have an awkward history, Shell and Gina. Because of her dad, Shell was a reluctant liaison to Jorge, and Gina hates relying on her for it. They have never gotten over their past. When they are left alone for too long without Ellen, it always butts in between them.

"I can't stay long, like I said. I have to go meet John at this party. I really ought to be there soon."

"OK," Gina grunts and picks up her keys and looks through the viewfinder.

"It was good then, wasn't it?" Shell says. "I miss us. We're all just so busy now."

"It was the best," Gina says, looking at the picture of the three of them at Coney Island five years before. Ellen is busting with pride—the excursion to watch the Freak Show sword swallower marry the glass eater was to celebrate her promotion, executive director of ArtNow after only two years. Shell was weak with longing for John, then. In the picture Gina and Ellen are holding her up, each has an arm around her, and, despite this, they are smiling wildly, all of them, hair whipping into their eyes from the ocean breezes; each is full of the fierceness of their bond and each holds up a bloodied hand in solidarity.

They had gone to different colleges, and for the most part lived separate lives. Gina and Shell would see each other when Shell's parents drove them back and forth to school and during winter recess when Gina came home to see Jorge, but Ellen disappeared after high school graduation. They knew she had gone to Vassar, but she never came home on breaks, nor was it acceptable for her to hang out with them. After Ronnie's death, her mother forbade it. But in a snowstorm in New York something miraculous happened: Ellen turned and turned, looking for a beacon, something recognizable in the snow-shrouded skyline and right when she gave up hope and looked down, there in the foreground stood Gina. They had tea. Ellen touched her blisters tenderly and asked after Shell. The next day they called around and found Shell in a basement apartment in Cobble Hill. She was temping and starving herself so her ex-boyfriend, John, would notice and love her again—she'd followed him to New York. Each admitted nervousness about getting together, but when they met up at a tapas bar they discovered something remarkable: an unexpected levity at finally being in the comfort of others who had known what she knew. They didn't exhume Ronnie; he remained in their past.

But in the picture from Coney Island, they are fierce. They had watched the sword swallower swallow his sword, they had watched the glass eater eat her light bulb, these were their vows, and they watched the wedding procession full of mermaids and tattooed men dressed like dignitaries march to the carousel where they took rides, cementing the union. Shell was distant that day. John had come back to her briefly, but had left again, and she stared at the broken glass on the beach. The waves washed up and shards tipped and turned in tidal moves. She picked up a piece and without knowing it sliced the web of skin between her thumb and forefinger. She had already been crying, but she pretended it was the cut. Blood poured down her hand, and Gina came to her side, took the piece of glass Shell was holding out, and sliced her own skin in the same manner. She turned and held it to Ellen. Ellen came and did the same and they held their hands together, letting their blood mingle, but also letting the past and all its demons know that their bond was forever and unbreakable.

Thus the wildness of that picture. It is full of a promise. There is nothing false in it: Gina knew Shell lay the blame for Ronnie's death at her feet; they knew Shell would sacrifice everything for love even when it was dangerous; and Ellen, Ellen risked everything, the love of her mother, to stand with her friends.

Gina puts the viewfinder down and looks at the jagged scar on her hand. Shell opens her own palm. "I don't think she's coming, Gina," Shell says gently.

"Of course she's coming," Gina snaps. "What time is it? We should text her."

"I did. I've heard nothing. I called and left her a message before you got here, too. It's almost half past eight," Shell says.

Gina looks around. Looks at the back of the bar at the out-of-town boys. And consciously or unconsciously she sends out some signal; it is as if she releases a hormone into the air unlocking an invisible hog pen, and they come. Gina lets them wash over her like waves. They push Shell away. Men and their single-minded search for a good time are what Gina can depend on. But she doesn't like this feeling she has. There is a force gathering in her and it is collecting in her throat. She swallows to keep it from coming out. What form it will take she can't imagine. Words? Gasps? Or will it be more physical? Will her body convulse like Jorge's, seized with the fits of his muscles and nerves? Nerves had a lot to do with this. The tentacle endings that connected her thoughts and her body—you killed Ronnie your friends hate you you are invisible again no one knows you exist no one cares you're alive according to your mother you are now dead your father is a prisoner you are only worth the spectacle of that you are only smart by accident you are dangerous you are a slut you survive on the whimpers and writhes of men you are alone—a chemical message sent into her skin, into the muscle of her belly, into the ligaments of her knees.

She had a boyfriend her freshman year at Brown. Matthew. He was good. Poor, work-study kid, like her. Gina and Matthew had sex whenever and wherever they could. He told her he liked school a whole lot more now that he was with her and she didn't say anything, but every once in a while a terrible feeling would pass over her and she would hold onto his hand tightly as if this might keep him from suddenly going away. She told him about Jorge being in prison; he told her he loved her, and each night she dreamed that she was standing alone, naked in an abandoned old schoolyard, the squeak of ungreased swings tormenting her as she looked frantically around for Ellen and Shell, who had just left her. She suffered in these dreams and woke in panic and sometimes cried out. Matthew held onto her and said, "It's OK. I'm not going anywhere. You're safe with me." She believed him until one day his roommate asked her, "So did your father murder someone or what?"

Gina never talked to Matthew again and he went crazy. He was desperate, he told her. Please, he said. But each time he came to her and she shoved him aside with her shoulder or turned and strode away from him, she felt a strange power. When she lost Shell and Ellen after Ronnie's death, she suffered their losses in every cell. Her miserable life, which she had been able to survive before their friendship, was unlivable after they were gone. Each day she longed for one of them to be walking down the high school hall and look up and just by accident or old habit say hello. They didn't. But if they had, would she have had the strength to turn them away or realize the great freedom that came from rejecting someone? Probably not. But she had no problem watching Matthew wither and gray. He came to her and told her he was going home. She pretended she didn't hear him and watched him limp down the hall.

After that, when men chased her down, she slept with them then watched them suffer and burn as she pushed them aside and moved onto another. Soon, the men on campus were not enough. She got the job dancing at Diamond Dolls and every night she enjoyed the smolder she could create in those sad men. She spun and danced and from that moment forward her life sped off into a high-octane game of cat and mouse. This is how she stopped the dreams of being left behind. This is how she short-circuited her nerves and their messages. This was how she met Arthur Fairchild. He brought her to New York, made her an assistant producer of the *Nightly News* and chased her around his apartment with an iron from time to time. Men are how Gina survives when her friends let her down.

There are names exchanged: a Kevin, Mark, Constantine, a Drew, always a Drew, and there are drinks ordered and paid for and the sticky smell of aftershave. There is the contest among men to outwit the others. Gina slouches on the stool looking bored, giving the boys something to work for. She doesn't answer their questions. What does she do? She waves them off. The men and their chatter, the men and their interest melt together into a hum. She recedes into herself. Usually, this is how she likes it, but tonight it isn't. She's lost track of Shell, only noticing her when she and a stranger turn her way, and again when Shell kisses her on the cheek goodbye, "I'm sorry I have to go. I told you I have to be someplace. Call me, please." Gina is far away and watches her friend walk out the door, and feels herself disappearing like spilled beer, the boys' chatter a sponge; she is getting sopped up, erased.

This is when the stranger stands up and leans against the counter on his forearms and looks right at her. (The boys bleat around her, *Hey, you into ménage à twats?*) The stranger looks out from under his heavy brow and finds her eyes. He doesn't smile. He looks serious, dangerous even. And this is when Gina loses her game. When she no longer appears to the swarming drones to simply be far off, but is clearly interested in something other than three-ways. She is straining because the stranger is talking to her. She swears he asks, "So how'd he die?"

Gina slips off the barstool, grabs her bag and her keys. The drones yell, *Hey, where you going? Don't go! Wait! Slut.* The door of O'Malley's slams behind her with a jingle of bells and she stumbles onto the sidewalk, falling at the feet of a passerby who looks at her like she is a piece of trash that has fallen too close to his lambskin shoes. She skins her knee.

"Be careful." The stranger from the bar holds her elbow, helps her up. "You're in no state."

"Leave me alone," Gina says and strides quickly up Second Avenue and turns on Seventy-Third. She walks as she always walks, head down like she has a place to go. It is safer this way, on the street by yourself or in the halls of a small-town high school where anything could happen to you once they knew about your dad.

The stranger follows.

He has a limp but it doesn't seem to slow him down. When she looks back he is gaining on her. She knows he will catch her, even if she runs.

PART II

That's who you are, a murderer.

HE IS LIVE AND HE IS COUNTED

MOSES SITS IN THE infirmary. The male nurse checks the swelling on his face, head and neck. Opens his shirt and presses on tender bruises that have turned blue. He peels back a bandage revealing a long slice in the skin just below his clavicle and says, "Looks like you're ready to go back. But you better figure out how to get along down there before you end up dead."

He's heard from the nurse that Corn has taken up his post in the mailroom and he's taking some time to learn the ropes. Lila has taken a leave of absence and the mailroom is all backed up; no one's getting the right letters. Corn's old and rheumy and never read well to begin with.

Miller arrives to bring Moses back to B block and the nurse says, "They ought to get him out of there. Transfer him."

"Nah. He'll be all right. He just needs to learn how to make friends." Miller looks past Moses when he says this.

BOTH OF MOSES' KNEES ache as he walks. He can imagine the hollows of his face. He loses his balance, catches himself. Luckily Georgy isn't here to point it out. He's never felt so old. Never felt so yellow, so sure this is his end. He follows Miller from the hospital into the summer sun. It blazes on him, exposing him: He is a different man. He doesn't remember the man who just a few weeks ago had the strength to reach out and grab Lila, the man who last week took off Don's ear in a quick bite and swipe of his head. What damage could he possibly inflict now? What could he endure that wouldn't kill him? The fact that he's been sent back to B block is his justice for attacking Don and a sure sign that around here his life is worthless. But somebody's got to ring the bell. This fight is over.

The block is empty. Everyone's killing themselves in the mess hall. By habit, he walks to his cell and waits for Miller to let him in. A sparrow with a delicate red thread tied to one leg comes and sits on his shoulder. It's Papito. Moses swipes him away.

"Get over here. You've been moved," Miller grunts.

Only then does Moses see that his cell is filled with stacks and stacks of microwave popcorn and smell the cheap movie theater stench emanating from within.

Miller calls him again, "Get over here, old man."

Moses turns and sees Miller standing by the guard station pointing to the stairs.

"You're up here. Let's go. I don't have all day," Miller says, looking over Moses' head.

Moses moves slowly and Miller waits until he is standing in the proper position next to the stairs before he unlocks the gate and ushers him into the birdcage.

Moses grips the stair railing. His hands are blue from a lack of circulation. Veined from the same. His fingernails are yellowed and thick. His skin is cracked and always raw. Since the beating, the bruised kidneys, his body doesn't know what to do with fluids. Instead of satisfying his insatiable thirst, or quenching his parched, papery skin, they speed through him, making him piss every ten Goddamned minutes, piss can or no piss can; mostly it's pink.

Before the beating, Moses sat in the hole for two weeks for what he did to Lila, and when he was sent back to B block, Miller kept his cell unlocked so the lowlifes could get at him if they wanted to. No one came, but Moses fingered and mashed the ball of Lila's hair in his pocket so often it was nearly gone. When he looked to replace it, he saw the Styrofoam cooler where he kept his collection of her hair had been discovered and removed. Misery flamed in him. He couldn't eat; he couldn't sleep.

Perhaps some sun would do him good, he thought the next day, so he joined the lowlifes at rec. He held himself at the back of the line trying to avoid their notice, and found a spot at a concrete table with concrete stools where he could sun himself and find something new to believe in. Then, Don came to him. His tap was casual, really. Don looked bored, as if he didn't much care about Moses or teaching him a lesson about how things were going to go now that he was back in B block. Don was just following orders, his visit a message from Collin.

Don is the size of a refrigerator. He has dark, dark skin with symbols Moses doesn't recognize branded onto his thick, muscled arms. He always wears a green state-issue shirt with the sleeves ripped off to show off his "guns." He calls them that. "Collin wants you to know," his voice was deep and lazy, "that around here, he's in charge." He picked his white teeth when he said it. He spit off to the side then reached down and took Moses under the armpits like a child and tried to make him stand up, but he wouldn't. He clung to the edge of the well-anchored table and kicked his legs out so Don couldn't get him to his feet. Just when Don was about to give up, Moses flew off his seat and was after him. Bit his ear clear off. Collin gave a signal, and a pile of boys jumped him. Beat him and left him for dead.

He longs to have that strength now.

At the top of the stairs, Moses waits for Miller to show him to his cell. It's the first in the row. Moses goes in and lies on the bed. Miller leaves the cell door open. Moses sniffles like a child. A sob slips from him. It's the sort of wail that wakes a man in the night and reminds him of his infancy. He squeezes his eyes closed and huddles in a fetal ball and suffers until he feels something next to him that makes him hold his breath. A presence. It's too delicate and light to be a man; it can't be Don coming to finish him off. He's sure if he opens his eyes it'll be Jorge's ghost. He feels a hand reach out. To kill him maybe? To soothe? It doesn't matter. Moses doesn't want to know Jorge now.

"Hey, Moses," he hears Jorge's ghost say. "Hey, Moses, you cryin'?" Jorge sounds different dead. He sounds young and stupid.

Moses opens one eye and sees Georgy standing over him. He plops next to Moses on the cot.

"Leave me alone, Georgy. How did you get up here?"

"Moses, can you read something for me?"

"Not right now. Read what?"

Georgy pulls his phone book onto his lap and opens it up, "This, right here. Her name. Can you read me her name and her phone number and I'll remember it. I've got a good memory, Moses. I just need to hear it a couple times."

"Georgy, how do you even know it's a woman? Even if it is, no woman is going to want to talk to you."

"That's not true, Moses. Randy from four told me lotsa girls had come to see him cause he called them and they started going out. Just this one, Moses. Can you read it to me?"

Moses looks at Georgy. Eyes not working together, small blue fingers with nails bit to the quick, right leg bouncing up and down so that he has to keep pulling the book back up onto his lap. "I'll read it to you," Moses says. "Give me the book."

Georgy pulls the book closer. His head jerks quickly to the right four times, and he says, "You have to give it back and you better not do anything to it."

"I'm not going to do anything to it. Let me see the book."

"Don't lose the page. This one right here." Georgy keeps his small, spitty finger on the name.

Moses holds the book close to his face, and then pulls it slowly away until the letters come into view—his glasses met their end in the beating. "Laughlin, L.," Moses says, "567...wait, yes, 567-1346."

"Laughlin, L. 567-1346. Laughlin, L. 567-1346. Laughlin, L. 567-1346. 567-1346. 567-13... What was it again?"

"Give me the book."

Georgy carefully hands the book over to Moses.

"Laughlin, L. 567-1346," Moses says.

Georgy smiles. "-46," he says. "That's right."

They hear the others returning from chow. Georgy grabs the book back from Moses and when Georgy looks back at him with a worried expression, Moses reminds him, "567-1346. Why didn't you go to chow?" he asks.

Georgy looks relieved. "I'm gonna call her tomorrow. If I can. If there isn't no problems tonight. Don said he's going to kill you, Moses. When he gets the chance," he lisps. "Miller's keeping the cage open for him so he can." Spit flies through the gaps where his teeth should be and his head twitches to the right four times. "I'm going to call her if there isn't no problems now that you're back," he says. Then he runs down the loud metal stairs to join the others. Anyone can get to Moses, if they want to.

HE DOES NOT SLEEP. The new cot. The open bars. The open stairs. No hair in his pocket to touch or caress to his cheek. No Jorge with his comforting rhythmic apneic breath. No job. No books. He is left for dead. He prays all night that he'll die a natural death, that morning will never come, the sun will stay hidden, his cell dark forever, but as if on cue, the moment the day begins to overtake the night, Jorge's Goddamned sparrows beckon the sun. The birds' calls ring out from their perches on the bars of the birdcage. He's never felt such failure. Even when he was a young man and was denied parole time and time again, it hurt less than this. Lila. Oh, Lila. What has he done? Her smell. Chocolate chip cookies, faintly orange, faintly cassis? He was free when he was with her. Transported out of his body. Out of this life. He loved to fill his head with her. And he blew it.

From the cell directly below, Moses can hear Corn waking early, running the water in his sink, brushing his remaining teeth, preparing for a day at his job. Moses rolls onto his side into a ball. His stomach grinds. Hunger. Humiliation. Horror of what's to come. Would they most likely kill him at breakfast? Or would they wait for lunch? He doesn't have to wait long to find out. A guard calls live count. Moses drags himself from the bed, finds the piss can, urinates, and carrying his aching head in his hands, steps out of his cell. At least for today, he is live and he is counted.

SHELL

As the car draws down Anders Avenue bringing Shell and her dog, Marty, home, Shell can see her mother inspecting the front of the house from the sidewalk. Shell doesn't know what Sid is looking for, but as the car gets closer she can see that the stand of larch behind the house is charred and dripping with foam.

"That's it up on the left," Shell says to Larry, her freckled-faced, feckless, redheaded, sweaty-palmed, down-the-hall neighbor who smells like bologna, always stares at her breasts, and offers her rides upstate whenever he is heading home to Rochester. She never accepts. He hadn't planned on going to Rochester this weekend, but Shell put on a tight tank top and said, "Any chance you feel like heading upstate?" Larry said no, then an hour later knocked on her door and said, "OK. Pack. I took tomorrow off. We'll leave at the ass crack." Shell didn't open the door all the way. She didn't want him to see that the power was not on.

"What happened?" Shell yells from the car. Larry wants a friendly kiss. Shell pulls Marty out of the car and waves him off. "I'll call you and let you know what time I'll pick you up on Sunday," Larry says. She ignores him and he pulls away. Her cell will be turned off by then.

"Mackey's controlled burn," Sid says, still in shock over the planned springtime incineration of brush and scrub that raged out of control in the cornfield in the back of her property. Shell walks to her mother with her dog and a single bag. "When did it happen?"

Sid looks at her and Shell thinks she can still see the flashing lights of emergency vehicles, a choking smoke, flames devouring the line of larch and all the expensive landscaping Sid invested in over the years reflecting in her mother's face.

"Yesterday. I came home to it. What are you doing here?" Sid asks, turning back to the house, as if it is too much of coincidence: her unexpected arrival; the fire licking the back of her house.

Sid and Shell stand near one another. Sid inspects. Say Claire D. hears the news, or someone who knows Claire D. well, one of the club ladies, say. What if perhaps one of them wanders this way to see how the house has fared? Would the front of the house reveal the truth? Or would Sid's carefully tended orchids in the bay window distract a curious eye away from the charred treetops of the backyard?

"Hurry up, boy," Shell says as Marty roots around for a good spot in the dark, neat mulch where he can crouch and get busy between the budding rhododendrons that cozy up the front of the house.

"He looks like a pig."

"He's a Boston terrier."

"Yes, but isn't there a better place for him to do that?" Sid asks keeping her eye on the house.

"Not really. If he goes in back, won't his feet get all covered in soot?"

Sid walks away before Shell can finish the word *soot*.

Sid is dressed neatly in a light gray summer suit. She wears a pink scarf tied at the neck and pulled to the side. It picks up the hints of pink in her fine-knit floral-print sweater. Her hair, still damp from her morning shower, is beginning to frizz out from her scalp in strawberry blond ringlets—wild hair for such a small and delicate woman who so requires order. As Sid walks up the stone path to the front door, Shell notices that her mother's hair is beginning to lighten. Hidden, new white hairs add an overall shimmering effect. While this doesn't make her look particularly old, Shell notices that her mother has changed. The soft pillows of her cheeks, for example, are beginning to lilt below her jaw. She lacks the layer of fat that is the telltale sign of youth.

She seems to be shrinking into a condensed version of herself. Shell had forgotten the lost feeling of standing next to her mother and she remembers suddenly what a shit situation she is in: Gina hasn't returned her calls, Ellen's absence that night at O'Malley's is giving her a terrible stomach ache, and without friends to call on in her moment of dire need, she's had no choice but to come home. She is desperate.

Her father, Ed, is sitting at the old rickety kitchen table with chipped yellow Formica and rusty legs and chairs with ripped leatherette seats. As Sid decorated every corner of the house like the inevitable coming of a tide, Ed fought back by insisting on keeping the table. He likes to have something worn out to look at. Something old and crappy he can sit at and spill food on. The table is the one compromise in the Cavanaugh home décor. Sid won't look directly at it; it is a symbol of what she worked so hard to erase: a worthless, rusty past with no beauty. She stands at the sink and washes the breakfast dishes and averts her eyes from him, from the table. Shell joins her father and crosses her feet on its top.

"What are you doing here?" he asks without looking up from his paper. Sid washes her dishes, dries her hands, and delicately fingers the petals of a bright Vanda, all the time avoiding the view of the backyard and its charred landscape, all the time avoiding the table.

"I promised I'd come home when the movie was done. It's done."

"Yeah, well, where's your husband?"

"He couldn't get away."

"That important, huh?"

Ed is in his underwear, as usual. He sits with his knees spread wide apart so there is room for his copious belly. He wears his slippers with dress socks pulled straight to mid-calf, and navy and white striped boxer shorts—so large they look like bloomers—pulled up over the front of his belly. He wears a white, ribbed, sleeveless undershirt, a wife-beater, tight and stretched to the limit across his stomach, confessing the dark cavern of his belly button. Tufts of copper hair spring insistently out at the neck and at the tops of his shoulders. His dark red hair is splayed across his crown so as not to reveal his shining scalp. His hair looks slightly metallic, as if perhaps it has been dyed, but the gray still shines through. He wears a well-groomed mustache that frowns around his mouth and the expression it gives him always makes Shell nervous. He looks permanently irked.

"Someone will burn that museum down," he says, turning back to his paper. "…If I don't get to it first. No business sticking their noses where they don't belong." Shell sees the article: *Museum Goes Behind Walls: Hardenberg Correctional Facility and the town that shares its name are subject of summer exhibition.* "Dave here with his Mexican yet?" Ed grunts and crumples the newspaper into a heap on the table.

"Dave who?" Shell asks. She is eyeing her father's leftover breakfast. Some egg scraps. A piece of toast.

"Kennedy. Says he knows you."

She knows him all right. Kissed him once in a bar before she married John. Shell calculates how to get Ed dressed before Dave arrives, but there's no way. His prison guard uniform hangs in the garage just on the other side of the kitchen door. Sid won't under any circumstances allow it or anything that has been worn inside the prison and might carry with it some smell or remnant of contaminant—who knows what's carried around in there?—into her hermetic and genteel home. Her father will swagger to the backyard in just his underclothes and his slippers to complain loudly about Mr. Mackey, and accuse Dave Kennedy and his Mexican of taking advantage of him before the work has even begun, and that is that.

Soon there is a knock at the sliding glass door leading from the family room to the backyard.

"Why does he have to come to the back door?" Sid asks.

Ed lumbers to his feet. At the door he asks Dave, "So? How much are you going to take me for?"

The door closes behind him, sealing out the conversation, and the house falls dead quiet. Perhaps it's her father's breathing that fills the space, or maybe it's the general sense that he's bothered by something all the time that makes the room feel pregnant with a problem.

"Your father is gaining weight again," Sid says. "It started before Jorge, but that's just going to make it worse." She vigorously scrubs the counter. "Are you getting a divorce?"

Shell looks up from her father's plate. She licks toast crumbs from her fingers. This little bit of food awakens a deep hunger in her. "What?"

"Well, here you are all by yourself, no announcement. Feels like an emergency," Sid says and ducks into the half bath off the kitchen to brush her teeth in time to get into her late-model Honda and arrive at her accounting office in Syracuse before her subordinates.

Sid comes out of the bathroom. "How's Gina? I've tried to call her all week since it happened and I can't get through to her."

"I saw her last Friday," Shell says. "She's Gina. I haven't talked to her since."

"Well, I'm concerned. She shouldn't be alone right now. Has Ellen heard the news?"

"Yes," Shell says. She suddenly fears Ellen's no-show had to do with her. Or that her mother might interpret it that way.

Sid turns to leave, then pauses by the door to the garage, one hand on her pocketbook, letters and bills she will send at the mailbox on the corner sticking out of it like the plumes of a bird, her back to Shell. Sid turns around and comes to her. Palms the hair out of Shell's face. Shell looks up and suddenly she isn't close to thirty; she is eleven and she can feel her mother looking at her, wanting to ask her to at least look happy.

"How long are you home for? You could use a shower," Sid says and leans down and kisses Shell on the forehead. Then she leaves, stepping gingerly around the uniform hanging on the other side of the door.

"I know all about you guys," Ed says as he opens the sliding door a moment later. "Sit around drinking beer all day, fertilizing my burnt lawn." Shell doesn't hear Dave's muffled response, but Ed replies loudly, "Who needs clothes? It's too nice a day for clothes."

Shell puts the newspaper down, but it is too late. "Don't let me catch you going to that museum. Not while you're in my house," Ed says as he walks through the kitchen, grabs his wallet and keys off the counter. "They're not so bad," he says about Dave and his Mexican. "But keep an eye on them anyway. You can't trust anyone these days." He shuts the door to the garage. A moment later he opens it again. "How about an ice cream sundae? I'll pick you up. 4:10. Sharp." He shuts the door, then opens it again. "Don't tell your mother."

Shell is hidden by orchids. From the bay window in the living room, she sees Dave Kennedy and his partner, whom he calls Pedro, carry the ladder from Dave's truck up the slope of the front lawn and disappear at the side of the house. She gets up from where she is crouching and sneaks into the family room, squeezes herself between the wall and the sliding glass door, and tucks herself behind the curtains. Marty, who thinks this is a great game, barks at her. "Shut up," she whispers. But Marty barks again. She hears Dave and Pedro right outside the door; she steals a glimpse.

Dave is dressed in swim trunks and work boots with white socks pushed down at the tops. He wears a brown t-shirt. It says *Missouri Loves Company*. He wears a sweatband and wristbands like a tennis player. He and Pedro carry the ladder past the sliding glass door and set it up in front of the kitchen window. She comes out from behind the curtain and darts to the kitchen.

The view through the kitchen window from the outside is obscured, she's sure, by the sharp glare of the morning sun shining from the east against the back of the house. Shell walks to the window. The men are just on the other side. Beyond them is the damage from the fire, the trees charred and draped in fire-retardant foam, the Alabama bluegrass and the patio bricks black with soot. It looks like a demented winter wonderland. Shell stands face-to-face with the men. She is pretty sure they can't see her, which is a thrill. Dave begins to climb the ladder. Pedro holds it. Dave says something to Pedro that she can't make out and then he stops moving up the ladder so that she is looking directly at his crotch. She smiles, can't help it, even thinks of reaching her hand out. To do what? She doesn't exactly know. So she does, as if waiting for someone to hand her a bouquet of flowers, and just as her fingers graze the petals of Sid's delightfully purple Vanda, Pedro looks up. A glimmer of acknowledgment flickers across his wide, dark face. He sees her. Sees something, anyway. She steps back into the kitchen, into the dark. His face returns to normal. He says something to Dave. She can't hear it exactly.

Upstairs, she turns on the shower and lets it run for a while to steam up the bathroom. When she opens the door to her parents' room, she looks behind her, as if someone might be there, but she is alone. Shell runs a finger along the bed then walks to her father's dresser. On it is the small piece of white marble broken roughly from some larger source that has always been there. She picks it up and runs it along her cheek like she used to do as a child. She smoothes the cold stone under her nose and smells it. It has no scent except the clear smell of water and something ancient and earthy. Rubbing it along her cheek calms her as she opens his top drawer, moves his socks aside to reveal a small leather box. She pulls it out, and reaches around knowing exactly what she is feeling for. Her fingers find a small key, simple like the one she used to have for her jewelry box. She pulls his birth certificate, the papers for his safety deposit box, and his parents' wedding rings aside and underneath she finds what she is looking for. She fans a stack of one hundred dollar bills and the air blows her hair from her face. She counts the stack. There are twenty-three. She slides five bills off the top, enough to keep John's phone on and for him to buy some groceries. She folds the bills and sticks them in her bra.

They hardly ever fought, Shell and John, and she never thought of John as an asshole, but that night at the party at the loft in Williamsburg where she met up with him after leaving Gina, Shell overheard John talking about their film, *Panoptic*, to a short, slim, red-headed man wearing a shiny Hollywood suit. John said he believed in ideas. "Ideas and art are king," he said to this slick young movie-executive type, who was at this party for precisely this reason: to see John, to hear what a genius he is, to get excited about *Panoptic*, to write Shell and John a huge, life-saving check upon which everything depended, and give them a promise to promote the hell out of the thing now that it is ready for festivals and, hopefully, wide distribution…but not too wide. John doesn't want the film to lose its integrity by playing at every cheap seat in America.

In the car on the way home from the party, John reached for her hand, and there in the back of the car she let him pull her pants down, rip open her shirt and they had sex with the driver watching, and it felt perfect because everything was going to be OK. But as the week went on and they heard nothing from their lawyer and no check came, they fought a lot. John wanted her to ask her friends for help. She tried to call Gina but couldn't get through; for some reason she was embarrassed to tell him that Ellen hadn't shown that night. The electricity was already off. Their phones were about to be turned off, and without them, no one could get hold of them, and they'd never finish the deal. They were hungry—Marty was getting wild with discomfort—and she feared what was about to become of them, so she packed Marty up and came home. Today, John plans to go find a free meal.

Shell lets the shower steam her clean. I'll replace it as soon as the check comes in, she promises herself.

"Go have a seat over there, and someone will be right with you." A bank teller points her to a circle of leather club chairs arranged around a coffee table with neatly fanned magazines and credit union products. Shell wired the five hundred dollars to John and while she was at the counter saw a discreet help-wanted sign. She inquired, even though she was damp and disheveled from her long walk. The teller looked her up and down.

Shell takes a seat in a warm corner of the bank in front of a large sunlit window with some very healthy plants. She peeks outside and sees Marty panting. He's tied to a handicapped parking sign. He needs water. Still, Shell is pleased being surrounded by productivity. It makes her long to be busy, to work in an environment where the rules are clear and the boundaries understood. For two years Shell's been immersed in *Panoptic*. As soon as she and John got married, the rush of the project swept them up and she found herself fully and happily involved in John's vision—he is like that: Compelling and smart and funny and people want to please him. At first she acted as a secretary so he wouldn't be disturbed while writing. Worked temp jobs and paid all the bills so he wouldn't have to worry. When money got low, she found she was really good at convincing people at parties to invest. She wrote pitch letters, found him representation, hired crew, organized the first shoots to put together a pitch reel; she bolstered John in moments of insecurity when he felt bereft of vision. One thing led to the next and she had secured the financing he needed to film the movie. And then she found Lorna Norris, *the* hottest new starlet, who just happened to be at a party they were at on the Lower East Side. In no time Shell was getting permits, greasing palms, and they were filming—a production that awed her. There were trucks of equipment, trailers for her and her production team, for John, talent, make-up, wardrobe, for catering. Whole streets were shut down, blocks blocked off, fake weather produced, and all of this, the production of it all, it had all been Shell.

Then one day, three months ago, it was over. Done.

A very professional woman with a painfully perfect auburn pageboy that doesn't move when she moves says, "Hello, my name is Dorothy Card. I'm the branch manager. Would you like to come with me?"

"Sure," Shell says and follows the woman to a desk behind a smoky glass partition on the other side of the seating area. The music soothes. Shell sits in a chair upholstered in eggplant jacquard and Dorothy leans forward with some brochures.

"What I would really like…" Shell leans forward, and so does Dorothy, "is a job."

"Well, we're looking for someone with experience."

"May I fill out an application, just in case?" Shell asks.

Begrudgingly, Dorothy reaches into her file drawer and pulls one out. "You can go sit over there to fill it out. I'll need the names of three *recent* references. You can leave it with one of the girls when you're done." Dorothy points her back to the seating area and walks away without saying goodbye.

DAVE IS WORKING ON the front of the house when Shell walks up. His dark hair is pushed up by his silly sweatband. His shorts are wet from a recent hosing.

"Hey, McEnroe. Hot day, huh?" she says.

"Actually, it's just too nice a day for clothes. I think I'll go nude."

"I'm sure Ed would be happy to hear you say that."

"I admire the man, frankly. Why not live in your underwear and socks? I think I'm going to give it a try."

"Well, keep it at home, please."

"If you insist," he says and raises his eyebrows. He reaches out to her and awkwardly, but gently, punches her arm. Shell looks away and feels for her wedding ring.

"You know, I've got to talk to your father about something," he says. His tone is serious. "I found pretty heavy termite damage, which is rare in this climate. It's all over the house. I am not looking forward to breaking that news to him. Any advice?"

"You could do it naked. It might distract some of his focus away from the news."

"You know," Dave says cocking his head. "That's not a bad idea." He throws Marty a stick. "Would you go all nude, or just go Ed-style with the socks and underwear?"

"I'd go all nude," Shell suggests. "Then he'd really want to get the conversation over with."

"Boy, am I glad we were able to have this chat. I feel so much better."

"Anytime," Shell says. "Glad I could help. Come on, beast." Marty drops the stick and follows her to the front door.

"Hey, Shell," Dave says and trots up behind her, "Do you have any interest in maybe catching a beer while you're around?"

When Shell kissed Dave Kennedy she was home for a weekend with Gina. They had gone to Lucky's, and Shell was drunk. She came out of the bathroom into the dark hallway and walked into someone. A man. Somehow—she's gone over this and she still can't imagine how it might have happened, but it did—their lips grazed each other. Out of impulse, or reflex, or maybe she might even admit desire, they kissed one another. It was Dave. In high school she used to search for him on the weekends in hopes they'd end up out on a country road tangled together in a prickle of raspberries. That night in the bar, the kiss shocked her. It jolted her awake. John, who had always been everything to her, seemed small and unhealthy, nervous and weak. Suddenly his every move was held up and compared to Dave Kennedy: A man of simple ambitions, chestnut hair and few words; a man without the heavy burden of ideas weighing him down. He had an easy sense of humor. But with time, she'd forgotten about him.

Thinking of it now just makes her miss John. "Maybe," she says. She has no intention of ever following through.

IN HER ROOM SHE sits in a white wicker vanity chair and she practices answering the princess phone that sits upon it. *Hello, Shell Cavanaugh,* she says in a business-like tone. She sits up straight and examines her face in the mirror. She imagines Dorothy Card calling at any moment. She is poised to answer the phone as if it is an imminent possibility. She looks out the window. The vanity chair is for a girl so her knees are near her chest. The house is quiet. There is a crow riding the summer breezes on a branch of the silver beech outside her window.

When she was a girl she had a dream that went like this: The princess phone would ring. There would be a man on the phone, a prisoner. She would know that he was hers and hers alone. He would love her the way she wanted to be loved, freely and without having to ask for it. He would arrive through the phone and climb on top of her. She could feel the weight of the prisoner's body. The weight is what she remembers best, how she longed to be that close to someone and how real it felt, almost too much for her small body to bear. She could feel his flesh against hers, his body between her legs. She was only a child then; to her this was sex.

Shell goes to the bed. She pushes Marty away. She puts her hand between her legs. She closes her eyes. She tries to escape into the smothering weight of someone's want. Shell disappears. Her body is no longer her body. Her life is no longer her life. This house is not her parents' house.

AT EXACTLY 4:10 AN anemic horn sounds Ed's impatience. Shell is waiting by the front door. She hurries to the truck, opens the passenger door and pulls herself onto the ripped nylon seat, her thighs scratched by the foam poking through. She wears a light summer dress. She has done her hair. She is wearing a little bit of make-up.

Without talking, Ed pulls the rattling truck from the driveway and speeds down their quiet, respectable street.

"What time did they leave?" he asks stopping short at the stop sign.

"Just a couple of minutes ago," Shell lies. They left at least two hours ago.

This old ritual of theirs, sneaking behind Sid's back to go to Happy's to eat ice cream sundaes, this is the only thing that Shell has ever seen that will break Ed's mood. They share a history of sneaking food. Aside from a genetic predisposition to gain weight under stress and a tendency to disappoint Sid, it is all they share.

Hardenberg is the same. But the way she sees it now is different. Shell, Ellen, and Gina learned Hardenberg by heart together. They learned the best bike routes—when to move from sidewalk to road, when to avoid cracks and potholes, how to speed across intersections and through lots. They learned how to time the lights so they never had to stop as they flew on their bikes from the lake to town, Shell on her blue no-name ten-speed, Ellen on her perfectly gorgeous new Schwinn, Gina wobbly on Ronnie's old bike. They could make it from Shell's house on the east side all the way across town to the sub shop next to the prison and over to whatever tower her father was working in that day in less than twenty minutes. They'd find his tower by standing beneath it yelling his name. "Dad." "Mr. Cavanaugh." "Sergeant Cavanaugh." Ed would lower a bucket on a rope so Shell could put a foot-long Italian, his afternoon snack, in the bucket and yell "OK!" Gingerly he'd draw the treat up, the girls watching as the bucket tipped and swayed until it disappeared through a tower window and his huge hand waved. Then they'd take off and ride laps around the ten-block length of the prison. Along the river, they'd stop and throw stones into the trees, sending crows flying up in black clouds, and Gina would ask, "Do you think my dad can see those birds? Next weekend, I'm going to ask if he saw those crows flying. I'm going to tell him it was us."

Even though Shell never met Jorge, the landscape appears altered now that he is gone. When they were in tenth grade, Ed came home and told her, "Invite Gina Padilla over on Saturday. Ask her to spend the night. Her father thinks she's dead." Shell looked up from her Math II homework. Sid looked up from her *Décor* magazine. He didn't explain.

"I don't really talk to Gina much anymore. We're not really friends," Shell said, and she tried to swallow the memory of the night they hid in Gina's house with the lights off so no one would know they were there, Ronnie out looking for them, all three girls squeezed around the receiver of a telephone, a prisoner asking them, "Tell me again what you girls look like?"

"Tell her Jorge knows she's not dead," Ed had said.

"Why on earth does he think she's dead?" Sid interrupted.

"Why did Marie marry a murderer? Who knows why Marie does what she does? She told Jorge Gina was that girl they found out in the swamp last weekend. Showed him the article and everything. Just tell Gina I'm going to bring her to see Jorge. Can you do that for me?"

Gina was foreboding in her ripped clothing and her dark flopping curls covering her face. She slipped through the halls of Hardenberg High quickly on long legs. Boys followed because she was beautiful, but she never let them near her. Shell walked behind her. Despite Gina's slouched shoulders, she was Amazonian. Normally, when she saw Gina in the halls, Shell turned on her heels and avoided her like a criminal. But this was different. Shell was trying to get her attention. She followed Gina and tried to see her face, but Gina worked to disappear. She was slouchy and broken, making it hard to place the blame for Ronnie's death on her wide shoulders.

"How are you?" Shell asked. Gina kept her face hidden behind the metal locker door. "I was wondering what you were doing on Saturday. Thought you could come over. Maybe spend the night."

"Did your friends ditch you?" Gina sneered.

"No," Shell said bitterly. "My father asked me to tell you that your dad knows you're OK. He'll bring you to him on Saturday. You can spend the night so your mother doesn't know."

Gina closed her locker, fingered a curtain of hair back and tucked

SARAH YAW

it behind her ear, and looked at Shell with piercing violet eyes. "What time?"

"Two."

Gina flipped her hair back in front of her face, and in two quick strides was out of earshot.

"My mother killed me off," Gina said, leaning back against Shell's headboard that Saturday night. Shell and Gina sat on Shell's bed in their pajamas. It was March, too warm for early spring. Gina wore a t-shirt that hardly covered her, and every now and then Shell saw flashes of Gina's underpants. Shell wore a frilly little cotton number. Sid was always buying her matching sleeping outfits that were a little too snug, and Shell was supposed to be prettier in them than she was.

"It's my age," Gina said. "I just turned sixteen. Marie doesn't like how close Jorge and I are, especially now that I'm older." She paused, picking at a thread on the creamy eyelet comforter. The contrast of Gina Padilla sitting there, perfect and fresh in her haphazard beauty, made the comforter seem like an old rag. "Or it has to do with the age of the girl Jorge killed," she said matter-of-factly. "She's protective? I don't know." She stretched back, laying her head on Shell's pillow, one long leg extended, the other casually crossed over her knee. "Thanks for inviting me over. You didn't have to do that," Gina said. "I miss how it used to be. With all of us. You, me, Ellen. I wish it could be like that again."

Shell looked down and pulled on the threads of the comforter. Gina spent Saturday nights with them from then on and Sid and Ed always picked the girls up from college and drove them back together. Shell ignored her mostly. She hasn't thought about that in a long time. She was unkind to Gina for many years.

Shell's window is down as Ed drives. The smell is surprisingly sweet compared to New York. They pull into Happy's parking lot and drive full speed into a spot.

The décor has been updated. It looks like a retro Fifties burger joint and smells like grease. A waitress with big, permed brown hair

88

and heavily sprayed bangs comes to their table and introduces herself.

"Camille," Ed interrupts. "We'll have a banana split, a cup of coffee, and a Peanut Butter Bonanza. What do you want to drink, kid?"

It takes a second for Shell to realize he is talking to her. "Diet Pepsi," she says.

"Coke OK?" Camille asks. Shell nods.

The food comes out quickly and soon they are lost in their routines of eating. Ed's face softens as he slices a banana with the side of his spoon and shovels a dripping heap of vanilla ice cream and chocolate sauce into his mouth. She considers telling him about the money, but instead she digs around in her peanut butter and chocolate and whipped cream and nuts. When she was eleven, these trips were her father's way of keeping her young, buying some time before she became a teenager. She loves him for this. She loves that her mother wasn't allowed to join them. When they are here, none of Sid's questions, none of her nags, none of her comparisons with other wealthier families like the D.'s, none of her talk about the future, or how a young lady brings the spoon to her mouth not her mouth to the spoon, none of this dominates the conversation. When they are here there is no conversation. Shell knows he won't ask her how she is doing or why she came home.

Coming here with her father makes her feel useful, as if she has some special power that helps the loosening of his brow, the relaxing of his features, the slowing down and quieting of his breath. It is a guilty pleasure, not sharing him with her mother, helping him distance himself with ice cream from the life sentence he is doing in eight-hour shifts. His words. She knows that even though he is quiet and doesn't talk much, he'll put his hand on her shoulder as they leave the restaurant. He'll steer her to the truck. She'll push her shoulder into his touch.

GEORGY

MOSES LOOKS DOWN THE stairs and considers tripping and falling. Ending it that way. But he's too scared. He takes it one step at a time and remembers running from Caruso, the words from "Death in Venice" relentlessly pursuing him. They roll around in his mouth now and he can feel the horrifying tug of his stutter, "Since human development is human destiny…" With each step down his own Bridge of Sighs he sees how this is a different sentence: He is facing true condemnation. He expects them to take their time sauntering over to him. He imagines they'll wait for him to reach the bottom just so he'll have to suffer down the last two steps then they'll jump him and beat him 'til he's meat.

But when he gets to the bottom Collin, Georgy, and Don, listless and half-asleep, remain seated in chairs in the gallery. Moses pretends not to notice them and stands near the guard station ready to march to chow, his intestines running ice cold. He can't help but steal a look at Don. A large white bandage covers his left ear. Moses can still feel the rubbery cartilage, the wiggle of it between his teeth.

He enters the mess hall and follows along the wall single file. Four rows of stainless-steel-topped tables run the length of the room. The seats are bolted to the tables and sit the men one across from the other. Across from Moses is Georgy. Collin and Don, the two Moses are most concerned with, sit a few seats from him. They are too blurry-eyed to bother with him.

When Moses spoons a forkful of watery egg into his mouth, he breathes easy. For the moment.

The first full day back in B block, Moses awaits his fate sitting on the edge of his cot all alone, trying to muster the will to face his death with a modicum of pride. The pride wavers. He periodically bursts into tears. But it doesn't matter. No one comes for him. And he is called for chow two times and final live count, and not one person gives him even a second glance.

The next morning after chow, instead of returning to his cell, he walks past the stairs, past Collin and Don sitting in their illegal chairs in front of their illegal television watching *The Price is Right*, and he takes a seat at an illegal picnic table nearby, on which sits the day's newspaper. Moses can't see the words, but it doesn't matter. He doesn't care to read it. Instead he pretends to look at it, while stealing glances at the men. Once, Don looks up while Moses spies on him and instead of coming to Moses and killing him, Don reaches to his bandaged ear, and returns his gaze to the TV.

Later that morning, Miller comes in and drops a box at Collin's feet, and then hands him something else and walks away. Collin shuffles through the box, gets up and throws a pack of cigarettes at Don and one at Georgy. Moses has never seen either of them smoke, but it wakes a longing in him that he's pretended not to notice since he ran out of commissary and hasn't been able to buy a pack of his own.

Collin walks over to Moses and stands at the end of the picnic table without saying anything for a minute. Moses quickly glances at Collin and right back at a newspaper ad for a Ford convertible. Collin looks down at Moses under heavy lids. He kicks the table. Moses thinks this is it and suddenly has to go to the bathroom. "Hey, old man. Heads up," he says, and tosses a pack of cigarettes at Moses. They land on the middle of the table and Moses doesn't dare touch them. Collin walks away.

At noon, when the men line up to go to the mess hall, Moses slips his palm over the pack and quickly stashes it in his pocket.

THAT AFTERNOON, AFTER THEY return from rec, before they go to chow, Collin takes the box that Miller brought to him earlier and, carrying it on his hip like a woman holding a baby, stops at the table next to Moses. He stares at Moses for a long time. Collin moves closer to him and puts the cardboard box on the bench next to Moses. Collin sits down on the other side of the box and waits for Moses to look inside. In it Moses can see a mass of brown hair, and silky pink fabric peeking out from under the hair. He looks back at his paper, and Collin laughs a high-pitched hyena laugh, and snorts loudly. He stands up and leans close to Moses' ear. He sniffs, and runs off with the box.

Georgy is sitting in Collin's chair, his leg bouncing like mad, the phone book open on his lap, his head bent low trying to make out what he sees. Periodically, he shakes it violently as if to right his eyes. Don is asleep. Moses feels for the pack of cigarettes in his pocket and slowly takes it out. He unwraps it, smells the cigarettes and that deep desire yanks at his body. If only he had some way to light one.

"Wanna light?" says a deep feminine voice just over his shoulder.

Moses turns slowly around. There is a wall of pink clinging satin, the large bulges of a man poking through in the most vulgar way. Moses looks up and up and there is Collin wearing an enormous brown curly wig and bright pink lipstick. He holds out a lighter and zips his thumb along the back of it. A high flame wags in the air. Moses turns back and slowly pulls a cigarette from the pack. He knows by doing this he's entering into some sort of agreement. He puts this thought out of his head as he places the cigarette between his lips and draws in deeply, catching the flame and lighting the cigarette.

Collin straddles the bench next to him and pushes his chest forward and thrusts out his hand, "Maxine," he says.

Moses takes his hand, but doesn't look him in the eye, "Charmed, I'm sure," he says snidely, and focuses on the long silky inhalations of his cigarette. His whole body relaxes as he breathes in the smoke, as it swirls through his nasal cavity and rushes out his nose. He feels light-headed.

"I have harder stuff, if you're interested," Maxine offers. "Just let me know," she says in a low, husky voice.

SARAH YAW

"No. No, thank you." Moses looks straight ahead.

"Or anything else. I like to take care of people. Maxine takes care of her people," she says and licks Moses' ear. Moses swats her away. Maxine giggles and gets up and loudly makes her way over to her chair. "Up!" she yells in the booming voice of Collin, and Georgy flies out of the seat and runs as fast as he can away from him. Moses can hear the frantic slap of his cheap shoes as he runs the whole forty-cell length of the block. Birds are awakened by it; they fly and chirp. "Shut those fucking birds UP!" yells someone high above.

Moses returns to his cigarette. He pulls the air through the paper, letting it burn quickly to his fingers, and uses the cigarette to light another one. Jorge would not approve of his new lifestyle. Taking cigarettes from Collin he didn't earn. Moses remembers the warning the night Jorge died: don't steal, no phone calls, *claro?* From behind he hears the approaching slap of Georgy's feet on the concrete gallery floor like a wildebeest. He comes running back full speed to the stairs, turns on his heels, and bolts past Moses, the sound bouncing through the open hall. As Georgy passes, Moses catches a whiff of himself and thinks perhaps a part of him has already died. But without a job, without commissary, he can't buy the good soap. Or the good toothpaste. He's out of everything and left with prison issue, which he refuses to use, convinced it's full of glass or experimental substances from the government. So his mouth tastes like bile. He'd like a few things, essentials. And there are other things he would like to have back: his typewriter, the *World Literature Anthology*, his beloved paper. Certainly Jorge couldn't fault him for wanting those.

He gets up from the picnic table. His ass hurts from sitting so long and he stretches before he walks over to where Maxine nods off. Standing next to her he says, "There are a few things. Soap. Toothpaste. You know, the good stuff. And I have some papers and books, a typewriter they took from my cell. I'd like those back."

Maxine doesn't open her eyes. Moses doesn't know if she's heard him, or if he crossed a line coming over like this. He looks at Don. Don covers his ear and looks away. Moses returns to his seat at the picnic table. He keeps an eye on Maxine to see if there's movement, a flicker

94

that indicates she heard the request. He promises himself he'll only ask for the essentials. Georgy comes flying back by, turns at the end of the gallery and as he sprints past again, Maxine holds up her hand and screams "STOP!"

A FEW DAYS LATER, Georgy is hopping around from floor to table to TV holding his phone book, head twitching to the right, leg bouncing up and down when he sits, asking questions, asking favors. "Collin, is you ever going to get me that hat and the Polaroid?" Collin is Collin again, quiet and sullen. Maxine hasn't appeared. Georgy is pissing everybody off.

Moses is sitting at his picnic table, the paper spread in front of him. This is the ritual that has replaced all other ritual in his life. The newspaper and a daily cigarette, his two remaining pleasures. Despite his withering vision he has become sure enough that he's not going to be killed anytime soon, so he has started to actually read the paper. Mostly advertisements for things he's never heard of. Cellular phones. MP3 players. Global Positioning Systems.

Georgy comes to him, phone book under his arm like a college boy and says, "I called her. I told you I got a good memory, Moses. And you know what? You and Don was dead wrong. She's a woman, Moses. Just like I said she was."

Moses isn't listening.

"And she's young and pretty. I could hear it in her voice," Georgy continues.

Just then, Miller comes in with a large box and drops it loudly next to Collin. There is a crash on the concrete floor. Collin jolts awake from his nap, and he looks mad as hell. Moses is curious, but he's afraid of Collin's unpredictable behavior, especially when he's come off a long high, so he waits for the box to pique his interest.

"Here's your shit," Miller says to Collin and walks away.

Collin closes his eyes again and his head bobs to the side. Then bobs to the other side. Georgy, who's sitting on the picnic table, leg going a mile a minute, phone book falling off his lap, brings it back up to his chest and hugs it like a teddy bear. He asks, "Collin, did I get my hat?" Collin's eyes shock open and he wipes some drool with the back of his hand. He gets up slowly, walks over to Georgy and lands his fist like a wrecking ball on the side of his head.

"Shut the fuck up, Georgy," Collin says quietly. On his way back to his chair he pokes Don in the head just above his bandage, just because. Don cowers. Georgy shakes his head, trying to right himself. Collin flops into his chair and looks over the arm and picks through the box. "Moses, come get this shit out of here," he says.

It's all there. The paper. His beloved typewriter. The *World Literature Anthology*. The stylebook. Some zesty green soap. Minty-fresh toothpaste. Moses spends two days cloistered, poring over the paper, making edits, inserting citations. He's embarrassed by the mistakes he finds. He realizes now that he wouldn't have done very well. It's not as good as he thought it was. But still he loves that he has it. That he wrote something scholarly. He decides to rewrite it. Maybe if he gets it just right, he'll send it to Wilthauser on his own.

Propped up on his bed, enjoying his cigarette, the book open on his lap, he looks up, and standing in the open door of his cell is a man wearing a gigantic brimmed hat. He can't quite see who it is. The man is lit from behind. Moses' heart pounds in his chest.

"Moses," says the man in a low, macho twang.

"Yes?" says Moses.

"Can you help me?"

"I don't know," he says cautiously.

"I need you to help me write a letter," the man says and steps forward into the cell.

The light hits the camera hanging round his neck first, then the thin phone book he's holding with his left arm, then finally his face.

"Georgy, what the hell are you doing in that hat? You look like a Goddamned idiot."

"Ain't I great?" Georgy grins. "Collin got it for me. It and the camera. Moses, will you take a picture of me in my hat and help me write Laughlin, L. a letter? I think if she gets my letter and sees a picture of me she'll talk to me next time I call."

"Nope," Moses says. "Turn yourself around and take that phone book with you. That's the devil's work, Georgy. I won't partake in it. You shouldn't either."

Georgy comes on in and sits next to him on his cot. "Here," Georgy says removing his gigantic ten-gallon Stetson so he can take the camera from around his neck. "Take a picture of me over here. I don't want bars in it." He leans over and hands Moses the camera.

"Are you deaf?" Moses asks, refusing the camera.

"No, I'm not deaf, Moses. I heard you, but I can't take a picture of myself. You've got to help me." He nudges the camera into Moses' hands.

"What do I do with this thing? I can't use this."

"Yes, you can, Moses. All you got to do is aim it at me and press right here. The picture will come right out the bottom."

"This is ridiculous. You look ridiculous in that hat."

"No I don't. I look good. I used to have one just like this when I lived in Texas. Now come on and take the picture."

"OK. Stop shaking your leg. Sit still, and smile, dammit," Moses says.

"OK," Georgy says, puffing up his skinny chest. He grins. Moses clicks the button and the camera digests and lo and behold a picture spits out the bottom of it. Moses looks at it. "It didn't work," he says.

"It did. It takes a minute for it to develop. See?" Georgy says, coming next to Moses. "I'm right there."

Sure enough a faint, ghostly image of skinny Georgy in that ten-gallon Stetson starts to appear. Then a clear as day picture of Georgy: toothless smile, small, just-bones body poking out of his white t-shirt, the cold concrete his backdrop. Somehow he manages to look sweet. Moses feels soft for the boy.

"Now can you write me a letter for her, Moses?"

Moses looks at him and throws the butt of his cigarette into the piss can. Georgy reminds him of himself when he was a teenager. He has a good heart. Moses had a good heart, until things went wrong with Sally. Surely Jorge couldn't fault him for doing this kindness for the boy. He pulls himself up best he can and makes his way over to his locker, pulls the locker up to his bed, sits, and rolls a piece of paper into the typewriter, securing it with a cocky flip of the lever. "So? What would you like it to say?"

"Well, I'd like to start it like this: Dear Laughlin, L. You don't know me but I called you a few days back and I think you got a nice voice. You sounded pretty on the phone. I sure would like to talk to you, so maybe the next time I call you could accept the charges. I'm in prison, so I can understand if you don't never want to talk to me. But if you did, I sure would like it. Your friend, Georgy Smith. Did you get that, Moses?"

Moses looks at him like he's crazy. On the paper he has *Desr L.* "Not so fast this time," he says to Georgy. "Not so fast." He rips out the paper and puts in another piece. He plunks away at the keys with his index fingers and finally makes it through a clean copy of the letter without making too many errors.

He pulls it out and Georgy looks at it and grins. He takes a pen that Moses has on the locker and he writes his name under the salutation. His signature is illegible, but he's so proud of the letter that when he looks up at Moses and grins, Moses grins back.

"Can you address an envelope for me?" Georgy asks.

Moses takes an envelope and puts it in the typewriter. "Let's make it look nice," Moses says.

Georgy laughs with glee.

When they're done, Georgy folds the letter carefully. His hands shake as he runs his small fingers along the creases. He carefully pushes the letter into the envelope, licks the flap and smiles. Then he folds down the flap and runs his finger on it to seal it. Moses hands him a stamp that he found in his box of books, and Georgy sticks it on. Moses is pleased. He didn't know it until now, but he's been lonely without Jorge.

"I'm going to go mail it," Georgy says running out of Moses' cell.

Moses hears his heavy child steps ring out. He looks down and sees Georgy has left his phone book. Moses looks at the front of it.

He reaches out to touch it, but pulls back. Moses used to spend all his free time dialing women, hoping one would be desperate enough to answer. But when he met Jorge and Jorge taught him the truth about punishment, he stopped and hasn't tried to escape his incarceration since. But Jorge is gone. And by the looks of him at his end, perhaps there wasn't much truth to all that. He reaches for the book again, but at the last minute thinks better of it and pulls out a cigarette instead. He lights it. His second-to-last.

A moment later, Georgy comes running back to the cell, alarmed. When he sees his book on Moses' cot and sees that it's just as he left it, he collapses onto the cot, grabs it, clutches it to his breast, and smiles. "Would you like to look at it, Moses?"

"No," Moses says looking at the cigarette quickly smoldering to smoke and ash.

"Sure?" Georgy asks. Carefully, he holds it out to Moses. Moses looks up at him. He is such an innocent boy, he thinks. What was it he did to get in here? Armed robbery, murder in the first degree. Moses can't imagine it. It's like a five-year-old boy is handing him his homework. Moses reaches for it. Georgy pulls it back and clutches it close and Moses feels a burn in him that he'd like to snuff. Shit, he thinks. He wants to grab the book from Georgy. Rip it from his hands. Then he takes a deep breath and when he exhales he says to himself, *I'm falling apart. Everything I thought I believed in is shit.*

"You won't hurt it. I know you won't," Georgy says, painfully pulling the book from his chest.

"I won't hurt it, Georgy. I promise."

"I know," Georgy says as he lets it out of his hands, and shakes his head to loosen his worry.

Moses takes the book and fans the pages looking for H. A dry sweet smell washes over him. He scans the page looking for H-A, but Lila is not there. And then he knows that the book means nothing to him. It was just the hidden promise that he could reach out and into her life that made it tempting. He almost chuckled at himself that he had been so afraid of it, as if the book itself were dangerous. He flips through aimlessly. For fun he looks up his own name, Singleton. There are a few. Buffalo isn't far. It's not hard to imagine some of his father's people living out this way. He never knew his father's family. He'd like to, perhaps. No. On second thought he wouldn't like that. He goes to the front of the book and looks at a map of the state. He looks at Buffalo and sees the area codes there. One of those would be his…if he weren't here.

BIRD

IN THE THREE DAYS she's been back in Hardenberg, Shell's discovered it doesn't take long to forget who you are. It is as though the person you are in your real life—wife, movie producer—is some sort of mirage, a thin, wispy rendering that since she's been home has been rearranged as easily as dust.

Marty crawls out from under the covers, jumps off the bed, paws open the bedroom door with purpose, and trots into the hall. He stands outside Sid's office, sniffing at the bottom of the closed door. Shell follows and hears a beating on the other side of the door. A frantic thud. A savage sound, like a heart, not a drum. The hair on her body stands at attention. Marty rears back and puts his paws on the door. There it is again. Thud. Thud. Thud. Thudthudthud. The beating of an arrhythmic heart. Is it coming from Sid's office, or is it coming from her? Marty looks at her, as if to say, What's the matter with you? Open the door.

She opens it slowly. The warm, moist air smells of fresh spring green growth, days and days of rain, and charred pine. It is a nauseating combination, the thickness of it. She looks around the room. Papers are scattered across the floor. The window facing the backyard is wide open. That is no mystery. She opened the window herself the other day when the weather broke and forgot to shut it. She nervously shuts the window and gathers the scattered papers and inspects them, trying to put them in some order, but they are covered in graphs and charts that have no meaning to her. "Shit," she says, and just as she does a bird flies into her face and hits her on the nose. She screams, of course. Her nose stings from being touched by something wild. She is brushed again by the beating wings. This time she feels a flash of wing flip the hair up off her neck. She grabs a pillow off the pullout and turns to swat it away.

She runs from the room, slams the door, puts her ear to it. The window is shut so the bird is trapped in the room. It flings itself against the door once more, then nothing.

She opens it again, cautiously. There is no movement. She creeps behind the desk and there on the plastic floor mat by a desk chair wheel is a small starling. It is black with iridescent flecks of purple, blues, and reds. It has a bold yellow beak. Its eyes are still, but its breath flutters quickly in and out. It is stunned. Shell reaches down and picks it up. The rapid beat of its heart in her hands and the quick breaths of an animal that is fully prepared to die frighten her. She moves carefully to the window, but when she removes one hand to open it, the bird shakes loose and frees itself. It flaps frantically around the room. Its display is hideous.

Back in her room, she dials Gina's cell. It rings and rings and rolls to her voicemail again, which is officially beginning to worry her.

Then the princess phone rings. And it startles Shell. It is loud and the fancy receiver shakes. Shell was twelve when her mother gave her the phone and her own line, and Ed said, If a prisoner calls you, don't you ever, I mean ever… And her mother cut him off, Not now, Ed. But as Shell reaches forward to pick up the phone to answer it, she remembers a prisoner calling. She remembers the operator asking if she would accept the charges. She remembers his voice.

"Hello?" a woman says on the end of the line. "Shell Cavanaugh? Is this Shell Cavanaugh?"

"Yes. This is Shell," she says.

"I know it's last minute," the woman says, "This is Dorothy Card, from Hardenberg Federal Credit Union, but can you come in tomorrow morning? We're short staffed."

"Yes! I can," Shell says.

"Good. Be here at seven o'clock on the nose for the morning meeting."

"Seven," Shell says. "I'll be there."

"Good," the woman says and hangs up.

John's cell rings too many times, as if someone were on the line and not picking up. In the vanity mirror, she looks pale. She pulls her dirty blond hair behind her ears. The skin around her gray eyes looks dark and unhealthy.

"Hello?" a woman answers.

"Hello?" Shell says. She dialed the wrong number.

"Who is this?" the woman asks.

"I'm sorry. I must have dialed incorrectly."

"Shelly? Is that you?" the woman asks. "It's Lorna! Oh my God, Shell. You better come home. Your husband is lost without you."

"He is?" Shell asks.

"Well, not really. I'm taking care of him for you. I cooked him a huge dinner last night. He looks anemic." Lorna's mouth is full. "I'm eating ice cream," she says.

"Is he there?" Shell asks.

"No."

"Where is he?"

"Oh. He's here. He just can't come to the phone. He's in the shower. Do you want me to have him call you?"

"That would be nice. How are you?" Shell's voice cracks. Her throat tight. She is trying to sound cool.

"I'm good. I've been busy keeping John company. He's so needy. You really must come home."

"There's a bird trapped in the house. I should go," Shell says.

"A bird? In the house? That's so gross!"

"Tell him to call me."

"OK. Bye bye!" Lorna sings.

Shell hangs up the phone. She looks in the mirror. She can feel her breath shallow and quick. She moves robotically through the hall to the office, opens the door and looks around. There is no bird. She walks to the open window and looks out. There on the ledge of roof extending below is the starling. It is dazed. It is free to fly away but it does not.

GHOSTS

THE WORST THING ABOUT seeing Jorge is the girl that has attached herself to him. She is young. Sixteen. Moses can only assume the mark around her neck, the blackish line that necklaces her, is the mark Jorge left there forty-eight years ago. Jorge looks the same. Pants stained from urine, his hair disheveled, his mouth twisted in death. And he is burdened. The girl takes up much of the space he needs for his left shoulder, so he's hunched over now, not straight like he was in life. He appears saddled and troubled. He hangs at the entrance to the cell and his circumstance tells Moses everything he needs to know: The girl has her knee in his left rib cage and she's squirmy like a kid. She is giving him a hell of a lot of trouble.

"Why are *you* here?" Moses asks but he's sure he already knows.

Jorge looks around as if he's lost something. He pulls the girl over to Moses' typewriter. He's searching and his eyes trace up the wall and Moses realizes he's looking for his daughter's diploma, her letters. He is agitated. He moves frantically around the cell. The girl is making it difficult. She claws at his back and pulls him in the wrong direction. He makes constant panicked adjustments for the girl but she insists on clamoring over his shoulder like she's trying to get to something. The rest of her life, perhaps. She looks like a real pain in the ass. But that's not the worst of it. The worst part is Jorge. Agitated. Worried. He keeps returning to the desk. To where the letters once were. He turns around and around, confused, frustrated.

"Why am I seeing this?" Moses yells suddenly and jerks forward on the bed. He looks around. Nothing is there. No Jorge. No girl. Just an empty cell. Just the typewriter, the discarded *Anthology* down on the floor. "Have I been sleeping?" he asks. "Haven't my eyes been open?"

A Goddamned dream, he assures himself and gets up and goes to the sink. He splashes water on his face. It was a Goddamned dream. But he's angry just the same.

Papito sits on the locker looking at Moses with his black-as-bead eyes. Moses tries to ignore him, but the bird does his best to be seen. He hops from side to side. He chirps a demanding chirp. Moses thinks he wants to be fed, and thinks he ought to know better: Jorge's dead. "Jorge's dead!" he says to the bird and returns to his cot. He pulls the *Anthology* onto his lap; it's open to "Death In Venice," but he's not reading. Each time he tries to focus on words, he's distracted because something deep down knows it was not a dream.

Don fills the door of Moses' cell and blacks out the light. His shadow grows across the small chamber as clouds float away from the sun and light fills the gallery windows behind him. Papito flutters from his perch on the locker, and Moses looks up in terror. His punishment. Perhaps Jorge came to warn him. Moses stands and backs up into the corner. He grabs the typewriter and picks it up, ready to throw it at Don (he's impressed with himself that he can do this), but Don steps in casually with his arms full of cigarette packs.

"Put that down," he says in a baritone. "I don't smoke," he says, emptying his arms of his booty onto Moses' cot. "I use 'em for barter, but I've got too many already. They're takin' up room. They ain't gonna be good anyhow if they just sit around getting stale. You might as well have 'em."

Moses stands in the corner of the cell holding the typewriter and can't believe what he's seeing. A year's worth of commissary just tossed on his bed. I'm too old for this, he thinks. He puts the typewriter down and stands in front of the cot. There must be thirty packs, at least.

"You look like you seen a ghost," Don says and leans back against the wall, crosses his enormous legs.

"Why are you doing this?" Moses asks looking at the floor.

Don shrugs. "No reason." His voice is deep and dark, but there's no hostility in it. "I like to cook," he says.

Moses shifts a bit so he can get a better look at Don. The bandage is still over his ear. It shines bright white. Papito flutters around the room then lands on the floor near Don's feet. Don holds his hands in his lap and looks down at them like a shy child. "I was running out of room for my spices. Needed to clean house."

Moses doesn't know what to say.

"I like to cook mostly one-pot meals. Rice and peas, oxtail if I can get it. I just got me some saffron, so I'm going to make rice. I got a few hot pots, you know. Work just as good as a stove. One holds grease for deep fryin'. The other I keep clean for sauté or frying up eggs, bacon. I got a third for boiling water. Makes good rice. And don't take long, neither. I sent my oxtails recipe to *Gourmet*. I'm waiting to hear if they'll publish it."

Don looks off into the middle distance. A pleasant look crosses his face. "I'd like to get me an ice cream maker," he says.

"You have a refrigerator down there?" Moses asks.

"Nope. Don't need one. The rice, beans, eggs, flour, bullion, sugar, spices, powdered milk's all good on the shelf. The meat I keep tied up in plastic and stuck in the turlet packed with frozen vegetables."

"It's that cold, eh?" Moses says and remembers the cigarettes. The bounty! He reaches forward and fingers a single pack, curls the plastic wrapper open, shakes the thin ribbon of plastic from his finger onto the floor, then peels off the foil. He smells the fresh cigarettes and slides the plastic skin from the pack, crumples it up and throws it on the cot. He's more interested in the sweet smell of the tobacco than Don's refrigeration.

"Cooler than a cooler. Better in winter, though."

"I'm sure," Moses says. "Cold as a witch's tit in here in winter."

"Sure it is, Moses. Sure it is," Don chuckles and slaps his giant hand on Moses' leg. "Sure it is." He pushes up off the cot. Papito flies up and out of the cell.

"Mind if I take this?" Don reaches down and picks up the

crumpled plastic skin from the pack of cigarettes Moses just opened.

"Feel free," Moses shrugs.

"Spices," Don says and saunters out of the cell, then stops, turns around looks on the floor until he finds the thin ribbon of plastic Moses threw there. When he finds it, he steps back in, picks it up, holds it up to Moses, showing him what he was looking for. "To tie it off," he says then turns and leaves with the slow, relaxed movements of a laborer on Sunday.

Papito flies back into the cell and lands on the floor. He tugs at the foil Moses tossed there. When he gets a good hold he flies out of the cell, holding it in his small beak.

Moses pays him little mind. He reclines on his cot, considers an unexpected thought: Perhaps he was ready for retirement. His eyes pull shut, his hand holding the cigarette droops to his side and he wakes up in a jerk. He throws the half-smoked cigarette into the pisscan, and stacks his cigarettes on top of the locker in ten neat rows, three high, next to his typewriter. He returns to his cot, settles in for a rest, his eyes pull closed. Somewhere nearby, Papito calls frantically.

MAXINE IS NEEDY THAT afternoon. She keeps grabbing at Georgy, pulling him into her lap and nuzzling him, trying to wrestle the phone book from him. Georgy pulls away. He keeps coming to Moses at the picnic table and hugs the phone book to his chest. He looks over his shoulder at Maxine every once in a while. And every once in a while, Maxine says, "Little bitch. You're a little bitch."

"Moses," Georgy says. "When you worked in the mailroom, how long did it take for the mail to get processed? How long 'til a letter got to a guy? If he was waiting for one."

Moses ignores Georgy because he doesn't want to get in the middle of this. He reads the paper. Apparently, there is a controversial exhibit at the local museum about the prison. It is causing protests and calls for resignations.

"Georgy, come here," Maxine demands. "I'm sorry, Georgy. I really am. Just come over to me. Please."

"In a minute," Georgy says quietly but keeps his gaze fixed on Moses for an answer.

"I don't know. A day, maybe more if it came in on the weekend or we got backed up."

"Oh," says Georgy.

"Georgy!" Maxine demands. "Come dance with me. Don, find us some music, won't you?"

Don doesn't look at Maxine, but he lifts the remote and flips the station to cable access and Maxine yells, "Perfect! That's perfect. Come on, boys. Let's dance." She claps her hands, "Don, up. Moses, up. You're partners. Georgy, you're mine. Come on. Snap snap."

They don't know the tune, but it's happy music. A young man sings of a love, of cars, of tragedy, yet the beat keeps beating, and Maxine beats that beat out on the concrete floor with her heels. "Onetwothreefour. Onetwothreefour. Come on! Face each other. Face me, Georgy. Put your hands on each other. Hurry! The song is going to end!"

Moses stands across from Don. Don does as Maxine says with the emotion of a doorstop. Moses is mortified, of course, but he's afraid, too. He's still shaken from the dream, from seeing Jorge in a bad way. Don plops his heavy arm over Moses' shoulder and grabs his hand, puts Moses' hand on his enormous waist, and begins to move slowly back and forth.

"Not like that. Not like that!" Maxine yells, leaving Georgy for a moment and grabbing Moses from Don. He pulls Moses close, arm round his waist, other arm outstretched in a tango, and he moves Moses like a rag doll round the floor. "Like this!" he yells. "Like this!" Then he dumps Moses in front of Don and runs to grab Georgy before the song ends. The men dance frantically round the gallery, Maxine yelling out in ecstasy, "Yes! That's it! That's it!" while men high above in the birdcage yell, "Faggots!"

They waltz, they twirl, tables get kicked, chairs knocked to the side, the television nearly falls. "Faster!" Maxine yells. "That's right! Faster, faggots!" And they follow her commands. Moses clutches Don. Don flings him artlessly through the air. "Dip him!" Maxine yells, and Don dumps Moses toward the floor and catches him right as his back is about to break. Maxine dips Georgy, then romantically rolls him up in her arms, holds him viciously close and says, "I'm better than her." She shakes Georgy. "I'm better than her." She squeezes him tighter each time she says it, "I'm better than her. I'm better. I am." Moses and Don stand nearby, Don still holding Moses in his arms until Moses rips away and they turn their backs to one another in disgust.

"I'm better than her, Georgy," Maxine yells out.

"No," Georgy says.

"You're not getting away. I'm better."

"No," Georgy says and goes limp under the pressure of Maxine's embrace. She discards him to the side. Georgy looks at her defiantly, "No!" he spits.

Maxine glances to the floor. She's quicker than he is. She pounces on his phone book. "Moses!" she demands. "Bring me the lighter."

"No!" Georgy screams.

"Bring it to me, Moses. Now! I gave it to you. It's mine."

Moses steps toward Maxine and holds out the lighter. Georgy says, "No, please, Moses. Don't. Please."

Maxine holds the flame to the edge of the phone book, the pages begin to darken and Georgy thrusts his head in his hands and takes off running. He sprints to the end of the block and back. He runs and runs and runs, head in his hands, and Maxine stands holding the flame licking the book until she bores of this. She tosses the lighter to Moses. Throws the book to the floor, sits in her chair, and when Georgy comes running past, she screams, "STOP!"

AT REC, GEORGY ATTENDS to the row of phones in the yard under the glare of both Collin and the sun. Moses sits far away and refuses to admit he's interested. Moses can't believe his bravery. He wouldn't defy Collin like this. Seeing Jorge scared him shitless. He fears showing the slightest interest in Georgy's exploits will be a punishable offense in the afterlife, or in this one. They seem to mingle more and more; his naptime dreams bleed into his awake afternoons. He's losing his hold on this life.

Georgy smiles at him like a boy waiting to get on his favorite ride. He waves, and Moses loves him just then. He does. He admits to himself sitting there in the blazing sun, that this boy makes his heart beat hard in his chest. He would not, could not deny him joy. Moses has to fight the urge to go make sure he gets the number right. He can hear Georgy laughing as he dials, and he's sure he's going to blow it. But Moses sees something is happening. Georgy's squeezing the phone to his ear. Then he hangs up quickly and bounds away and runs through the yard. He does not hide his excitement.

Georgy comes to him. Falls to his knees on the concrete and puts his small hands on Moses' waist, turns him around so they are close, face to face. Georgy smiles so hard it looks like he's going to bust open and Moses is filled with a feeling he's never imagined and right there under the scrutiny of all who are watching, of all who would kill them both in an instant, Moses has to resist the desire to kiss this boy's cheek. "She answered, Moses! I heard her voice. She said no, but I heard her. Moses," he says looking nervously toward Collin who glowers at him from under an angry brow. "Moses, if something happens. You know, if I can't call her, just keep trying. Please," he begs and looks over at Collin again.

HARDENBERG

SHELL CALLS GINA'S CELL. When she doesn't answer, Shell hangs up and finally calls her office. Her assistant, Veronica, answers, "Newsroom!"

"Hi, Veronica. This is Shell Cavanaugh. I'm looking for Gina. I've been trying to reach her for weeks. Is she in?"

"No," Veronica says. "Can I take a message?"

"Well, yes. Has she been around? Her father died. I don't know if you knew that," Shell says, and remembers the out-of-town boys swarming Gina. The gulf they opened between them. The boys had wanted to know if Shell liked to party and once they determined she did not, they squeezed her out of the way once and for all, and a man reading the newspaper next to her looked up. "Happens every night. I guess it's a good time for her," he said.

"She likes to be in control," Shell said, knowing she shouldn't have. He was a stranger. "I wish she wouldn't. At least not tonight," Shell went on.

"I come here because of her," the man said.

"Does she even know you?" Shell asked, taking a closer look at him.

"No," he said. "Someday she'll know I'm here." He had a mouth that slanted and he spoke out of the side of it. He hunched over in the way of a man of great strength and build. He sipped a pilsner and read the financial pages. He said ma'am, as if he had at one time worn a uniform, and he had a look in his eye of someone who had seen something unimaginable.

"Make sure nothing bad happens to her tonight," Shell said. "Her father just died. He was everything to her."

Veronica asks, "What's your number?"

"I guess I'm just wondering if she's OK?" Shell asks, helplessly.

"Number, please," Veronica demands.

Sɪᴅ ᴄʟᴇᴀɴs ᴀs sʜᴇ cooks. Efficiency is paramount in the kitchen. Shell joins her for a change. Ordinarily she hides in her room, guilty that she is full from Happy's, only descending when it is absolutely necessary, the dinner already on the table, candles already lit, the salad plated, the food beginning to get cold, and with the dissipating heat, her mother withering at the table waiting for her good-for-nothings to come join her as she sips wine.

But tonight, Shell wants to be near someone. Today scared her. When she sat across from her father at Happy's she said, *Gina is missing and I think John is in love with Lorna*, and Ed said nothing. He just spooned banana, nut, and ice cream into his mouth. He shifted in his seat, and she thought this might have been the beginning of a response, but he exhaled a wind as big as a horse's and his response went nowhere. By the time they left, she doubted herself. Had she said anything at all?

She watches her mother move easily through the kitchen. Lemon. Oil. Salt. Tomatoes. Cucumbers. Fish fillets. She wants to tell her, too. But she is afraid. She works a hard butterscotch around her mouth with her tongue, the sugar burning it, the shards lodging themselves in her molars as she crunches.

"This will all be over before third quarter corporates are due. It has to be. Nothing should take this long," Sid says to the knife.

"What will be over?" Shell asks.

"This," Sid says, looking up as if she just realized she is not alone. She waves the knife toward the backyard. Sid looks at Shell and her eyes land on Shell's chest. Shell looks down. Her breasts are falling out of her tank top. She pulls up her shirt. A headline on the newspaper in front of her reads: *Hazy, Hot & Humid: June Breaks All Records*. Shell looks up and sees her mother looking at her again. This time at her arm. Then a thigh. Sid's eyes fall to the floor on a fat foot.

"Your father is killing himself," Sid says as she chews one skinny *haricot vert* at a time.

"What do you mean?" Shell asks.

"The ice cream. I mean all that ice cream. He's going to die," Sid says. "I just hope he's home when it happens."

"It would be terrible if it happened at work."

"It would be terrible if it happened at his girlfriend's house."

"What are you talking about?" Shell asks.

"I mean he's getting fat. Whenever he gets fat like this, it's because he's hiding something, that's all. I'm not dumb. I know how this works. It's Jorge. He refuses to admit it. He's doing what he usually does. Runs away. Eats. Cheats. You remember this."

"No," Shell says. "I don't."

"Yes, you do. When you were eleven he pretended he was taking you out for ice cream after work. I guess he did because you both blew up like balloons then too, but then he'd drive to his girlfriend's house while you slept in the car."

"He did that?"

"Yes. It was his mother then. She had just died. You don't remember? You weren't young. You were the one who told me. He's never been very bright, you know. I mean who would think an eleven-year-old is going to keep her mouth shut?" Sid takes a quick, angry sip of her wine.

"Why didn't you get divorced?"

"For you. I just don't know what he's up to now, that's all."

"I don't think he's up to anything. It's just him and me. We go out and come home, that's all."

Sid doesn't respond, as if she knows better. Shell recognizes the worry in her jaw. She reaches for her mother's hand. It is so small. Like a small silk sack of bird bones. It is cold from holding the wine glass. "I know how you feel," Shell says.

Sid squeezes her hand but lets go abruptly. She is over it. You can't get stuck in it or what will your life be like?

Shell gulps down some wine. She can't be weak. Look at her, she thinks. She's steel. Shell's chest hurts and she wants to crawl into her mother's lap. But they have never fit together. As an infant Shell was awkwardly large. In her first year too heavy for her mother to carry, even. Ed used to have to rock her to sleep because Sid buckled under the weight of her. Still, Shell longs to nestle in and find comfort somewhere. She looks at the skinny beans, the modest portion of fish, the small mound of lightly dressed greens her mother places in front of her and it is all so insufficient.

"I spoke to Claire D.," Sid says.

Shell looks up alarmed, "Oh? What did she have to say?"

"Things with Ellen are elegant. She is planning a large party in the Hamptons. Are you and John invited? I told her I thought you two were having some difficulty."

THAT NIGHT SHELL THINKS of the worst things. For example, she thinks of John and Lorna wrapped in one another's embrace, pulling each other's clothes off, lost in the romance of love. Shell is tormented by a wretched desire.

AT THE CREDIT UNION, she waits in the solitary confinement of the drive-through to be fired. Shell's been missing closing time and leaving her drawers unreconciled each night—the receipts just don't add up. She decides she has to do better. She needs this job. She needs to send the money home to John. Doesn't she? She hasn't heard from him, and no matter how she slices it this is a bad sign.

The cars pull in to her window and Shell tries to be professional but she thinks about John and makes hideous faces at them. When someone asks her for change for a hundred, Shell says, "Sure. Fuck you." The driver just nods. When an old lady pulls up, Shell makes a gagging face. A woman with a young child pulls up; Shell flips the girl the bird. The world pulls in; Shell tells it to go to hell; the world ignores her. She holds up her arm at one point and asks herself, *Is this thing real?* Dorothy never comes, and once again Shell forgets to close up.

A small white American economy car pulls in. It is the woman with the glowing hair, a prison employee she met on her training shift who told her about a leave of absence, about an assault by an inmate she trusted. She pulls up and Shell watches her, awed by how the woman seems illuminated, despite the gray pavement, the rust on her car, the heavy heat that Shell knows is weighing on the world outside of her icy glass cell.

"Oh, hi, Shell. It's Lila," she says. "I can't believe you're here. I thought for sure you'd be closed. I couldn't believe my luck when I saw your light on. I thought it was a mirage."

Shell thinks Lila is a mirage.

But Lila keeps talking. "I hope it's cooler in there. I can't believe this summer. Started so wet and cold. Now it's unrelenting."

"You can see me?" Shell asks.

"Oh yeah. I can see you just fine," Lila says, sending her canister through the tube.

"Oh," Shell says.

THE AIR OUTSIDE IS damp and murky. There are a few crows hopping among the branches overhead. One of them shits on the sidewalk right in front of her. She steps around it with her head held high and an air befitting the dress she wears, refusing to find meaning in this. She has decided to come home from work, dress up so she can feel good about herself, and bring Marty for a nice, leisurely walk. But he begins to pull her, desperate as he is for attention and exercise, and she stumbles down the stone path to the sidewalk as he strains and wheezes. She is at a crossroads. Her clothes are ripping at the seams. She is covered in stains. She has taken on a slump and an awkward shuffling walk. She is exiled at work. Exiled by John, her friends. All of this has to change. Wardrobe, for one. She searched her closet and the only thing she found is the ever-tasteful bridesmaid dress she wore in Ellen's wedding.

It barely zipped, but it did zip, and she feels this is a good sign. She is made up; she is hope-filled; transformation feels real and possible.

Two houses away, an elderly neighbor looks up from her gardening. She pats her rake at the earth while she smokes. Shell holds her head up high and tries walking Marty with purpose; Marty walks her with a vengeance.

She follows Alden Avenue to the end and makes a left on Main. She'll end up walking the loop around the duck pond in the park, but she promised Marty she'd take the long way. Cars pass her quickly, swooshing her dress; wind pulls at her wrapped-up hair. The cars' quick passing makes lives like hers feel small and separate. The effort it takes to move one foot in front of the other gathers and slows her. A truck pulls next to her. Dave Kennedy peers at her from the driver's seat. He is driving her pace. Cars begin to honk and speed around him. The driver of a small green sportster guns past, gives him the finger and yells *Asshole*.

He stops the truck, leans across the seat and rolls down the window. "Hey, Posh Spice."

"I remember you," she says wishing he hadn't seen her. "You're the guy from that erectile dysfunction commercial."

"That's me. I was never quite the same after Ed Cavanaugh got hold of me. Not the best advice, by the way. Telling him naked didn't help at all. On your way to a wedding?"

She looks down. "No," she says.

"Well, you look smashing."

Shell smiles at the patchy ground, embarrassed.

"Come on. Get in," he says.

She holds up the leash, "I have Marty. This is a walk. We're supposed to do this on foot."

"Good point," he says. He pulls to the curb, turns the truck off and gets out. "I could use some exercise," he says adjusting his shorts like an old man.

Quietly, they follow the sidewalk to the end of the block and make their way across the road to the park. When they enter, the birds sing and a cool air washes softly down from the trees.

"You know?" Dave says after a while. "You do everything they tell you to do. Play sports. Go to college. Get a good job. Believe in yourself. You end up back here anyway. It's really not so bad. Hardenberg, I mean. Kind of surprising, huh? It's not such a bad place. There are a lot of people still around," he says and steps off the footpath to the edge of the pond. Marty follows him, dragging Shell across the grass in her heels. Dave reaches into his pocket and pulls out a wad of napkin and opens it up. Inside are the uneaten ends of a hotdog roll. He smiles sheepishly, "Lunch," he says and tosses them to a gathering of mallards who go mad over the offering. "You'll be OK," he says. "Promise."

"I am OK," Shell says. "Everything is going to be fine," she insists because it is, as soon as the deal goes through.

"Oh. OK. Good," Dave says.

HER FATHER IS STANDING in the upstairs hall in his underwear.

"You coming?" he grumbles.

"No," she says, having just returned from her walk.

"I didn't think so." He turns and walks across the hall to the bathroom. He looks old. Smaller even. Not in the stomach—he is quite fat—but in the shoulders. Less broad. More defeated. Shell thinks he looks like someone who's just been dumped. He starts the shower. And then moments later shuts it off, returns to his room, dresses. When Shell hears the rumble of his old truck firing up, she goes to the window and watches him pull out and drive down the street. At the stop sign, he turns left. He isn't going to Happy's. The fact that there are parts of her memory that are blacked out make her mistrust her version of everything.

She calls John on the princess phone. The deal, which was imminent, is delayed now by lawyers' vacations. Her paycheck from the bank is just enough to keep John's cell phone on. He answers, "Look, we need to talk. I've been thinking," he says, and she knows what is coming. "I think I have feelings for Lorna," he says.

Shell looks at herself in the vanity mirror. She looks older, fatter, surely, and scared. "So you love her?" she asks.

"It's complex, Shell," he says and she knows this means Lorna is an opportunity he just can't pass up.

Shell steals the DVD player from downstairs and hooks it up to the small TV in her room. She sits in the middle of her bed and keeps turning up the volume. She wants to fill the air, all the space of her room with the sound of the movie, the sound of Lorna's feet slapping the wet streets of a summertime Chinatown.

She turns the volume up louder. She forwards to her scene, the one she wrote. She catches it late. The scene is ending. The camera pans the crowd. It finds the face of Lee Hawley, who plays the young gorgeous cop, his dark skin glistening with exertion, and zeroes in. The crazy distorted music cues her to rewind.

The room empties of sound like the last swallow of water down a tub drain. The silence intrigues Marty, who looks up and barks. When the scene comes on again, its sound pierces the room right through with the terrific noise of traffic, the urgent rush of Lorna, wrapped up in a long wool trench despite the summer heat. She is hiding her body. She moves quickly through the crush of Chinatown. Everything is made harsh and confusing by the music.

Shell can smell the streets. The rotten puddles of street water. Urine and decomposing vegetables and rats. That sour smell of New York when it's hot. That city grime that covers the body and coats the inside of the nose. All this is in the scene. All this and Lorna's perfect, naked body.

Lorna trips on a curb and her shoe fills with that juice freshly squeezed from the Department of Sanitation truck. Shell jerks in the bed like she is the one who tripped. The camera shows Lorna's ankles. How her skin is like a hammered copper pot. Mottled. Each dent self-inflicted. The pain of cutting her skin keeps her from losing touch with reality, keeps her immune to the paranoia inflicted by the gaze of the plainclothes guards.

It is about the evolution of identity, their movie. How one's perception of self is formed. The forces that play on the body. The movie is based on Jeremy Bentham's panoptic prison, in which the prisoners can't see the guards. Don't even know if they're being watched or not, so the prisoners always behave. John intended the movie to build on Foucault's postulate that the panoptic prison is a metaphor for the self-policing society at the heart of modern social control. It's smart, but it's got good action. There are five different characters like Lorna who rip at their skin to stay free. The pain reminds them to fight against the control inflicted by the gaze of the undercover guards.

Right as Lorna's shoe fills with sewer juice, she sees an old Chinese woman looking at her and she knows this look: This is a guard. This is important. The music swells because for the first time in the movie Lorna doesn't run when she sees the guard. She walks right up to the woman. She stands in front of her, eye to eye; she returns the gaze and unties the tie on her trench and opens it right up. She shows the woman her body, dented and scarred. But what Shell sees is not the distorted body of Julie, the character Lorna plays. Shell sees Lorna. Long, silky blond hair. Perfect, thin, self-assured legs. If legs can be self-assured, Lorna's are. She pauses the movie here so she can look at her.

This is the scene that frustrated John the most. He complained for days how Lorna wouldn't let him make her ugly. Shell looks at her body. She is not ugly. She has a beauty so perfect and easy it can't be ruined. Shell sits forward on the bed, shoulders rounded, and the straps from her tank fall down her arms.

She presses play and the camera pans, finds the chiseled face of Lee Hawley. The music clamors and bangs. The scene ends. Shell rewinds. She wishes she could rewind all the way. Past the beginning of the movie. Past the filming of it. Past Lorna agreeing to take on the project. Past the big financing deal she brought with her. Past the workshops where John perfected the action, hammered out the issues of believability that exist with these sorts of smart films that play on reality. Past her wedding and its promises. All the way past Shell following John to New York after graduating from college and maniacally dieting so he would notice and love her again. Past all that. Past John leaving Albany to go to film school. Past the year they spent together at Albany as young philosophers, to that first moment, the first time she really saw him and took notice: Short. Skinny. Smelling of smoke. His khakis too loose, hanging below the waistband of his boxers, cuffs down so far he walked on them, his small nervous fingers, his skin anemic and college-cafeteria gray, his hair matted and dirty, his few chin hairs unshaven, his glasses crooked, his fantastic blue eyes, his air of tremendous importance, as though he was just in the midst of a conversation which got to the heart of it all, and for this he was forgiven everything: his chronic lateness, his nervous demeanor, his vibe that he'd rather be somewhere else doing something more important with people more significant than present company. When he came to class, even the professor got giddy, as if a celebrity were among them.

Shell wishes she could rewind back to that moment. To when she first noticed him loping into class late, the whole semester nearly already passed. What was it that made that moment the one? It doesn't matter. To Shell he might as well have ridden into class on a horse, a white one.

LUCKY'S

"FREEBIRD" PLAYS AND SOMEWHERE in the empty bar someone tries unsuccessfully to sing along, catching up with the chorus too late, holding it too long. Shell can't see the singer. The back of Lucky's is poorly lit and she is blinded by the overwhelm of her senses: ears packed with the music and the tone-deaf singing; nose full of the scent of urinal cake. It is too dark to see anything clearly. She is next to the men's room and the electric chair.

She would not have come. She wouldn't be sitting here in the shadows in the back booth at Lucky's if Carla, who trained her at the credit union, didn't scare her a little. If Shell didn't have a bizarre need to please people who were downright mean to her. All Carla said was, "Meet me at Lucky's. Eight o'clock. Back booth." Shell protested, but Carla didn't hear her say she couldn't make it; she'd already hung up.

The bartender, with pierced lobes so big you could shoot a grape through them and a face tattooed in constellations, emerges from the dark, slaps two pints of stout in front of her and disappears. Shell looks out of the booth quickly to see if there is some explanation for the delivery, but a dart whizzes past and she pulls her head in like a turtle. The beer sits on the table, sweating. The pint closest to her starts to move on its own, pulled by the moisture that has pooled at the base of the glass. It nearly dumps into her lap. She catches it. Takes a sip. The cool, tart beer cleanses her mouth. The beer turns hot in her belly and loosens up her muscles. She is able to sit up straight without effort. She even slides out of the corner of the booth and peeks around the high wooden sides to see what Dave and Pedro are up to now. They have their backs to her as they talk to someone she can't see. She finishes the beer, grabs the other and downs it.

The bar fills. It is loud and stuffy. Carla isn't there yet and Shell's legs already feel like rubber. Her head is light. She hangs her legs out of the booth, lies down and flings a forearm across her eyes. Her bare legs feel funny and loose and she enjoys swinging them back and forth until someone says, "Those are dangerous." Dave points to the empty glasses.

"What's in them?" she asks, pulling her arm from her eyes.

"Whisky. Jed drops a shot or two in the pint and it knocks you on your ass."

"Where did they come from? You?"

"No. I'd have warned you. You always take naps in bars?"

"What time is it? I'm meeting someone."

"Eight-thirty. Can I buy you that beer?"

"I'm meeting a girl from work."

"Wanna hand?"

"No. I just want to lie here a minute." She is drunk. It feels good.

"So how about it? Want another?"

"Of these? I don't know." She takes Dave's hand and lets him pull her up. Dave smells good. Familiar because he is a man and men have that smell, but there is that part of him that is uniquely his and this worries her because she likes it, which is confusing and sad.

"Just a beer, none of Jed's funny stuff. How about it?"

"OK. Just beer," she says.

Dave walks away and Carla slips out of the dark and into the booth with a piece of paper and a pencil.

"You're really late," Shell says.

"You're really drunk."

"No, I'm not."

"I've been here for an hour. I just didn't feel like doing this until now. How'd you like those beers?"

"Why did you ask me to come here if you were just going to leave me sitting here? You don't have any reason not to like me."

"So do you want to know the trick or not?" Carla asks.

"What trick?"

"The drawer trick, dummy."

"You do have a trick?" Shell asks. "I knew it."

Dave shows up with the beer and puts it down.

"Busy," Shell says.

"Hi, Dave. Tell Pedro to order me another. We'll be done in a sec," Carla says. Dave puts Shell's beer on the table and retreats, hands in the air.

"Yeah. There is a trick to it. It takes a while for tellers to give it up, though. We're really competitive."

"I've noticed," Shell says.

"But you've caught on fast, so I'll tell you. Ninety-nine percent of the errors made are inversion errors, meaning you invert two digits when you add it to your running tally. So when your drawer doesn't add up, instead of going through each transaction one by one, you can subtract the difference from your drawer and your receipt and divide it by nine. If the difference divides by nine, it's an inversion error. I don't know why it works, but it does. Once you know that, you just look back at the deposit and withdrawal amounts and make sure you input them correctly. You usually find the error really quickly once you know what you're looking for."

Shell grabs the piece of paper and pen and makes Carla go through it again. She tests it out, and sure enough it works. "That's amazing!"

"Can we sit?" Pedro asks. He slides in next to Carla, Dave next to Shell. Dave clinks his glass to hers. Pedro clinks her glass, too, "Hi, Shell. I'm Pedro. We've never actually spoken because your father doesn't believe I can speak English, but I've seen you in a towel."

Carla punches him in the arm and Pedro grabs her and pins her against the back of the booth and kisses her. "Give me my beer, Professor Gonzalez, or I'll report you to the dean."

"I'm her geology prof," Pedro explains, as he slides Carla the beer.

"And my boyfriend," Carla points out.

Shell is surprised.

"So how do you know each other?" Shell asks Dave and Pedro.

"Lacrosse," Pedro says.

"Cornell. We played lacrosse as kids. Pedro's from Skinny-And-Assless."

"He's my rich boy," Carla says referring to the town he's from. "His daddy's Doctor Gonzalez, Central New York fertility God," Carla says.

"I started working with Dave on houses when I decided I too wanted to be a huge loser."

"Pedro's getting his PhD in rocks," Dave says. "He's slumming it with me for the summer."

"And teaching part-time at the college," Pedro says.

"That's how I met him. Too many lab hours talking bedrock," Carla says.

"Where are you in school?" Shell asks. It feels good to be out with people in a lively conversation and she doesn't notice that her bare knee is touching Dave's bare knee, until she does. And when she feels his skin to hers, she can think of nothing else. She doesn't hear where Pedro is studying. She just knows that Dave is pressing his leg into hers and she smiles at him for it.

"Hold on a second!" Carla puts her hand up and stops the conversation. She jumps up onto her seat, and carefully looks up and over the booth. She pops back down and her eyes are wild. "Dorothy's here," she says to Shell. "And she's with her guy. Two booths down. I'd recognize that guy's piece anywhere."

"They're made for each other," Shell says.

"What do you mean?" Carla asks.

"I mean Dorothy wears a wig. I'm sure of it," Shell says.

"No she doesn't!" Immediately Carla is scheming.

"Carla, you're being rude. Explain," Pedro demands.

"I can't. Not yet," Carla climbs over Pedro's lap and disappears out of the booth. Moments later she is back, flushed with mischief.

"I don't want to know what you just did," Shell laughs.

"I ordered them a round. I told Jed to bring them a round of whatever they're drinking and to tell them it's from Cupid."

"I don't believe you. That's too tame."

"Believe it," Carla says. "I'm drunk. And even an uptight bitch like Dorothy Card deserves to get a little, don't you think?" She snuggles up next to Pedro. Kisses his nose.

"Did you finish that paper for Gupta?" he asks in a caring and private voice.

"Please don't ask me, Daddy."

"I'm not being your daddy. You need it to transfer."

"I know. I'll get it done." Pedro squeezes her close to him.

Dave nudges Shell in the side, "They're cute, aren't they?"

"Yes," she says and downs half a beer all at once.

"Hey," Dave says. "You still see Ellen and Gina? You guys are still close, aren't you? You were always together."

"Gina's dad just died, didn't he?" Carla asks. "My dad told me. But she's tough. She can handle anything."

"How's your dad feel about the exhibit?" Dave asks changing the subject before Shell has to speak, and she is glad; she worries about Gina.

"I know the guys are pretty pissed about it," Carla chimes in. "My dad said he was going to burn the place down. Big topic at the credit union. Apparently there's all this stuff about guards. How they drink too much and hit their kids. Ha! I could have told them that. If your dad's like mine," Carla says to Shell, "he's all fucked up. My dad used to hit us something awful when he'd come home from work. But he lightened up when he stopped drinking. He goes to meetings every day inside. It's the only way my folks are still together. Or that any of us talk to him."

"My dad never did that," Shell says.

"You're lucky," Carla says.

"What do you think?" Dave asks Shell. The conversation around her has grown louder.

"I don't know. Ed's nervous about it. The COs have hard jobs. They sure don't appreciate everyone sticking their noses in where they think they don't belong. It's probably a good thing, though. We grew up like it wasn't there. I grew up like my dad went to some office every day. My mother never even let him wear his uniform in the house. Though when he's nervous in social situations it's all he talks about. It's complicated. I'd like to go. He told me he'd throw me out if I did."

"You want another beer?" Dave asks.

"Sure," Shell says. She is numb from the beer, which is good because every so often she remembers that John is leaving her and the panic is enough to overtake her, but the alcohol is doing its job, keeping her anesthetized so that she could also, if necessary, just as readily give up a leg.

"OK. The woman wants another beer. How about you two?" Pedro and Carla look slumped and ready for bed. "Nah. We're beat. We're taking off."

"Suit yourself. Shell, it's just you and me." He disappears into a sea of shoulders. Lucky's is packed.

The hall where the bathrooms are located is so poorly lit the only light comes from the red glow of the emergency exit sign at the far end and the low eerie light shining up at the electric chair, which is on display in a closet walled off by bars. Shell has to feel along the filthy bars to find the bathroom door.

She is surprised. In the mirror she looks good. She still has the hot burn in her eyes and nose from crying about John, but the beer has blushed up her cheeks and made her lips full and attractive.

When she opens the bathroom door, she feels someone moving through the darkness in front of her. They don't collide this time. Instead, she holds back and lets Dave go on ahead. He has a beautiful, confident gait. He pauses at the end of the hall and turns. He walks back toward her. She stays in the shadows so he doesn't see her. She watches as he reaches into his pocket, pulls out a handful of change and shakes it. He picks out quarters and drops them into a machine hanging on the wall. He presses a button and the machine dispenses a strip of condoms. Shell steps back, and steps back again, and slips out the emergency exit.

ELLEN

ELLEN AND ICHIRO HIRED a kitchen expert, Chico Giccardi, who for thirty thousand placed a prep sink and a cooktop on the kitchen island and refrigerators underneath like cupboards so Ellen could cook and still share in the conversation. The sum pleased her mother, Claire, endlessly. She reveled in her daughter's wealth and lifestyle, even if she had married a man who was half Japanese. During intimate gatherings like the one Ellen is having tonight, when she is expertly preparing salads and pouring wine and slicing bread and placing cheese on a cheese stone and not once breaking the conversation with her well-heeled acquaintance, Lillian Worthington-Chance, or losing eye contact for more than a well-placed second, she knows Chico was worth his weight.

Her mother has a new career now that Ellen is married: helping orchestrate the perfect household for a woman who can and does have everything. Ellen knows that the details of her life give her mother something to live for. Claire never gets these sorts of social opportunities living in Hardenberg. She is always being tortured by pig roasts with the county Republicans—farmers who smell like chicken coops—to whom she's been beholden all of these years as the wife of an elected state judge, so Ellen includes her in the planning and calls her at the end of every gathering for a recap.

They are closer now that she is a wife.

Ellen listens to her guests recount tales of their single lives in New York and pours Sancerre and catches glances of Rosaria in a stupid maid's outfit given to her by a former employer (she insisted on wearing it and it keeps bothering Ellen). Rosaria is circulating with fennel, goat cheese, caramelized onion tartlets and skewers of bufala mozzarella, basil, and a sweet yellow tomato topped with an oil-cured kalamata olive like a finial. It is fresh that evening because they have the patio doors open to invite in the view of the river and the Statue and the financial district where Ichiro and all of his friends work. The fire and the night air are the perfect combination, candles flicker throughout, potted gardens adorn the apartment, giving it a courtyard feel, the lights low, Stan Getz and Jobim a compliment to the warmth of summer. The whole soirée an homage to the beautiful weather.

Rosaria arrived that day armed with a home decorating magazine she stole from her OB's office with an article detailing how to make the most amazing arrangements of potted grasses, ferns, vegetables, herbs, succulents, stones, and fruit. *Bring the Garden In!* the article's title instructed.

They set out early that morning to Long Island and bought six rustic concrete pots shaped like wide, low bowls, bags and bags of soil, fertilizer, exquisite grasses, early-start greenhouse currant tomatoes, purple-striped eggplants, bright lights Swiss chard, lemon cucumber, okra with a flower like a small hibiscus, tomatillos, young chiles, red lettuce, chocolate mint, strawberries, pansies, frisée, arugula, purple kale, and a variety of succulents Rosaria said looked like they were grown on the moon. They sat on the patio covered in dirt, drinking, arranging, and planting. These small, delicate plants, so full of potential for the season, came together in rustic palettes worthy of the most exotic hacienda. They laughed at themselves when the party was only hours away and black dirt was ground into the concrete of the narrow balcony, and streaked on their faces. Oh my God, your ring! Rosaria laughed. Even in Ellen's ear, she pointed out. Ellen sat back, leaned against the glass of the sliding door, put her feet up on the railing and lost herself in Rosaria's easy laugh, the sound of the traffic moving smoothly ten floors below along the BQE, the calls of the ships coming into the harbor, and the din that is New York. It sounded to her like competing radio stations, like the whole place was plugged in. She imagined a small child finding a mysterious plug in the back of a closet in a tenement in Bushwick, pulling it, and the whole place going down under a blanket of silence. This thought was accompanied by worry. She's been having moments of passing discomfort like this. Waves of anxiety that pass over her from time to time. She often has to resist the desire to get up and walk out of the room. Shhhhhhhh, she said to herself quietly so Rosaria couldn't hear her.

Ichiro is the most handsome among the men at the party. Loose-limbed, tall, beautiful olive complexion, the perfect hint of his mother's Japanese blood in the shape of his eyes, chestnut brown hair, he comes to her post in the kitchen to refill his glass and kisses her on her cheek and she feels badly for being short with him earlier. She still considers herself lucky that he came along and saved her from her lonely, pack-rat lifestyle three years before.

The conversation around her has turned to the fate of the freak show. "I've been to Coney Island once," Ellen says returning her attention to her guests. "With my friends from home." She says this breezily and times her entrance in the conversation so that she doesn't appear to be too involved in her husband's affections. "We crashed a wedding. The sword swallower married the glass eater on the beach. Their attendants were the mermaids and the best man was tattooed in maps. The groom swallowed a sword. The bride ate a light bulb."

"That sounds about right," says her guest, Trudy Levine, and they all laugh loudly. Except Ellen. She sips her wine and thinks of the note that came from her mother-in-law, Sakamoto Collins, today in a box of books. It said, "Name one thing you did today to make your life worth living and drink to it." The box came when she and Rosaria were still covered in dirt. Ellen drinks to that.

Twice a year Sakamoto sends Ellen a box of books she's read in the last six months. Mostly they are about death and dying and what comes next. Sometimes there is a book of philosophy. In the box were the following: *Sir Mix-a-Lot's Mixology 101*, the pages of the drinks she liked the most dog-eared, *The Feminine Mistake,* Gramsci's *The*

Prison Notebooks, Many Lives Many Masters, Children's Past Lives, and *Lady Chatterley's Lover.* Ichiro came home from the office and found Rosaria and Ellen drinking a *Swedoise.* Sakamoto's invention. She'd handwritten the recipe and a note and stuck it in the book: vodka and Orangina—sexy and a little hairy like a *Swedoise,* the note said. They were covered in dirt, sitting on the floor of the balcony, drinking, laughing, poring over the books.

DURING DINNER ELLEN HEARS Rosaria clinking in the kitchen, cleaning up prep dishes and preparing coffee, gathering desert plates. They are having fruit tart. This is what her mother meant about a divide between the workings of a kitchen and the guests. Rosaria turns off the sink and Ellen hears the phone ringing quietly in the office—they forgot to turn that ringer off. She hears Rosaria hurry down the hall.

Below the dinner conversation she hears Rosaria excusing Ellen for not being able to come to the phone. May I take a message? Rosaria asks in a hushed voice. Rosaria is quiet but Ellen hears her say, Hold on. I'll see if she can. The conversation has turned to Ichiro's work. There is a new boss who seems promising. There is palpable relief that the old boss has been transferred overseas. "The farther away the better," Kristen Bauer says and lifts her glass for a toast. Just then Rosaria comes respectfully to Ellen's side and kneels by her and whispers in her ear, "Miss Ellen, it's someone named Gina."

Ellen looks down at her plate annoyed. "Did you tell her I'm entertaining?"

"She said she must speak with you now."

Ellen removes the napkin from her lap and wipes the corners of her mouth. "Excuse me," she says to her guests and Ichiro looks concerned. She dismisses him with a wave. She is relieved when the conversation resumes easily.

"She is a friend of yours?" Rosaria asks.

"From home. Knowing Gina it's nothing. Please don't call me Miss Ellen."

"I'm sorry. It's just habit from my last job."

YOU ARE FREE TO GO

"I know."

She doesn't talk to Gina right away. She takes the phone to her bedroom and stands at the wall of glass, looking for a moment at the city glimmering like a diamond.

"Hello, Gina," Ellen says, "I'm in the middle of a party. What couldn't wait?"

There is no response. "Hello?" Ellen asks. Through the phone, she can hear sirens screaming. "Gina, are you there?"

"What's your excuse?" Gina asks in a husky voice, as if she hasn't spoken in some time. "I just want to know," she says, "how long did it take you to forget? A minute? Two, tops?"

"I have no idea what you're talking about…" But as Ellen says it, she realizes that it isn't at all true. A month or so ago Gina called and said she'd be at O'Malley's and asked Ellen to meet her there because her father died. Ellen had hung up the phone and completely forgotten. She is stung and shocked by this. It can't be true. This is not like her. Her throat tightens and burns. What had she been doing that had stolen her attention so completely that she might forget something like that? She tries to remember back. These days she's been having a hard time remembering things. Days seem to blend together and it has been giving her some worry. This reminder—What on earth had been on her mind that she could hang up the phone and just walk away?—makes her question herself. She is a good friend. She is known for going out of her way. Suddenly, she is gripped by an uncharacteristic anger at this rude reminder that she made a mistake. She doesn't want to admit that underneath it there is something else: more evidence that she doesn't quite recognize herself these days. "Have you spoken to Shell?" Ellen asks flatly.

"Is that it?"

"No, Gina. I was just wondering if…I didn't know your father. You didn't see him a lot, did you?"

"Shell didn't know him, either. No one did. All you had to do was be honest with me, say you couldn't make it. Ask if there was anything you can do. That seems like the appropriate response when someone's father dies, don't you think?"

Ellen feels hot and lightheaded. She places her hand on the window. Her warm, moist palm makes a ghostly mark. The cool window, the vibration of the city, that sound that fills her days, calms her. "I'm sorry, Gina," she says. "Gina, are you alright? Gina?" The phone clicks dead.

Ellen can hear her guests laughing, the music louder than before. She looks around, doesn't know what to do. She begins to dial Shell, but can't remember her number, which also surprises and upsets her. Her jaw is tight and she feels as though she might pass out. She places the phone on the nightstand and crawls into her bed. She curls into a fetal position and presses her ear to the pillow. It is like putting her ear to a conch. The sound of everything is in there. She closes her eyes and lets this sound wash over her. It calms her. She wonders if the sound that she finds so soothing is really the city or if it is the growing sound coming from her. And she drifts off into it and in that way that a dream lifts you up like a wave and deposits you somewhere, she is looking at her mother and feeling in every part of her—her eyes, her fingers, her belly, every cell—a calling out for her embrace. She is reaching her arms out, a child asking to be cuddled. But the memory is fuzzy. And it makes no sense because while she is reaching her arms out to her mother looking for that comfortable place that she longs for with all of her heart, she is standing tall, eye to eye to her mother. She is in a woman's body, reaching out for the loving comfort she once knew well. She longs for that now as she rocks herself in her bed and the sound coming from within grows louder. Claire had a wonderful enveloping hug that Ellen and Ronnie, even when they were too old to fit in their mother's lap, would revel in. Somehow she'd hold them both, rock them together, soothe them even when they didn't know they needed soothing. Her mother. That mother. Chasing her children through the house saying *I'm gonna get you.* Holding them and tickling them until they peed. Ellen longs for her. The vibration of her breath, her words echoing through her ribs, the deep thud of her heart, heavy, loud, reliable, her body an instrument that played and calmed Ellen. She reaches. Everything pulls toward the ever-present match, cell-to-cell, so that when she reaches out and they plug into each other as mother and infant, mother and toddler, mother and child, they are one. Ellen's ears tune to her breathing so that they already hear it as if it were as close as mouth to ear, her body already feels the vibration of her words, "It's OK. Everything's going to be alright. Shhhhhhhhhhhh." She already feels this, standing there, eye to eye, anticipating the comfort she reaches out for. But in this memory where she's been dropped, there is no response. Her mother's arms hang by her sides, her eyes are already stoned, cold. The doctor called in to prescribe something as soon as they'd heard the news. By the time Ellen reached her home and learned that Ronnie was dead, her mother was gone. Claire turns away. There is no comfort, no calming sound. Not then. Not ever again. Ellen stands. A statue of a child reaching. When she lowers her arms, they crack and hurt like they are breaking. Mechanically, she puts a foot in front of another. She walks through the cold and empty kitchen. The only sound her shuffling feet. She climbs the servant's stairs and somehow makes it to her room. She shuts the door, climbs into her bed as she is in her bed now and she pulls in her knees as her knees are pulled in now and she rocks herself side to side as she is rocking now and she listens to her breath, the sound it makes, and she makes it louder and louder until it is a shhh shhh shhhhhhhhhhhhh so loud so deep she can't hear her mother's wails. She can't hear the screaming in agony of her father over the loss of his boy. She can't hear the death-like silence that entered their house after the anger of grief dissipated.

"Stop that sound!" her mother yelled at her.

"Is that you?" her roommate at Vassar asked before requesting a room change.

Whole years of her life were dropped down into it.

When she thinks back, she doesn't have memories of activities, skiing down white hills or flying over aquamarine waters and white sand beaches. What she remembers is just the enveloping totality of that sound. That is, of course, until the morning she sat at her easel in her kitchen in Manhattan, Gina asleep in the bed behind her. That morning it took her some time to realize that the strange thing about her wasn't the presence of another—though she had been lonely for so long there was an electricity to the room by virtue of sharing it with someone—it was her silence, which she only noticed when from the bed behind her she heard a sound, someone awakening.

Gina. What has she done?

She can't imagine lifting herself from the mattress, joining her guests. She feels dizzy. Her face is wet. Rosaria pokes her head in the room, "Ellen? Is everything OK?"

Ellen takes some time to speak. Clears her throat. "It's fine," she says, finally.

"Would you like me to put out dessert? I think people are ready. Ichiro asked if you were OK."

"Tell him I'm fine. I'm fine," Ellen says, staring straight in front of her at a clean floor and a clean, light, wood-paneled wall. There is no extraneous furniture. Just clean lines, and it occurs to her just then, looking out at her room, that something seems missing. As if there had been furniture there and someone came in and stole it all.

HER GUESTS ARE ENJOYING the fire when she rejoins them. Rosaria is serving the coffee and the tart. Ichiro walks to the sliding doors and closes them and Ellen feels suddenly starved for air so she walks through the room, slipping between warm bourbon conversations—the guests are embroiled in talk and none seem to notice her return, or her absence, for that matter—to the doors and steps onto the balcony. The cool breeze off the water is a relief. She breathes. Fortifies herself, listens to the sounds of the city, and walks back inside. The kitchen is clean and it is time for Rosaria to go home. They had agreed she would leave the dessert plates and the last of the glasses. "Are you sure you're all right?" Rosaria asks as Ellen swiftly walks her to the office. Ellen takes out her wallet and pays her for the week. Rosaria says, "Thank You. Good party, huh? Are you going to give the pots away? That was so much fun. I felt like a kid."

"Oh, thank you for reminding me," Ellen says absently, then she turns back to her wallet and takes an extra hundred-dollar bill and gives it to Rosaria. "For today," she says.

Rosaria takes the money. "Thank you, Ellen. I feel weird.

Sometimes it just feels like fun, not work. But I really do need the money. I'm not rich enough to just have fun all the time."

"I know," Ellen says. "I appreciate and value our time together." And the minute she says it she knows it was wrong to say.

Rosaria takes a moment to say goodbye to Ellen's guests and though her mother wouldn't like this—Claire would think it an intrusion— Ellen is pleased because it shows that there isn't such a staunch and stifling hierarchy in their relationship. The moment Rosaria closes the door behind her all the guests talk about her. Kristen Bauer asks, "Can I get her number? She's gorgeous!" Her husband Jonathan says, "I'd like to go on record that it was my wife, not I, who asked for her number."

"Well, she's not for sale," Ellen says loudly. Her voice sober and angry. The guests quiet and look around at one another. "We ought to get going," one couple says. "It is getting late," says another. Ellen stands at a quiet distance watching them leave. She forgets to give them their pots. Ichiro eyes her, asking in his own way, What the hell is wrong with you?

When the guests are gone, she sits on the couch with the fire crackling, filling the air with its rustic smell. Ellen watches Ichiro as he leans against the balcony smoking a cigarette. He is drunk and angry with her. She can see this in the way his body slumps over the railing and she imagines him tipping forward and falling a free fall to the street below. She dials her mother. She holds the phone to her ear and listens to it ring. She wants her mother to sound excited to hear from her. She wants her mother to tell her what a wonderful hostess she is and how lovely her life is. She knew just how she would please her: She'd report on the success of the Brazilian casserole; she'd report how perfectly dressed her friends were; she'd lie and say the night was a success, how they loved the pots she and Rosaria had planted.

Claire answers. Ellen can hear her cheek pressed against the pillow. Her mother has been drinking, of course. And trying unsuccessfully to keep herself awake so she wouldn't miss the call.

"How clever," Claire slurs when she hears about the pots. "But before we get to the good stuff," Claire says. "I have something awful to tell you. I broke my leg. In two places. Now don't worry about me, but my summer is ruined. No more tennis. I'll be leaving the ladies high and dry. I'll have to pull out of all my fundraising activities because I can't get myself around and your father is campaigning and he won't be bothered with me. I don't want to be a brat, but that's the way he is. I'm not cut out to be a burden. I have a very busy schedule. I don't know what I'm going to do, Ellen. I could hire Daisy full-time, I suppose."

"I'll come home," Ellen says.

"Oh, but you can't!" Claire says. "The big party is next week!" Ellen pauses for a moment and remembers that the night Gina called she had been planning the party that she and Ichiro were hosting at a rented house in the Hamptons. When she hung up with Gina, her mother called and Ellen was quickly distracted by their debate over menus and caterers. They needed to make a decision that night and it took much of the evening. Gina's call simply slipped her mind. She is appalled with herself. "Shh," she says, and her mother asks, "What?"

"Nothing. You need me. I want to come home."

"You would do that for me?" Claire says quietly. She has two speeds when she drinks: bitter, angry, and mean, or sentimental. Tonight she is sentimental. She begins to cry softly on the line. "You're a good girl, Ellen," she says. And Ellen feels the evening's grip loosen.

"Oh!" Claire exclaims, interrupting her self pity, and Ellen can see her adjusting herself in the bed. Ellen imagines her mother in her dressing gown, robe, her hair set, a breathing strip plastered to the bridge of her nose, a glass of Scotch and water in easy reach on the night stand, leg elevated in a sling. When she speaks, her voice is raspy and intimate. It has none of the dignity of her up-and-around voice. "I can't believe I keep forgetting to tell you this. *Update from the lives of the poor and the unknown*: Shell Cavanaugh has been dumped by her husband after only two years. I ran into her mother yesterday before my accident. Shell is home. Sid says that she's concerned about her. That girl is trouble. It's the father. He's a buffoon. And they always had that strange relationship with that girl whose father was incarcerated. What was her name?"

"Gina," Ellen says, even though she knows full well Claire remembers her name.

"Right. I knew it sounded trashy."

"Her father just died," Ellen says and wonders why on earth she mentioned it. Discussions of Shell and Gina never went well.

"Oh, Ellen, please! Father. He was in prison. What kind of father is that? Don't defend them, Ellen." And Ellen knows she means: let's not go through *this* again, shall we? "I'm just glad you've moved on," Claire continues. "Now you have friends with class, like the Worthingtons."

Ichiro opens the balcony door and comes to her. He stumbles on the coffee table. As he leans down he kisses her neck and falls onto the couch next to her. He strokes her back. He has forgotten his anger. Ellen stiffens, though she wishes she hadn't. He points to their bedroom and raises his eyebrows. She forces a smile and holds up her finger telling him she'll be a minute. She wishes she wanted to throw the phone on the floor and chase after him, but she doesn't. "How did you break your ankle?" she asks her mother.

"Leg, dear. Tibia and fibula. Nasty spill on some wet stairs at the Club. Your father wants to sue, but we've worked too hard building up a reputation there; it would be suicide."

CLAIRE

ELLEN SITS ON THE cold leather couch in the study, the night she arrives in Hardenberg. The windows are open and for July the evening has a chill. She felt the drop in temperature the minute her father's car pulled from the Thruway onto the county route south toward town. The lush green fields of the country had pulled the heat from the air and made it fresh as water. When they hit a canopy of trees, the still, cold silence of the night made her feel like crying. She didn't know why. She had to swallow to keep from doing it in front of her father.

In the study, her mother sits in a leather armchair with her cast leg elevated on an ottoman; she gossips about the prison exhibit at the local history museum, and Ellen's father, Judge D., grunts they should leave enough alone, and the cool breeze blows in off the deep lawn from the dark stand of trees that surrounds the house. Ellen hears a truck's chains rattle as it lumbers down South Street and the chill bores into her.

When it is time for bed, her mother instructs her to go and be comfortable. She doesn't mention how she will find her own way upstairs into her bed, nor does she request that Ellen help her. So Ellen says goodnight, and ascends the large sweeping staircase in the front hall. She finds her way to her childhood room, which is now a guest bedroom, no evidence of her childhood left in it, which probably is a good thing. It is appointed nicely to please her, as a hotel would be. Her mother doesn't treat her like a daughter anymore. She treats her like a woman she'd like to impress.

THE NEXT MORNING SHE wakes with the distinct feeling that something is wrong and she is very cold, but she doesn't know why she feels this way. She does not recall any dreams, but she is left with a heavy, miserable dream hangover that weighs her down. She considers going to her mother's room, but worries what she might find. Will her father still be there? What if he is dressing? Will her mother be sleeping? Ellen would be embarrassed if her mother woke up and knew Ellen saw her looking old and disheveled. But how is she supposed to take care of her otherwise? She dares go down the hall to her parents' room.

Walking this walk is familiar. Even now she adopts the game of silent movement that signified her life after Ronnie died. If she can move from one room to another without making a peep—no shhh!— then she will not disturb her mother and it is a good day.

The door is closed. She reaches her hand to the knob, but hesitates. She puts her ear to the door then slowly turns the handle. The curtains are drawn, so it is very dark. The door to the bathroom is cracked and she can see light coming from within. The shower runs. The room smells moist and the air is thick. There are the dark oriental carpets, the stately cherry bed with high, carved posts and matching dressers with brass handles. There is a gold brocade chair in the corner in front of the large window overlooking the backyard, and a delicate brass leaded-glass-topped table next to it. The room is clean, of course. But the air is stale and the dark furniture and the dark of the room which hangs heavy with sleep and injury repulse her and make her wish for a breath of fresh air. Her mother sleeps with her mouth open and snores. The skin on her face sags, revealing the bones beneath. She is ashen and looks dead. Ellen steps quietly out of the room and shuts the door and when she does, there is a loud click.

"Ellen?" she hears from within.

She looks around, as if looking for someone to blame. She opens the door and looking at the floor says, "I'm sorry I woke you."

Claire runs her hand over her hair, and gathers herself in the way she would if a friend from the Club were standing there. "Not at all, dear," she says. "Come in." A breathing strip straddles her nose, a sleeping mask hangs from an elastic around her neck. "How did you sleep? Well, I hope. Daisy made the beds and I didn't get to inspect since I haven't been able to move. I hope it was acceptable."

"It was fine," Ellen says. "Very comfortable." She is relieved by her mother's tone.

"Open the curtains, will you, Ellen?"

Ellen grants her wish and Claire says, "This will never work. I am going to be such a burden."

"Not at all," Ellen says. She looks out on the deep green of the thicket and the tall trees of the backyard. She feels cold and moves away from the window.

The shower stops running, her father grumbles something to himself. "I'm in here!" Ellen yells. And at the same time her mother yells, "Judge, your daughter is in here."

"Well, scram!" he says from behind the door. "I'm late for Goddamned court."

"One minute, you angry old goat," Claire says. "Dear, do you have what you need for a shower?"

"I think so," Ellen says. "Do you need anything before I get ready?"

Claire looks toward the bathroom door nervously, and Ellen thinks she ought to get out of there before her father comes out. She steps out into the hall and then remembers she needs a bathrobe. "Mom," she says. "Do you have a robe I can borrow?"

"Of course, dear. Judge, you wait just a minute. Ellen has to step back in."

"I'm late! You women don't understand responsibility."

"In my closet, dear," Claire whispers, and Ellen runs to her mother's closet, opens the door and on a shelf to the right is a long terrycloth housecoat, laundered and folded. "Take that one, Ellen. I have plenty of others." Ellen knows this is true.

THE BATHROBE IS WARM, long to the floor with a zipper, and sweet-smelling. Despite its dowdy look, it is the most comfortable thing Ellen has ever worn. She lets the water in the shower run a long time until it is hot and when the room is filled with steam, she steps in and it feels renewing. The cold that hooked her on the drive from the airport is boiled out. Her skin turns red; the water scalds her scalp. It is wonderful. When she turns the water off and steps out, the large marble bathroom is still warm. She wraps her hair in a towel and dries herself and puts the robe back on. She thinks to check in on her mother, but knows that Claire will find her more appealing if she dries her hair and dresses first. So she does her hair in a smooth pageboy and her lovely two-process blond mane sweeps under with the perfect amount of bounce. She still marvels at the improvement in her looks, no more glasses, no more dishwater hair, as Claire used to call it. It's as if simply by Ichiro walking through the door of the party at the home of some of her Vassar friends and into her life she became a more attractive version of herself. She dresses in a lovely outfit. Green twill shorts, a pink poplin shirt with a demure rounded collar rimmed in red grosgrain ribbon, a low skinny red leather belt, pink slip-ons with a red bow. She puts on her rings and polishes the big flat table of her diamond so it has extra sparkle because she knows it makes Claire very happy to see it shining on her finger. She hangs the bathrobe on the hook on the back of the bathroom door, and a slight suggestion of a body's smell lifts up and out of it and it catches her and makes her unstable on her feet for an instant. She rights herself, and goes on to her mother's room.

This time she doesn't try to be quiet. She doesn't hesitate as she puts her hand on the handle and begins to open the door. But as she turns the knob Claire growls, "Don't you dare!"

"Mom?" Ellen asks through a crack in the door. "Can I come in?" Ellen hears movement. Something falls to the floor. "Shit," her mother says.

"Mother, I'm coming in. I came all the way home to take care of you. You have to let me..." Ellen steps into the room.

There is a smell. Her mother hangs half off the bed, the heavy cast anchoring one leg in bed while her other leg, bare all the way to the waist, hangs stiff and straight with her foot pointed, toes touching the floor. A brown drip rolls down her leg and lands on the oriental rug. A glass lays on its side on the floor, its contents spilled. The smell is overpowering. Claire is twisted in sheets and a soaking wet nightgown. She buries her face in her pillow. Ellen takes a step closer and says, "It's OK. We can clean this up."

Claire lifts her red face from her pillow, and in a cold and quiet voice says, "Call Daisy. I don't want you."

ELLEN WALKS DOWN THE stairs silently, but her muscles are jerky and mechanical. The walls are covered in pictures of herself, but mostly of her brother. She looks up at the portraits, mostly formal, and he looks down on her. Dated images of a boy who lived only in their dreams. He was the most mythical of boys. Four years older than Ellen, he wasn't beautiful in the traditional sense, but there was a certain quality to him that made everyone look at him in wide-eyed awe when he happened to be in the house between practices, so strong in his baseball whites, scabs on his tanned arms, roping muscles that seemed impossible on any body, let alone a boy still in high school. He was an All-American. He was going to the big leagues. He was known in every house in Hardenberg as Ronnie D. His vocation as a baseball star had permanently shortened their name, the most prominent name in town.

But of course no one loved him like Claire. No mother had ever been so perfectly awed by the child that came from her. In his presence, she floated. When he passed through a room like a celebrity or auspicious ghost, she glowed, and when she turned her attention back to her daughter, Ellen basked in this warmth and love. Ronnie only ever passed over them. And they received this blessing like grounded onlookers gazing up at the magic of a dirigible; the joy made them feel consecrated just from having been in his proximity.

Ellen forgot that it was her habit not to look up at those pictures.

IN THE KITCHEN, THERE is the evidence of breakfast, some crumbs on the table and on the counter. There is hardly a cup of coffee left in the carafe, and the newspaper looks like it has been torn through by an angry dog. The kitchen is quiet and haunting.

It has been remodeled several times over since she was a child. A fact that always relieves her. The spot on the floor where she stood when she learned of her brother's death literally no longer exists. She also doesn't know where anything is. She doesn't know where to begin looking for Daisy's number and stands at the windows for a moment looking out on the lawn. She shivers and turns away. She looks through cupboards and drawers for a phone book. She doesn't know Daisy's last name, so she hopes to find a clue. She does not.

In her father's study, she checks his desk and sees a picture of her father standing behind Ronnie—he couldn't have been more than seven—and her father holds his son's hands on the bat in the proper position as Ronnie learns to take a pitch. She looks away from the picture and opens the desk drawers. She looks over her shoulder a few times, as if her father might find her there and she might get into trouble. There is nothing helpful there. Checkbooks, bills, bank statements, calculators, pens, paper clips, rubber bands, a stapler and stacks of boxes with staples inside, no phone book. No personal address book. She glances at the picture again and realizes she's saying shhhhhh. She moves quickly into the front hallway as if she were escaping a conversation she wishes weren't happening.

She finds herself standing beneath the gigantic crystal chandelier where the front staircase swoops into the foyer. Normally, she enjoys noting how everything in her mother's home is freshly scented and despite corners of disarray, there is a casual elegance to the lived-in home. But she remembers her mother waiting half off the bed. Her words: *Call Daisy. I don't want you.*

A glimpse of a familiar picture draws her into the living room. She walks to it and picks it up. It is her wedding portrait. In it she is smiling foolishly, like a child. Ichiro is beautiful and looking at him she longs for him in a way she never does when he is near her. She wants to call him and right then remembers her mother's phone table in the corner of the living room. There it is, an old rotary telephone on a narrow stand covered in a fine piece of embroidered linen. Under the linen is the Hardenberg phone book and Claire's personal book. Ellen opens it and small pieces of paper fall to the floor with the names and addresses of people Claire intends to add to her Christmas card list. Ellen flips through the book and finds Daisy, no last name, listed under the D's. Ellen picks up the phone and dials the number.

"OH, I KNEW YOUR mother wouldn't make it a day without me," Daisy says as soon as Ellen introduces herself. "I have my grandson with me. Your mother won't like it, but he'll have to come with me. I have him for the week."

"That's fine," Ellen says. "We just need you right away."

"I'm sure you do," Daisy says, as if she'd been waiting for the call. "I'll need a ride. My daughter has the car."

"I will come get you. Where are you?"

"Oh, I'm just on the other side of town on North Street. Just run straight down South Street and when you start up the hill, you'll hit North Street. You can't miss us. Big blue side-by-side with a beige minivan in the driveway. Minivan belongs to the neighbors."

"Ten minutes," Ellen says.

She hangs up the phone and runs upstairs. At her mother's door she says, "I'm going to get Daisy. Just a few more minutes." Claire does not respond.

Ellen runs back down the stairs and finds her mother's keys in the key box by the back door. When she sits in her mother's large, plush car, she has a terrible thought: What if I just left her there? What if I drove back to Brooklyn and never came back?

ELLEN FINDS THE COFFEE filters and pours the last dregs of the morning coffee into a cup, then starts another pot. "Do you drink coffee?" she asks the young man sitting at the kitchen table. He sits slumped facing the window, his back to her. He wears a large sweatshirt and the hood is pulled up over his head. He rocks forward and back ever so slightly. Perhaps he didn't hear her. His grandmother called him Ty. She hears the coffeemaker come to life and is relieved at the break in the silence. She takes the cup of leftover coffee and fills it with milk and sweetens it too much. She hears water running upstairs and muffled voices and begins to hum quietly so the boy won't hear her, but enough so the sounds upstairs disappear. She takes her coffee to the island and dials Ichiro's office number. Karen, the receptionist, answers and tells her he is in a meeting. She asks Ellen if she would like to leave a message for him. "I'll be sure he gets it," she promises. Ellen is angry at the way Karen says it, as if Ichiro might dismiss her and not respond to her call. Ellen says, "No. Thanks. I'm sure he'll call me on his own," and hangs up and calls his cell instead. It rolls immediately to voice mail and she says, "Just wanted to call and tell you I'm thinking about you. It's cooler here. My parents send you their best. Have you looked to see if you can join me this weekend or next? The doctor says she will be in bed for a month. But all is well. We're having a good time together. I think this was the right thing to do. The party can happen anytime. Getting time with her like this is rare, you know?"

She watches the young man as she speaks. She half expects him to turn around and look at her with that knowing look people give when they've just heard someone tell a lie. But he continues his slight forward and back rocking, gazing out at the lawn. She wonders if she ought to be scared. He is large for his age. His grandmother said he is only thirteen, but he has to be older than that.

THE NEXT MORNING DAISY arrives bright and early. Ellen's window is open a crack so she hears her car with its loose muffler pull up in front of the house and park directly under her window. She hears the car doors open and close and she hears Daisy speaking to her grandson. She is saying, "You stay out of trouble today. Don't let me hear you was messin' around. These are good payin' people and I don't want to lose them. You be good, now." Ellen doesn't hear the boy. She is glad Daisy is here. She had been having a lovely dream about the ocean and a beautiful beach house like the one she and Ichiro and their friends rented last year out on Fire Island, but of course it wasn't that house exactly. This one had a widow's walk and Ellen stood on it and the warm ocean breeze blew and covered her face and hair in mist. She rolls over and closes her eyes in order to reenter her dream. She is loathe to admit how inadequate she felt the day before, but is relieved that Daisy has agreed to take on the heavy lifting. Ellen thought she had more pluck than this.

As she drifts off to sleep, she does not return to the widow's walk. Instead she falls into a dream that feels an awful lot like reality. She is just as she is now, staying at her mother's house, having just awakened from a much-needed night's sleep. She is wearing her mother's housecoat and she is walking into the kitchen for coffee. At the table slumps the boy. Like yesterday, all she can see is his back and his hood. She walks to the coffeemaker, opens the cupboard above it for a cup, and pours herself some coffee. Like yesterday she asks, "Do you drink coffee?" And, like yesterday, he does not respond. She walks to the refrigerator for cream and she pours in too much. The coffee turns almost completely white. She adds sugar by the spoonful. One after another. When she takes a sip the coffee is a thick syrup. She turns to look out the window and the boy's head slowly turns to her. She prepares to greet him, and looks forward to seeing his face again, but as the head turns, Ellen sees that the hood is empty. It is nothing but black shadow. There is no boy.

Ellen wakes with a throbbing headache. She pulls the housecoat over her fine linen pajamas and walks to the large marble shower at the end of the hall. She lets the water steam and when she reaches forward to turn down the scalding heat of the water, a small whiff of a deeply familiar odor, something of her mother, comes up and out of the fabric of the housecoat and Ellen just makes it to the toilet before throwing up.

Migraine. Ellen is prone to them. This is no way to see her mother. She kept her distance all yesterday. Daisy left after nine at night and told her Claire had just had one of her pills and would soon be sleeping comfortably. So Ellen went to bed early. Despite the rest, this headache is clamping down on her and she barely thinks she'll make it through a shower. She looks in the mirror. She is pale and sallow. Her cheekbones are protruding and her eyes sunken in. Her hair looks good enough, she guesses. She brushes her teeth and slowly makes her way to Claire's room. When she opens the door, the curtains are open and the sun blazes into her eyes and she makes it to the toilet in her mother's *en suite* just in time.

"My god, dear." Claire says. "Tell me you're pregnant."

"Migraine," Ellen says and her mother's face falls.

"Let me call Daisy. She can get you some coffee." Claire rings the bell that sits on the table next to her and the high-pitched peals tear through Ellen's head. She closes her eyes and feels her way along the wall to a straight-backed chair next to her mother's gold brocade armchair at the window.

Daisy comes soon and before she can enter the room Claire demands coffee at once. Ellen would have been appalled by her mother's lack of respect, Daisy is a person, after all, but the urgency of the pain makes her glad for it. She misses Rosaria. On days when Ellen gets her headaches, Rosaria knows exactly what to do. She draws the curtains shut, brings her black coffee, a little dark chocolate, gets a large bowl and places it at her bedside and gives her a dose of her medicine. She wishes she were home. She longs for her bed, for the smell of her fine sheets, for the deep hum that she could lose herself in and leave her body and the pain and float up and out and into a drugged slumber. There is no sound. There is a self-conscious and imposed quiet in the house. Every once in a while there is the rattle of a truck rumbling down South Street. But the in-between spaces of those staccato sounds put a point on the pain. She tries to make her breath sound like the ocean, to get lost in that, but there isn't enough to envelop her and take her where she wants to go. She doesn't dare make a sound loud enough to soothe herself in front of her mother.

Daisy brings her coffee with lots of cream and sugar, which is not what she wants.

"I've never seen you like this," Claire says. Disappointment obvious.

"I get them now and then," Ellen says quietly; it hurts to move her jaw.

"You ought to go lie down. I was going to have you keep an eye on that boy downstairs. But you're in no shape for that. Go to bed and sleep it off." Claire says. She wants Ellen out of the room.

Ellen nods, "I will. I'm sorry."

Claire shrugs.

Ellen makes her way to the large bed and takes off the bathrobe and lets it fall to the floor. She slips her legs along the cool sheets, spreads herself out like a starfish trying to get as much contact with the cool fresh feeling as possible. When her body heats up a spot, she makes small, slow movements so as not to disturb the moments of relief. When she moves, there is the warm musky smell of her mother's body that imprinted itself onto her from the bathrobe. The smell is like a wave that crashes over her head. Each time, there is an insecure moment in which she doesn't know if she will be OK or if the pain and nausea will worsen and she will simply die. But then comes traffic, cars blend with a truck's rattling chains, and Ellen begins to hum. It isn't a melodic sound. It is just enough to fill in the spaces, enough to merge with the sound of the cars passing by, with the sounds of a house, the hissing of the lawn, water running, water coming to a stop, the refrigerator buzzing on, the garage door lifting, the sound of a distant lawnmower fading in and out. She falls into the world and she is safe and finally at peace.

ON HER THIRD DAY home, things finally work out. Ellen is up early and is dressed in time to greet her mother cheerfully. Claire is thrilled to see her and have someone to talk to. They talk about the canceled party and Claire says, "I can't believe you'd do that for me." Ellen smiles at her, happy she is happy. Then they talk about shopping. Claire says she likes Ellen's pocketbook. Ellen says it is quite chic and hard to find, but she'll look for one for her when she gets back to town. Claire says, "I don't think I could use it. It's really too young for me." But Ellen disagrees, and she can tell this, too, pleases Claire, which in turn pleases her. She relaxes and takes a deep breath and thinks this is right. This is why she came home. Things feel normal again. For the first time since

Gina's call, her head is clear; she doesn't feel divided against herself.

As it turns out, Claire had a visitor the day before. Milly came and brought her some flowers and asked why there was a large, hooded black man sitting at her kitchen table. "Is he really that bad, Ellen?" Claire asks.

"I'm not sure what you mean, exactly," Ellen says trying to pretend the conversation isn't happening. She wants to hold onto the good feeling, but it is slipping.

"Well, is he scary looking? Milly said she was terrified to come in here."

"He's a boy, mom. He looks older, but he's only thirteen. Oh, I forgot to mention I have a new sweater that I think you'll like. It's beautiful, but I think it will look better on you. I have it in my bag. I'll show it to you."

"That's what Daisy *says*," Claire says. "You can't trust that. For all we know he's thirty. You can never tell with these people."

"I don't think Daisy would lie. She has no reason to. Besides, if he were older, he wouldn't need to be watched by his grandmother all day. He's really quite quiet," Ellen says.

"Well, I'm probably going to have to let Daisy go after this. I just don't like it. I'd do it now if I didn't need her. I'm very uncomfortable in my own house. And your father isn't too keen on it, let me tell you. What did he do in my house until nine o'clock the other night? Did she feed him my food? I imagine she must have had to. Why don't you go down and see what he's doing right now. You can get me one of my pills and bring it back to me. My leg is killing me."

Ellen wants to say that she doesn't think spying is necessary, but she is thrilled to have a task she can accomplish. When she returns, she gives Claire the pill and a fresh glass of water; her mother takes them and says, "Now let me see this sweater you think I might like." Ellen hops up cheerfully to get it.

When she returns, Claire is dozing. Her head has fallen to the side and she is snoring lightly. Ellen walks to her side and kneels next to her chair. She looks at the delicate, melon colored merino sweater in her hand and places it on the arm of the chair. She hears a quick catch in her mother's breathing. It is accompanied by a small snort and then her breath deepens and she falls into heavy sleep. Ellen leans toward her and puts her ear to her chest. She listens to her mother's breath pulled in with heavy effort and thrust out, leaving her chest sounding empty save the big, isolated beats of her heart. Ellen closes her eyes and lets the parts of her body that long to be connected to her mother's body find that match. Her head quivers in an involuntary nuzzle, an old reflex she didn't know she ever had, and she takes her mother's hand and places it on the side of her face. She falls asleep like this for a time until Daisy wakes her asking about lunch.

CLAIRE LOVES HER SWEATER. She has Ellen help her put it on right away. When Daisy brings them a late salad, Claire says, "Look at this lovely gift from my daughter. She is the best shopper."

Ellen reaches for her mother's hand and Claire squeezes it. They eat the light salad Daisy prepared for them in silence and Ellen feels calm and peaceful. She closes her eyes every now and again to remember the sensation of her mother's closeness. Her hand on her face.

"Ellen," Claire says as Ellen stares off. "The phone."

"Oh," Ellen says and reaches over to the phone on the table next to her mother's chair.

"Hello," Ellen answers.

"Hello," says the woman on the other end of the line. "This is Sid Cavanaugh."

When Ellen hears the name, she considers hanging up the phone and pretending it is a wrong number, but her mother looks at her with interest so she says, "Hello."

"Is this Ellen? How nice to hear your voice. We heard about Claire and just wanted to give her our very best and tell her we are all hoping she recovers quickly. Did you know Shell is also home?"

"No. I did not," she lies.

"Well, I'm sure she'd like to see you. She's having a bit of a hard time."

"Oh," Ellen says. Her mother is following the conversation with an eagle's eye, looking for some clue as to whom it might be. She is keeping score, granting approval for those who call or send flowers, discounting anyone from whom she has not heard.

"Is your mother well enough to speak? I'd like to tell her I wish her a speedy recovery."

"Hold on, Sid. I'll check."

Claire rolls her eyes, clearly disappointed that it isn't someone better, and draws a line across her neck with her finger, as if to say she'd rather die.

"Sid," Ellen says. "My mother's just taken a pill and is about to doze off. Do you mind if I relay the message?"

"Not at all. Please tell her we're rooting for her. I hope she'll call if she needs anything."

"I'll tell her. Thank you."

"All right, then. I'll let Shell know you're home. She'll be thrilled to hear it."

"I don't know if I'll be able to get away. My mother needs me right now," Ellen says.

"I understand. But I'll mention it. I'm sure you can find the time for a phone chat," Sid says, sounding disappointed. Ellen hangs up the phone and just as soon finds herself walking toward the door.

"Wait. Where are you going? What did Sid have to say?" Claire asks.

"She said she hoped you're feeling better and she hopes you'll call if you need anything."

"Isn't that nice. Nothing about Shell, then?"

"She said she's home."

"Sid has always tried to make nice with me ever since the accident. I don't care for her, you know. Though, she has tried to make something of that family. She really has. It's no wonder her daughter's marriage didn't last. I could use another pill."

Ellen thinks it might be too soon for another pill; it has only been two hours, but she gives her one anyway because she wants to make her happy, and Claire asks, "You're not planning to sneak out to see Shell while you're here, are you?"

"No. I don't have plans to see her while I'm home. I'm here to take care of you," Ellen says, looking off to the side. Claire has a tone that tips Ellen off to what is coming next, and what is coming next is not good.

"Well, you do have a tendency to sneak off with that girl. And you know what happens when you do, don't you?"

Ellen nods, yes.

"You know what happens when you do that, don't you, Ellen?" Her mother's words are slippery. The pill is taking effect and Ellen expects her mother to slip off to sleep at any moment, but somehow she is still awake and rather energized, perhaps by the subject. The vitriol. "Why did you do it, Ellen? Why did you sneak off with those girls and let Ronnie die?"

THE NEXT MORNING, DAISY can't come. Ellen brings her mother two pills and gives them to her even though Claire says, "I really ought to just have one, but I am in such pain."

"Take them," Ellen says. "They will make you feel better. You are in an awful lot of pain."

Claire takes the pills and looks over at her daughter. Claire's eyes are lopsided, one lid falling lower than the other, and the breathing strip that straddles her nose pulls and widens it, making her look odd and distorted.

"Daisy can't be here today," Ellen says.

"That's because we paid her yesterday," Claire slurs. "They get a little money in their pockets and they go crazy."

"She said she needed to bring her grandson to the doctor's in Syracuse."

"She lies a lot. She always leaves me when I need her most," Claire says and falls asleep with her mouth open in mid-sentence, her brow furrowed, as if she is going to say something else.

Ellen turns the shower on full blast and gets in. She scrubs her skin until it is raw. She steps out of the shower, quickly dries off and throws Claire's bathrobe over her shoulders, stretches her arms into it, and Ellen is overtaken by the smell of her mother's body, overtaken by her mother as she was for a solid year after Ronnie died, turban on her head, a cigarette hanging from her long fingers, a drink in hand, her nails maintained meticulously because this was how she spent her grief: grooming, smoking, drinking. She'd lie in bed, the room dark and full of the burn of acetate, full of the heady smell of Scotch, full of the charred smell of cigarettes lit one after the other, and she'd drink, she'd file, she'd paint, she'd stare off into the day of Ronnie's death, Sid's call asking if the girls had arrived OK, the revelation that they were missing, her request of her boy to go out and look for them, the final dive off the lake cliff. She clicked her long nails to the timing of the events, the phone call, the worry over her daughter's whereabouts—how could you follow those girls, Ellen, and let your brother die?—the loss of control, the Range Rover's skid, its tip, its roll, its hit at the edge of the cliff, its bounce up and over, its soar to the shallow lake bed, her son hanging, neck broken, only his hair touching the water. Or at least this is what Ellen imagined Claire was seeing when her mother was looking far off, cigarette burning down between her fingers. Ellen would say, Mom. Mommy. Mama. *Mama?* And finally Claire would stop clicking her nails, she would turn her head, her eyes would refocus on the room, on the child she had left. She would take a drag of the cigarette, then snuff it out and say, *Come here. I need you.* And Ellen let Claire wrap herself around her. She let Claire wrap herself so tight around her that she thought she might not be able to breathe, and she let her call her Ronnie. All this is in the bathrobe.

Ellen dresses. She perfects her hair, her clothes, she looks just the way she knows her mother wants her to look.

Claire is sleeping still. Her jaw has fallen to the side; she looks like a corpse. Ellen leans down on her knees and puts her ear to her mother's mouth. She is breathing. She climbs into bed next to her, takes her mother's arm and wraps it around her. She pulls the arm over her so the embrace is tight, the way she remembers it.

Her mother stirs and Ellen holds onto her arm, pulls it tighter, closer, but Claire rolls over and frees herself. Ellen sits up. She looks at Claire. She looks old. She no longer looks like her mother, no longer looks like the woman Ellen has been longing for. In fact this woman lying here looks like a stranger, and Ellen sees that the mother she is wanting has been gone for a very, very long time.

FROM WHERE SHE STANDS in the kitchen, Ellen can hear Claire ringing her bell. Ellen turns from the window where she has been looking out at the backyard. She walks to the key box by the garage door and takes out the key to her mother's car. The bell rings again. Ellen opens the door and walks out.

Her mother's car floats along the streets, cushioning every bump with brakes that slow and stop the car without any roughness. She speeds down South Street right out of town, drives south along the lake, past the cliffs where Ronnie fell to the shallow lake bed below, past the beautiful houses with the stately lawns, past the farms and the pastures of cows and horses, past the hamlets of trailers and broken-down cars, past sheep grazing at the roadside, past the first small town that leads to the next small town that leads to the interstate.

SHE ARRIVED IN BROOKLYN and told Ichiro not to ask. He agreed. Her mother has not called, which she knows means she never will. Ichiro has gone to work and she is in bed staring at the ceiling. She holds up her hand and looks again at the faint, lacy scar between her thumb and forefinger. She sits up suddenly and throws the covers to the side. She wants the old viewfinder from Coney Island so she can see herself with Shell and Gina smiling a real smile. She rushes to her closet because she is sure the box should be in there. She opens the door and turns on the light. It is beautiful. Like a room-sized curio chest. Teak drawers. All her clothing hanging perfectly by color and length. She looks around and remembers that there are no dark corners in that closet where a box could hide. She feels foolish having done this again, but it seems impossible that a closet might not have a dark corner.

Nevertheless, this one does not. She flips out the closet light and turns back to the room and sees the picture on her dresser from their senior prom. Ellen and Shell in satin off-the-shoulder prom gowns, Gina in a torn t-shirt, hair hanging in front of her face. She is hopeful because she remembers, suddenly, that the picture had once been in the box with all her things from her life before Ichiro. She opens her top drawer and feels around. She finds a mahogany box, opens the lid, and inside there is a small silver dagger with a beautiful ivory carved handle, given to her by Sakamoto Collins when she married, in case things didn't work out. She shuts the box. Shuts the drawer and looks at the photograph again. She remembers taking the box out from the bottom of her closet a few weeks before her wedding. Yes. Where did she put it? It always stood out in the closet; that came clear to her now and she looks around the room as if she could have missed it next to a dresser or up against a wall. It was a tattered cardboard box with old useless things in it. Old hair ties and barrettes. Old journals with only scattered entries. Small paintings of hers that she kept when she emptied her apartment. The poster of the avant-garde German dance troupe she had brought to Vassar. And the viewfinder on the metal ball chain with the picture of them all smiling, wind whipping hair in their eyes, holding up their bloodied hands, behind them the Cyclone, the beach, that night they celebrated Ellen's big promotion: executive director of ArtNow after only two years. It was her happiest day. She called her mother from the restaurant and Claire said, "Dear, I'm not disappointed, *per se*. We were just hoping for something more stable." The viewfinder was in there with that picture. Oh, God, she thinks bringing her hand to her mouth. She remembers now. Taking the picture out, setting it on her dresser, declaring that nothing in that box had any place in her life anymore. The apartment clean and tailored, nothing unnecessary, everything with a place and a function, there was no good place to put that meaningless junk. That was what she told herself when she took the box (all on her own, not at the suggestion of the decorator or Ichiro or Claire) down to the basement and hurled it into the trash.

She shivers. She covers herself in blankets, burrows deep into her bed. Presses her head into the pillow in search of the sound, but it is gone. The sound is gone. There is an eerie silence. There is the small whine of sirens but no steady hum, no sound that soothes her. She makes the sound, thinking she can find it inside, but it just sounds like a lonely voice. She imagines the small boy sitting in the dark closet in Bushwick, finding the plug that powers everything and pulling it. This is what that would sound like: dead silence.

"Ellen!" Rosaria comes running into the room. "You're home? Why so soon?"

Ellen doesn't acknowledge her.

"Ellen?" Rosaria says quietly. "Don't worry. I'll get the bucket and some coffee."

"Come lie with me." Ellen speaks so quietly that Rosaria has to come closer to the bed.

"What did you say?"

"Lie with me. I'm cold."

Rosaria hesitates. The chill moves in stronger. Ellen is freezing, despite her body's best efforts to shiver it out, to heat itself through perpetual motion. She feels Rosaria's weight on the bed. First one knee, "Ellen? Are you OK?" Then another. "Why are you shivering? Are you sick?" Rosaria lays next to Ellen. "It's OK," she says and wraps her arms around Ellen. "It's OK," she says and rocks her. "Shhhhhh," she says, like she'd calm a baby, and Ellen feels the chill fall out of her. The soothing sound of the mother's shhhh in her ear, she loses herself in that. She is a baby, her cheek on her mother's shoulder. "It's OK," Rosaria says rocking her, holding her, warming her.

But it only lasts so long. Ellen pulls herself away. "Thank you, Rosaria," she whispers and rushes to the front hall and finds a gigantic wool winter coat. She slips on snow boots, grabs the keys to her mother's car, and Rosaria yells to her, "Where are you going like that? It's, like, eighty degrees outside!"

She doesn't feel the heat. She doesn't notice the looks from the strangers who pass her by and look her up and down. She runs with her long black coat flapping open and her floppy snow boots unbuckled and loose. Her hair is snarled up on one side, brittle and frizzled. She doesn't notice the looks people are giving her.

She is nervous standing on the corner, turning around in circles.

She fingers the car keys in her pocket. Where did she park? Where is it she intends to go? A young teenager walks by and asks, "A little warm? Lady, go home. If you've got one."

She's afraid. It's insane, she tells herself. I'm acting insane. She wishes she could go somewhere. Not to her apartment or to her mother's house, but somewhere.

She runs to the Promenade. She walks right up to the railing and places her hand on it and the sound, the vibration of the city moves through her and she feels her whole body let go a little. She takes a deep breath and looks around. Mothers play with their young children at the swings. One reaches her hand tenderly to her daughter's face and Ellen feels the gesture. She brings her face to the metal railing and leans into the city's vibration the way the child pushed her cheek into her mother's hand. Shhhhhh. She is a child. The house is warm. Shhhhhhhhhh. She extends both of her arms along the railing so she can feel it in her chest. Shhhhhhhhhhhhhhh. She is a baby. Claire rocks her. Ellen looks over her mother's shoulder, eyes clouded with tears. *I know, I know*, her mother says and Ellen loses herself in the steady rumble and bump of the trucks and cars that move through town down South Street along the length of their deep front lawn. Loses herself in her mother's shhhhhh.

The traffic on the BQE crashes below. The sound of the city, its traffic and digestion, the rattle of the trucks on South Street, *I know, I know* vibrating from her mother's chest into her, the wind blowing off the water, a helicopter swooping low across the harbor toward a pad on the southernmost tip of the island where Ichiro is probably snapping shut his briefcase, preparing to join the masses as they empty into the streets in search of a good lunch. A tug sounding to port, car horns blowing below, echoing in the trap of cement overhead, there it all is: Shhhhhhhhhhhhhhh. She wants to lean forward into the sound. Shhhhhhhhhhhhhhh. She wants the air in her ears. Shhhhhhhhhhhhhhh. She wants to reach out her fingers, stretch out her toes. She wants the sound to rush her like water and take her home.

GEORGY

SOMETIMES, IN THE MORNING before he fully wakes, Moses catches a view of blond, blood-matted hair just over his shoulder and he knows what that is.

In the beginning, when he first arrived, he saw Sally all the time in dreams. He'd meet her for dinner, take her out for ice cream, then to the movies, and so on. At the end of the date they'd return to their apartment and she'd ask him the question: Did you get the milk I asked you to buy a hundred fucking times? He'd answer Wha-wha-what? (That ugly stutter.) And she would laugh at him. Call him stupid. When she saw that there was no milk, she'd come to him casually and hit him like he was a woman. Moses blocked her blows, protected himself with arms, protected himself with legs. But she'd keep getting at him, calling him names for never fighting back, landing upper cuts on his ribs, jabs at his kidneys, gruesome kicks to his balls. Until she got bored and walked away. In the dream, just as in life, he reaches for the light, comes up behind her and wraps the cord tightly around her neck. He drags her to the floor, then to the car, then to the woods. A few hours later the police arrive at his apartment.

The dream always ends there because his life on the outside ended there, he figures.

The dream stopped after he met Lila and began working in the mailroom. But lately it's been coming back. At times, like this morning, he swears he's awake.

Moses lies on his cot and tries not to imagine what's lurking around him just on the other side of the fine line between this world and that. What gore awaits him. What burdens he'll carry. And then Jorge arrives. He looks at Moses in panic. He gesticulates wildly, brings his hand to his heart. He's looking for the letters again and when he doesn't find them, he falls to his knees in front of Moses. The restless girl pulls at his neck as Jorge struggles to stay on his knees, struggles to keep Moses' gaze and puts his hands together like he's praying, imploring, begging for help.

"Leave me alone," Moses yells at Jorge. When he yells his voice is startling, the way a normal voice can shock after one has been quiet and alone for days and days. He is beginning to have that way about him, he knows it. The way of the old men who have stopped living in the world of the prison and have ventured in—into a world of their own. Moses has one now. In it he has fallen in love with a boy. In it he has found himself. And in it he believes Jorge is just a product of his imagination. But alas, he has spoken to him. And he sees, as if for the first time, that Jorge is really here. And he is really desperate. He looks at Jorge there on his knees, imploring Moses to help him, and he thinks that he ought to have more compassion for his old friend, his protector. But he doesn't. He doesn't feel badly for him at all because Jorge is here to punish him, isn't he? Punish him for the phone calls, for cavorting with Georgy. "Go ahead and kill me, you old fuck," Moses says. "You had love. You can take your burdens and go somewhere else. Find someone who cares, Jorge."

Moses walks to the sink. He washes his hands and splashes water on his face. He fully expects to turn around to an empty cell, but Jorge is still there. He's sitting on the floor with his head in his hands; he's weeping. The girl yanks his neck as she reaches for something behind them.

"Oh, God damn you, Jorge," Moses says. "Can't you see we were wrong? Look at you. You killed her. You *killed* her. That's who you are, a murderer. No matter how good you try to be, you'll never convince yourself it's true."

Outside the cell a guard yells, "Live count!"

COLLIN GETS UPSET AT morning chow because Georgy asks Moses if he wants his piece of bread. "There's already butter on it," he tells him, as if he is selling it. "I'm full," he says, "and I don't want it." Collin, who has been moody for most of the meal, reaches across Don, knocking his spoon to the floor, and grabs the piece of bread like it is someone's shirt collar. Then he throws it clear across the room.

The birds chirp wildly and a fight breaks out among them as they tear the bread in small buttered pieces with their tiny greased beaks.

Moses doesn't see Collin or Georgy all day.

THE NEXT MORNING, MOSES closes his eyes but it doesn't stop the gathering of the ghouls. They're here to remind him how he's not long for this world. They arrive one by one. First Jorge and his girl. They hang by the bars, Jorge looking out like he's waiting for something to happen; the girl looking over her shoulder like there's something she's missing. Then Sally comes into view. Sally with the blond, blood-matted hair stuck to the wound on her neck. She's been taking on shape, getting her form. Looking at her now, Moses remembers the first time he saw her, the brown streaks of beef blood down her tattered and torn deli whites. She was the girl from the burger joint. When Moses ended up at her counter and saw that soft set of nearly white curls trapped in her hair net and her clean white smile, he liked her right off. She was the perfect lady.

She has a light cord around her neck. She looks a little blue, but other than that, not bad. Her flossy hair, braided and neat like it always was, has held up well, considering. And she's dressed real nice. Her clothes flawlessly pressed and clean, save a few grass stains from the field where they found her. And there's the soiled spot on the back of her skirt from when she lost control of her bowels. All Moses has got left are his kidneys; his bowels have already said *sayonara* so he doesn't feel badly for her about that spot. Once his kidneys fail, he'll be with Sally full time. Like Jorge's girl, she'll hang all over him, and he'll have to drag her ass around for eternity. He squeezes his yellowed hand and can't make a fist. There go my Goddamned kidneys, he thinks, and tries to avoid Sally's confrontational stare. She reminds Moses first of his bladder and how each night it fails him, then of his heart and the thick, heavy pain he's been feeling there, keeping him from catching his breath since Georgy went missing. He knows Sally's here to tell him he's near the end. A warm trickle of piss pools around his thigh.

He gets up to get ready for breakfast. This doesn't happen easily. Standing takes a few tries and he usually passes gas and leaves some kind of mark in his shorts. He hasn't bothered to get a proper haircut. His hair has turned nearly all white and has grown down below his collar. He combs it back with his wet fingers. He washes his face with water and rubs the last of a sliver of the good soap to a lather for under his arms and between his legs. The cell is filled with the mingling mangled and a little decayed; he'd blame the stench on them, but he knows what he smells like. He'd need more than this lousy piece of lye to cut the odor that has permeated his clothes.

It's difficult for him to get the room he needs to wash.

He elbows in the direction of Sally and says, *Move it, Toots*. She ignores him like Jorge does.

He stands naked. His legs white like a Goddamned plucked chicken, his breasts hanging like a native, his dick shriveled to a raisin. He takes the sheets from the bed and in front of this beautiful, rotting woman, in front of his friend, he cleans the stains he made in the night. It's humiliating. But he's gotten used to this. He only gets fresh linens once a week, so he does this every morning. *Enjoy it. Go ahead. You deserve a good laugh over it,* he says to them as he scrubs the sheet with cold water and the soap dissolves to nearly nothing and his hair falls into his eyes.

When he dresses, his clothes are stiff and only slightly dry. Nothing ever really dries in a concrete cell, not even in summer. He shivers pretty much all the time because of it, and the chill that catches up with him when he least expects it could be the one that kills him. He hangs the sheet over the sink and the toilet and the bed in hopes it will dry enough before night. He nearly falls on his ass a couple of times because he's afraid of touching them. Afraid he might feel them or his hand might go right through one of them or, worse, get stuck.

He folds the thin, smelly blanket and hangs it at the end of the cot so his mattress can air out and hopefully dry.

It is going on five days since Georgy and Collin went missing and B block is being run like a real jail. While Moses is locked up and unable to go downstairs and read the newspaper, he sees all the guys released for school and Industry, released for their jobs as porters, released for jobs in the administration building, in the hospital, in the mess hall. Corn, he watches him. Released. Released. Released. They are all released.

When Miller calls him for chow, he steps down one step at a time. He tries to focus, but if he takes a stair at the wrong angle, he could take a tumble and that will be the end of it. He can think of about ten other ways of quitting this life that appeal to him more than a broken neck.

On his way downstairs, he sees Georgy's phone book still on the picnic table and he loses his breath and his appetite.

LOCKED IN HIS CELL for the afternoon, Moses falls asleep and in his dream he believes he hears a girl's voice outside of his cell. She's protesting, saying she must get to him; she must find him. Moses wants her to come to him. He's looking forward to seeing her face, to touching her hair. He wants to get out of bed, to go stand at the bars. In his dream, he believes that if he gets to the bars, it will help her find him. He can hear her calling for him. *Moses?* She calls. Her sing-songy voice familiar in a far-off sort of way. And then it comes to him all at once: the voice is his sister Estella's, and he's terrified. Pinned to the mattress. He wants to escape, yet Moses can't help but give into a sad moment of missing her. He remembers her. He suffers that gleaming blond hair of hers. Those blue, innocent eyes. And even now at this old age, on this tippy threshold where he performs the daily balancing act between life and death, he can still remember what it felt like when she let him hide with her under the blankets in her bed and the shelter that was her body—young and sweet—from the storm of their mother. He can't move. There she is. A chubby girl of ten or so. Hair the color of sun. It hangs low and loops around her kid breasts. She looks at him. Holds up a hand, as if to say, Ah! I've found you, and as she comes closer, Moses tries frantically to get away. He scurries and crumples himself in a ball in the corner of his cot. She keeps coming. Moses? She asks innocently. For a young girl in Albemarle Projects, where they lived, the choices were simple: join a convent or become a prostitute. She was twelve when Moses watched a man pull her into his car and he remembers the soft ten-dollar bill she took out of her pocket and showed him. That night she invited Moses into her bed, made the fort of blankets, pulled him close to her, but she didn't wrap herself around him and make herself a safe harbor; instead she pulled down his shorts to practice. He lunges forward and grabs her neck. Still, while he holds and shakes her, she reaches out to him and Moses wakes himself with a glass-shattering shriek.

BEFORE REC THE DOORS unlock all at once. The cranks turn. The levers pull. The doors open. They are released, some of them. Others, for various reasons, are not. And they gather, stiff at first, shocked from real days behind bars. They look like travelers unloading off a bus, taking a bathroom break. They mill about. Moses finds the paper on the picnic table, as it always is, only there's a pile of bird shit on it. Georgy's phone book is still there too.

Don comes from behind and says, "Quick, meet me at my cell. I have some tasty fried chicken I cooked up in my hot pot." And Moses, who hasn't eaten well in quite some time, follows. Moses loses him quickly among the men milling around. There are more than usual. They find excuses to delay Miller, bombard him with requests for passes to the hospital, for grievance forms, for follow-up information on previous grievances. The men are stir-crazy. Restless. Miller yells, "Line up!" But no one listens.

Moses steals along the line of cells in Don's direction. He doesn't know exactly which one it is, but he knows it is far away from the OIC office and therefore one of the best rooms in the house. Moses moves sneakily down the row. Some cells are neat, with laundry strung up, cooking utensils gathered in old tissue boxes, painting palettes strewn about, clear plastic typewriters set on lockers like his, clothing neatly folded on high shelves at the far wall. Others are in total disarray. Deathly smells emanating from them. He glances in each and continues down the row, until he stops, realizing he passed a cell with a large slumped form on the cot. He steps cautiously backwards until he is standing in front of Georgy. He is lying on the cot naked. His eyes open but not seeing. Moses can't tell if he is dead or alive. Collin is wrapped around him tightly. Collin sleeps, yet he holds Georgy with the grip of a wrestler. His leg is slung over his small body, pinning him down.

Moses, who tracks Georgy's eyes like a hawk, sees a flicker of movement. A moment of recognition. Georgy glances at him, tries for a smile.

Miller calls them to rec. "Too late," Don says, coming out of the cell next to Collin's. And though the smells in his cell are heavenly, Moses is sure he couldn't eat after seeing Georgy. As they line up to march to the yard, Moses grabs the phone book and slides it under his sweatshirt.

He slumps as he dials. He is so consumed with his troubles he doesn't entertain what he might say if she answers, if she accepts the charges. He gives the operator Georgy's name and bats aside images of Georgy and what Collin might do to that boy. His boy. His stomach lurches as the phone rings in his ear. "Hello?" says a woman and he is stunned into silence. "Hello?" she says again and an automated voice says, "You have received a collect call from Hardenberg Correctional Facility from Georgy Smith. Will you accept the charges?" In the background somewhere behind the voice, he hears the plaintive whine of a child. It whimpers and begins to wail and Moses is both jealous and pissed off as he listens to the whine slowly morph into a high-pitched and persistent sound. What is that? He pushes the phone to his ear. "Yes," says Laughlin, L. She says *yes!* And there he sits on the line with a real, live woman. He can hear her breathing. Slowly the sound takes form and he understands it's the sound of a dog barking. A dog! He smiles and presses the phone harder to his ear. He doesn't want to miss a thing. "Shush," Moses hears her say. But the dog keeps barking insolently. "Hello?" she says. "Are you there?" Moses loves this. The sound of the dog, hearing her speaking freely and loudly, he feels like he's in the room with her. He wonders what room she's in. A kitchen? No, there is no echo, no open sound from a hard floor. It's a carpeted room. A bedroom. He imagines a hairbrush filled with her hair. He imagines windows. A view of trees. He imagines lawns cut and smelling fresh, flowers filling the air with their bawdy scents. He imagines the life he pictured for Lila, a fairytale cottage, a garden, a tool shed, muddy boots by a door. The barking continues. "I'm hanging up now," Laughlin, L. says. The line cuts and she is gone. And so are the room and the dog and the sound of life outside of the prison. Moses hangs on for a moment, pressing the phone to his ear.

He is slightly stunned as he walks away and considers her voice. There was huskiness to it, like she is someone who's resigned herself to a certain misfortune. And he likes this. He thinks there's intelligence in suffering. She knows how to be sad. "I'm hanging up now," she said. She said to him.

That night, during the free hour when they are allowed to mill around and mingle with one another before live count, Georgy runs out of Collin's cell, naked and small. He hurries to his cell, sits on his cot, and shivers.

Moses, who is at the picnic table when he escapes, comes to him. Don comes, too. He looks in at Georgy and says he'll be right back with a plate of food. Moses moistens a cloth and wipes off the lipstick smeared on Georgy's face. He shakes like a child as Moses cleans and dries him, eases a soft sweatshirt over his head, pulls on underwear, sweatpants, and socks. All the while, Georgy's eyes lock on something far off.

"She talked to me, Georgy," Moses says. "I called Laughlin, L."

Georgy doesn't break his gaze.

Don arrives with plastic plates overflowing with rice and peas and fried chicken, slightly sweet flatbread that Don says he made at the bottom of the hot pot like a pancake or crêpe. Georgy eats slowly at first. Don holds a cup of water to his lips, and he drinks it down fast.

"She really talked to you, Moses?" Georgy asks in a raspy whisper. "She really did?"

"She did."

Georgy chews a small bite and then another. "Tomorrow I'm gonna call her again," he says. His body, deprived for too long of food and water, begins asking for more. It growls loudly, and Don rushes off to fill another plate.

"Moses!" Georgy says in alarm. "My book!"

Moses holds it up to him. "It's right here, son. Right here." He pats the book by Georgy's side.

"Moses," Georgy says. "You just called me *son*."

THE NEXT DAY, COLLIN is back in his seat in front of *The Price is Right*. Don is seated beside him, and Georgy is back to his old self. But emboldened. And the block is back to normal. The men are allowed to wander; the bars of their cells stay open. The sparrows dance, even they can feel the new day. And the day moves quickly. Moses had a night without dreams, a morning free of ghosts, his speech is clear, and he feels healthy and young. He reads the paper, he goes to chow, he chooses to believe that Georgy's return, his apparent good spirits, mean that all is well again.

Georgy calls during rec, but doesn't get an answer. When they walk away dejected, Collin says, "No one wants to talk to you. Look at you, you stupid, ugly shit. And you, you old man. Fucking fools," he says, and the men around him laugh because he laughs.

"Not true," Georgy says. "Moses talked to her yesterday. You're just jealous, faggot." And he bounds off with the carefree bounce of a child. Moses cannot fathom the guts in this boy.

That night, Collin says, "Keep it down, dumbass." But Georgy pays him no heed. He makes Moses stand next to him, book open, reading him the number because in this excitement he cannot remember it for the life of him.

"567-1346," Moses says.

"What was it again?" Georgy asks.

"567-1346. No. You hit the seven, you want the six."

"Moses, you do it," Georgy says, handing him the receiver. Georgy takes the book from Moses and he holds the page open.

"Back up, back some more. A little more, OK! Right there, 5...6...7...1...3...4...6... It's ringing," Moses says handing him the phone.

"It's ringing!" Georgy giggles.

"Here. Take it. Say your name," Moses says.

"What?"

"Take it! Say your *name.*"

"Keep it down," Collin says from behind them.

"Hello?" Georgy says into the phone.

"Your NAME," Moses says.

"Oh. Yeah. Georgy Smith. My name's Georgy," he says real loud as if the person on the other end of the line is hard of hearing. "Operator's trying the call," he says to Moses. "She's calling her! It's ringing. Moses, it's..."

He goes quiet and listens.

"OK," Georgy says and waits. Then he quietly asks, "Hello? Laughlin, L.?"

"I said keep it the fuck down!" Collin yells from close behind.

"This is Georgy. Georgy Smith. I sent you a letter," he says, and right then Collin pulls the phone from his hand, slams down the receiver, and yells, "I SAID KEEP IT THE FUCK DOWN."

Georgy's eyes are wide as plates. His head twitches to the right four quick times and he sprints away holding his head in his hands. He runs and runs and runs; he cries while he runs. Moses stands close to Collin, clutching Georgy's book to his chest.

"Give me your lighter, old man."

Moses looks at the floor and shakes his head, no.

"Give me the lighter!"

Moses refuses. Georgy runs by and takes off again, hands to his head, *nonononononononono* he yells; his feet beat time with his words. Sparrows dart above, following him the whole length of the cell block in urgent dips and bobs.

Collin takes the phone book from Moses' arms, reaches into Moses' pocket, takes out the lighter, and pushes him down onto the floor. When Georgy comes running by again, he holds the lighter to the book until it's in flames and throws it on the floor in Georgy's path. Georgy stops in front of it, falls to his knees, and clutches it to him. His cheap clothes go right up, engulfing him in flames.

THE STRANGER

THE STRANGER FOLLOWS TOO close. When she looks back at him, he appears quite casual, like he too is walking the exact route he walks every night of his life. At first he is menacing, then he is not. He is stable, surefooted, square-shouldered. He has the limp. A newspaper held lightly under his arm, briefcase by his side. A few blocks and Gina looks back again. He keeps pace, but hasn't bothered to overtake her, which she's been waiting for since she left O'Malley's. At York she stops and waits. When he steps up the curb, they are eye to eye.

"You don't look yourself. That was a nasty spill."

"How do you know how I do or don't look?" Gina asks.

"I know you."

"No, you don't." She turns to go, but he takes her elbow. "Let me walk you home. Your place is nearby, isn't it?" He kisses her. But kind-like. As if he wouldn't have done it if she hadn't leaned into him at exactly the right moment.

So there they are, in her apartment.

"Water," the stranger says when she offers him a drink after they stumble into her place. "Just water." He drinks all of it in one gulp and when he bends to kiss her she tastes the minerals; she tastes the metals. The clean, washed-out mouth, wet, cold and stony like prison walls, like the cell where her dad died that morning or the night before. Her mother didn't say when; her mother doesn't much go for details.

"Wait," the stranger says in that slow, quiet voice spoken from the side of his mouth. "Slow down. I want to take you in."

So she, who doesn't like to be told what, who likes it when her men keep their mouths and eyes shut, says, "OK," and puts her shirt back on because tonight is different.

"In front of the window," he says, propped on a bed pillow with the enthusiasm of a boy. His wallet tossed and fallen open on the side table, his briefcase and newspaper over on the coffee table, tie, shirt and pants on the grass mat in front of the door. He looks like he should be some kid's dad, but no ring. And he has asked to come here instead of an alley; he is not rushing. He has a broad, smooth chest, and his shoulders have the look of someone who lifted a lot of weights once, the muscle built, the shoulders rounding forward and the arms strong and beautiful. But that doesn't matter. They are all beautiful when they are like this, waiting. He looks at her with gray eyes and rubs his hand over his shorn hair, nearly all silver.

She does it. Moves in front of the window. She knows once he's in her, his eyes will close. Roll back. He'll look into himself and she will watch him move like a ghost, then she will tell him to leave. Until then, she doesn't mind him watching.

"Come here," he says, tender. She is in the window taking off her shirt. He is watching. He could have been speaking to a little girl. "Get over here," he says and he could just as soon have put her on his lap and tapped his foot and sung a song that sounded like a horse galloping across the desert. She gets over there. He puts his hands on her face. He kisses her lips. He places a hand on the back of her head and his soft tongue finds a way in.

And then he is lifting her up, and she is wrapping her legs around his waist; he is carrying her like a child to her bed. Her head rocks on his shoulder with each of his father steps. His smell is something she knows in an old way. Her nose is not nestled in his neck; it is nestled in Jorge's.

Then he is over her, looking at her as he moves into her. So much life coming from him in waves, filling her up, washing away that which she can't stop seeing: her father on a cold slab. With each wave crashes moments. There are not too many. There were exactly six weekends in the trailer in the yard. On those nights her mother put her to bed too early and as she lay awake a girl child inside the walls of a men's prison, she heard the deep and desperate moans of her parents' lovemaking through the cheap and flexing trailer walls. When she heard her mother's breath catch in a snore, she tiptoed to the living room to find her father awake, waiting for her. *What is your homework?* He would ask her as she climbed under his arm, and the walls fell away, the razor wire and the watch-towers disappeared, the guard standing outside the trailer, and the screams echoing from the cell blocks dissolved into ordinary night sounds as they recited times tables, talked science, and she admitted to him that she didn't like reading books because she didn't like things that were made up. Make believe scared her, she told him. It was impossible to imagine that he had ever killed a girl.

She fell asleep on him, he on her. Each breath she took was filled with him. In the morning, before her mother woke, they snuck back into their beds. Jorge tucking her in, kissing her eyelids closed.

Then the stranger moves out and there he is again. Jorge. Father. Dead on a slab.

The stranger kisses her eyelids closed. She doesn't tell him to leave. He kisses her knee where it is scraped. They sleep wrapped up in each other, and Gina dreams she is in a trailer in the yard, tucked under her father's heavy arm.

THEN THE LETTER ARRIVES from Jorge. When Gina sees his addled penmanship, she shakes and the letter falls to the floor. When she reads it, there he is: The up-and-down rhythm of his Spanglish. Words written in that hand like a whisper from the dead, and he begins to take some form for her. A flickering in her periphery, like a projected image shown in too bright a light. She squints her eyes. She turns to unlock the door to her flat, and out of the corner of her eye, she swears she sees something.

She strides to the kitchen counter and dumps her bags: a few necessities, a bottle of vodka. She opens the vodka and gulps from it.

She dials the number she knows by heart. There is the voice of an old man, "Hello?"

"It's Gina."

"Oh, child, your heart is heavy. I can hear it in your name. But he is at peace. He is with his God. He will live on in Glory. He died a peaceful death."

"His life was not peaceful, Father. I don't believe his death could have been, but that's nice of you to say. Can I see him?" she asks. "I just want to see him one last time. I can come home…"

"I'm sorry, Gina. That is not what he asked for." *Don't try to come and find me*, he had written. *I am not here*, it said. *I have never been this body, but I have always been your father. And now I will fill the air around you, my love, m'ija. By the time you receive this letter, my body will be dust, and I will be just love for you.*

"Why didn't they ask me?" Gina says.

"It was for Jorge. Not for you, dear. I'm sorry."

"What about Ed? Didn't he tell them to wait for me?"

"He did. I gave him his rites and when Ed and I returned to find out what would happen next, he was gone. Those were his wishes. He's with you, child. Just close your eyes."

"It's not like that," she says. "Not for me. We were never together long enough to remember the details."

"We must discuss the services."

"There is no rush now."

"He must be put to rest soon. We don't want anything to happen to him."

"He wanted you to hold onto him until I come up, can you do that? He was afraid my mother would leave him in the back of the closet when she moves to Florida."

"Has she left?"

"If not yet, soon."

"I can hold onto him here. But you will have to come inside to get him. They won't let him leave unless he is received by kin. You must not wait."

"It doesn't really matter now, as I see it," she says.

Gina's gaze falls on a business card that sticks out under a grocery bag. She puts a finger on it and slides it out. The card is fancy letterpress, professional. There are the letters Esq. after his name, which is Jack Harding.

JACK HARDING WAITS FOR her at home nearly every night of the next two and a half months. She has stopped bringing people back to her place, which is probably his intent, so in this way he has wormed into her life more than any man ever has before this, including Arthur, including her father. Though in death, Jorge has become more of a presence.

There are things she can't explain. In the middle of her days when she is sitting in writing sessions at the *Nightly News*, or even when she is on the phone arranging interviews with guests, scooping and landing newsmakers, whispers of her father's form gather in her periphery. She is missing beats because of it. It worsens with the arrival of Jorge's belongings. Her letters have his fingerprints on them. They are worn at the edges where he once held them, leafed through them, looking for moments to revisit. They are all there. Thousands of pages of her life. Some written in crayon. Some written in pencil, faded and smudged, over which Jorge traced the disappearing letters in blue ink to preserve her perfect child words. There are her diplomas. Her new-hire letter from the *Nightly News*. There are pictures of her from magazines; there is a photo of her receiving an Emmy. The night they arrive, she stays up all night reading through the letters.

At five a.m. the next morning, as she brushes her teeth, she feels a soft flutter of fingers across her cheek and her curtain of black hair blows open, exposing her face in the mirror. She looks up and sees that her face is becoming more rectangular and the skin over the bridge of her nose is tightening and appears almost polished, like Jorge's. She looks around. There are no open windows. Nothing to account for the sudden gust.

At work, she drops the phone and loses the line to Iran because she is sure that someone has snuck up behind her and put their warm hands on the curve of her lower back. No one's there. But there is a lingering warmth and stirring inside of her, so she picks up the phone and calls her doctor.

Things with Arthur go badly that night. She falls asleep in the shower and he can't find her, until he does, and when she is too tired to get up and run, he kicks her out and tells her he is disgusted with her. Jack is waiting for her when she gets home and she decides to tell him this is quite enough. When she nears him, the air turns into a curtain of light silk and her vision gets cloudy; her balance is lost, and from nowhere there are hands holding her under her arms, softening her fall to the sidewalk so that it feels like it all happens in slow motion. She lands unharmed. Jack Harding, who is still at a distance as she falls, arrives in time to give her a hand up.

He doesn't say anything, which is the right thing to do. Instead, he holds her elbow as she brushes off her knees. He kneels down and picks up her lipstick and her keys. She feels light-headed. He walks her the rest of the way home, opens her door, leaves her on the couch, puts her phone where she can reach it, spreads a blanket over her, and leaves his card again, in case she needs someone to call.

And she does need someone to call, because she feels as though her heart is going to explode out of her chest and the couch rocks like she is on a rough sea. But she doesn't call Jack. She calls Ellen. She insists the maid get her, despite the fact that she is entertaining. How could you forget? She asks, and she can't quite remember the response except that she is left with the feeling she should have known better than to call and falls asleep with the phone to her ear and dreams that she hangs on a swing on the elementary school playground, the world darkening around her as her head falls slowly to the earth. She watches the ground as it comes closer, as the swing turns her in eights. Ellen is far off in the distance. Shell, too. They both ignore her, as if this is perfectly OK. This sudden turning away from each other is part of some sort of an understanding that they all prearranged and Gina just didn't get the message. She can feel all the heartache of losing them. In the deepest part of her dream, the empty place in her chest where she was once filled by a father and friends pulls her down closer and closer to the ground until all she can see is the scratch of the earth, the points of small pebbles, and the truth that there is nothing left.

She wakes on the floor bathed in a surreal light. The apartment is flooded with a soft and beautiful glow. She sits up and gathers the blanket under her chin. Through the light she can see that out on the street it is still night. She looks around. The empty feeling has made its way through all of her limbs. Her bones are hollow like a bird's. She feels light and insubstantial as she rolls back onto the couch. She tries to turn herself away from the light and close her eyes, but she can feel it warming her bones. She has not been returning Shell's calls. She is telling herself it's on principle; she is punishing Shell. But in the middle of the night, in the bath of this warm and loving light, which melts the chill that filled her with ice while she was on the floor, she wonders if she isn't cutting off her nose to spite her face.

The light gathers and strengthens. She half thinks it might take some form, that her father might suddenly walk out of it. But he does not. Instead, it becomes a small sun that moves into her and settles into a hot center at the bottom of her belly and she falls asleep with a clear sense that she will never be the same. What this means is too hard to pin down, but as she drifts off to sleep, she thinks, *I don't want to be alone.*

THE NEXT DAY THE Iranians are there and she walks out on Arthur as he is beginning to pitch a fit. His voice cracks when she tells him that the show is all set, she's approved the script, so have the Iranians, he shouldn't need her, the staff is able to take it from here. This is an easy night because it is just one long interview. These big shows are hard on the front end, but the night of is a piece of cake. "I have to go to the doctor," she tells Arthur and he yells at her, "What's so fucking important that you can't go tomorrow?" She gives him the finger and walks out the door. As she leaves, he says, "I made you; I can break you. Don't you dare leave me."

She leaves.

Dr. Wildman's office is under a limestone house on East

Eighty-Fifth Street. She is a short, thick, blond woman who wears blue eye shadow and who understands the situation. "There are a lot of options," she says. "Nothing we can do in the office, but I can refer you to a place downtown that can take care of this. You will need someone to take you home. Do you have anyone?"

"I can find someone," Gina says. "When will it be?"

"Let me talk to Nicole and ask her to call down there. Do you have a minute to wait, or do you want me to call you with the details?"

"I can wait."

"OK. It might take a minute. You can get dressed. The falling will continue and the other physical stuff will persist until after the procedure."

"What about the visualizations and the taste in my mouth?"

"The taste will stop as soon as it's over. The visualizations are something else. I don't know what to tell you. Have you lost anyone close lately? I have a cousin who had similar things happen after her mother died."

"No," Gina lies. "I don't think that's it."

"I could refer you to a psychologist. It could be the stress. You work too much. I've told you that before. You should take a vacation after this. The exhaustion you're feeling from the hormones could be making it hard to keep up with your normal pace. I'd take it easy until all this is over. You'll need to take a long weekend to recoup afterwards, anyway. You should go away. Come see me or call for a referral if the other stuff continues."

In the cab on the ride home, she holds the card with the date and the time and the address of the office where it will be happening next week because anything later wouldn't be good for anyone. Jack Harding is standing like a sentry at her building door. When she sees him, she has a flutter of anticipation in her chest, as if she has forgotten all the circumstances of her life. She remembers waking on the floor, the light, the strong sensation that everything has changed. So foolish. Here in the daylight when everything is harsh and sad, she knows that she is going to tell Jack to go home. If he doesn't, if for some reason tonight is the night that he sees something in her face that makes him want to stay, she'll tell him what is about to happen to his child. She puts her hand on her belly. She doesn't know she's done this until the cabbie asks her to pay and she has to remove her hand to give him the cash she's clutching there.

She steps out of the cab. When she looks at Jack, who never betrays his stoic resolve to be nothing to her until she invites him to be more, she wonders what he would do if she walked up and kissed his cheek. Would he smile and say he'd been waiting, or would he stay reserved until all her armor had been removed? She walks to him in her long-legged way, but slower than usual—she has learned to be cautious from all the falling.

As she walks to him, she sees his eye pulled from her to the street. He raises his arm up (as if he can do something) in the exact fraction of a second that the brakes of the cab engage and the tires scream and the scream echoes up the sides of the buildings up, up, up into the air, and they all—Jack, Gina, the child's mother—hear that horrifying thud. And Jack, who is trying to move, is trying to get his legs to move one in front of the other, who is stuck in one of those nightmares when the horror is upon you but your body just can't respond and you can't save yourself no matter how hard you try, turns white, looks at Gina with his eyes wide, pupils dilated, and begins to convulse in a way only a soldier would when proven, once again, that he can't reverse the course of things. His knees buckle; he falls to her feet. She kneels, puts her hand on his shorn head, on his cold, wet face. The blood has drained from all his extremities and is coursing around his heart the way the body keeps itself alive when in shock.

"The kid's up," she says. But he doesn't hear her. "He's with his mother. He's not dead." He shakes his head. He can't hear. He looks at her as if his ears are full of the ringing of post-mortar.

She slings his heavy arm over her shoulders and lifts him. She holds him up while she finds her keys, opens the door, and helps him up the stairs, taking them one at a time, like with a child or an old man. As they ascend up the simple staircase, she thinks it better not to tell him any details.

She helps him into her place. He drops his bag on the grass mat, just as he had the first night, and when they look up, they see the apartment is filled with the white swirl of her letters tossed as if by a wind.

"What's happened in here?" he asks. "A window open?"

"Must be," she says as they trudge over letters she wrote in fifth grade, letters she wrote in twelfth when she was already dead, over letters she wrote last year in which she told her father that her life was exactly as she wanted it because she got to call the shots and didn't have to answer to anyone. "Ha!" he'd said when she saw him at Christmas time, "Being free to imprison yourself in work is not free. You deserve love, *m'ija*. More than my love. The love of a real family of your own. You must listen to your father who knows of these things." He held her hand and looked her in the eye when he said this, so she didn't protest. She kissed him, thinking it would reassure him, but he knew her better than that. The kiss, holding his hand, those were both lasts.

She brings Jack Harding to the couch and helps him down. She props a pillow under his head and begins to gather the letters. There is a stiff breeze coming through the window, which is slightly cracked. Despite it, the letters don't so much as flutter.

She is about to ask him if he wants some water, but his eyes are closed. In her bedroom, she sits on the edge of the bed, and dials the phone. "I need to see you. Tonight," she says.

"You know what to do," he says.

"No, Arthur. This is different," but he's already hung up the phone.

She changes her clothes, finds something comfortable and loose fitting and brings Jack Harding a glass of water. He opens his eyes when she touches his arm.

"Water?" she asks.

"Water," he says. He props himself up and sips at it slowly. She takes the glass from him and kisses his wet, cool mouth. Then she climbs onto the couch and puts her face in his neck. He wraps his arm around her and drifts off to sleep. She slips out of his arms, "I'll be right back."

SHE'S LOST TRACK OF when that was. At first, she tried to count each time it got dark and each time it got light. The blindfold over her eyes allows at least this much. According to her stomach and the body that is growing inside her, she hasn't eaten in over a year. But, of course, that could mean she's been here a day or a week. She doesn't know. She slips in and out of consciousness a lot and is starting to believe what was just a passing thought the night Arthur took the whip to her: she's been left for dead.

When she arrived and asked if they could talk, he screamed at her to *RUN*. To hide if she knew what was good for her, and then he began to cry. She said, "Arthur you know as well as I what's happening here…"

"Run!" he screamed in her face again. Spit flew in her eye.

"I can't run, Arthur. I'm tired. I want to say goodbye."

"You belong to me!" He screamed like a child having a tantrum. She brought her hand to his face, to comfort him. "Don't touch me!" he said, slapping her hand away. Then he ran from her. She followed, thinking she would find him on his bed; maybe she would hold him. But he had anticipated this. He leapt out of a closet, grabbed her, tied her up with a strength Gina had never felt in him. He put her on the rack, put the gag in her mouth, and beat her until he was too tired to go on. She slipped out of consciousness and when she came to, the room was silent. There was no sound except the sirens on the streets and the creaks and cracks of his apartment.

At first, she thought there must be a housekeeper who would come, or that he'd tire of this and return. But no one came. She has stopped trying to hold her head up. Something is happening. There is the beginning of something terrible going on inside her.

PART III

Snow

MARTY

THERE IS A LOUD bang on the front of the house. Then the low, busy voices of men. A crash. A screaming machine. Shell hears heavy boots climbing up a metal ladder. A voice on the other side of the wall. "I'll take the front, Pedro. You take the back. We'll have the rest of this knocked off by noon." There is a splintering crack of wood. Then another. She moves quickly from the window to the middle of the floor. She squeezes between the foot of her bed and the vanity chair. Marty barks. She looks out the window and there he is. His hair pushed up by the stupid sweatband. If he sees her, he pretends that he doesn't.

Shell woke that morning from a sorrowful dream of John to Marty standing on her chest, his long claws digging into the soft skin at the base of her neck, his impertinent face hanging in hers. There was a smell that she was sure after her second sniff wasn't something her mother was preparing in the Crock-Pot. She turned her head to where the smell seemed strongest and there was a pile of dog shit on her pillow, and this reminded her that today the divorce papers are due and the exterminators are coming. The house is to be tented; there will be bombs.

Outside, she hears the warning beep beep beep of a large truck backing onto the lawn to deliver a dumpster. The fact that the entire façade was pulled off the house and now lay in debris piles lacing the front of the house among decapitated rhododendrons, creating general havoc on the lawn, has destroyed both her mother and her father. During the previous night's dinner, they had the most civil conversation they'd had in months; they shared their grief that the dumpster had to arrive at all, mourned the near demolition of their home. "It was just bad luck," Ed said to Sid as they stood nearer than usual and peered out over the orchids onto the lawn.

From the floor where she sits avoiding Dave, the shit on the pillow, the divorce papers on the vanity, Shell hears the truck lower the dumpster, issuing the final deathblow to the grass. She hears Dave and Pedro begin to clean up the mess.

There is a large manila envelope on the vanity, and inside there are twelve tabbed places where she must sign her name. She is supposed to return them right away. John called and said, "I think it's best for both of us if we make this quick and painless, like a Band-Aid." She asks aloud, to someone else, God maybe, Why does he win? In the dream, he belonged to her still, and she had been glad about that until he announced matter-of-factly that he was dead. Then he simply receded from her and became smaller and smaller. She suffered this the way a wife would, her chest heavy, her breath deep, her grief mounting until it woke her. When she awoke, she pitied herself a widow. It felt wonderful. Her heart filled with all the longing she hadn't had the guts to let in.

But there is the manila envelope waiting for her.

Lorna is an experience he needs to give himself, like a gift; he has no remorse; he's found his path, if only Shell can find hers.

There is no good in holding on.

Her head throbs. She gets up, sits in the vanity chair and pulls out the papers and signs each one. She tries to make her handwriting look peppy and strong in case John cares to interpret it. In the mirror, she is framed in wicker. She can see that her face is that different face, the one John used to tell her about, the one she'd shrivel into when things got bad. She brings her finger to her mouth and chews.

Sɪᴅ ɪs sᴇᴀᴛᴇᴅ ᴀᴛ the kitchen table dressed in her work clothes—a lovely khaki suit, a color she wears on warm September days in lieu of white—unconsciously holding the handle of a cup of black coffee inches from her chin. She holds up the waistband of a pair of Ed's pants that are draped over the chair next to her and shows Shell the waistband, points to the size. Forty-eight.

"Where did he go?" Shell asks. She is waiting for her mother to tell her she looks nice. She dressed in one of the sweater sets Sid purchased for her, and a pair of respectable slacks and pumps. Sid doesn't say anything.

"Where do you think," Sid says. "I wish he'd just have the guts to come out and tell me. That's all."

"Maybe there's nothing to tell," Shell says.

"Where has he been? Of course there's something to tell."

Shell shrugs.

"You have too much make-up on. You look like a clown, but the clothes I bought fit you nicely." Sid gets up and washes the dirty dishes and inspects her Vanda, which has seen better days. "Ellen's in town. Why don't you call her today?"

"Ellen?" Shell asks, stunned. "Come on, Marty. Let's get this over with," she says, grabbing a bowl, a jug of water, his leash and a bag of food. Marty hops from side to side. He's been pent up in the house for months. "Don't be too excited, beast," she says. "You're spending the day in the car."

Shell steps into the cool garage and is startled by the guard's uniform that swings in front of her like a hanged man. In the car she looks in the mirror and feels like she can't breathe. Call Ellen? By the end of the week, she'll be divorced. She pulls out, ignoring Dave and Pedro.

From the street, she steals a glance back at the house. The guys are hard at work, and her mother stands alone in the driveway. She has just moved her last orchid to safety on the side lawn and is looking up in disbelief as a worker fires a gun of some sort and out flies a heavy object attached to a string dragging a giant blue tarp. Sid watches her home disappear as it is wrapped up like a sloppy blue package.

ON HER WAY THROUGH town that morning, this is what Shell sees: Thirty thousand crows flying in from the North. Despite the warmth, it is now their season. They are on their way to roost along the river and the highest points in the city, the trees in the cemetery, the high branches on Pine Avenue. They are bringing with them fall, and eventually winter. There are freakishly cold temperatures predicted for the weekend, maybe even snow by Monday. So this is it. The crows will do this now every morning and every afternoon 'til spring. Shell drives and is damp from sweat, but the birds darkening the sky invite a chill in her when she sees them. There are more crows than people.

She drives with the windows down. Marty stands on her lap and hangs his head out the window. In the side mirror, she can see his tongue flipped up and his joker's smile. She pulls up to a mailbox and drops in the envelope containing her divorce papers, then quickly pulls away, without looking back to see if they made it into the belly of the box.

DOROTHY LOOKS HER UP and down during the morning meeting, and Shell thinks, I'm getting canned. Instead, she invites Shell to rejoin the girls back up front. Shell lands next to Carla.

"Got sick of solitary confinement, decided to finally do some shopping?" Carla says.

"More or less," Shell says.

Every half hour or so, Shell pretends to use the bathroom and runs outside to check on Marty. The day is cool from the breeze, but the sun is bright and the car is hot. He is panicked and his breathing is violent. She rolls the windows all the way down, and ties the leash to the steering wheel, but fears he'll jump out of the window and hang himself. At lunch, she sits at the edge of the forest that slopes down from the parking lot and he is joyous rubbing his face on the grass, stretching out comfortably in the shade. She ties him to a tree and leaves him there for the rest of the day. The afternoon is busy, so she doesn't get out much, but she's sure he's fine in the shade with water and food, out of sight of customers, far away from the four-lane service road in front of the credit union.

Lila comes in late that afternoon and skips past Carla and comes straight to Shell.

"They let you back inside?" she laughs. "Can I get a crisp hundred-dollar bill for my son's birthday card?"

Carla asks, "How are you doing on that paper?"

"OK. Not great. I never know what he wants. His assignments are like a page long. I'm pretty sure he's saying the same thing over and over again."

"I know, right?" Carla leans out her window.

When Shell gives Lila the money, Carla says, "She's Cavanaugh's kid."

"Oh, yeah?" Lila looks at Shell. "I can see the resemblance."

Shell can see the slightest blush rise to her ivory cheeks.

"Your father's a flirt," Lila says.

And when she says it, Shell remembers a house, small and dirty white against black-edged snow, over on the west end of town near the Ukrainian Club. She remembers being cold from the ice cream and from the frigid winter that blew the snow in spirals outside the truck. The truck's heater didn't work well, though he left it on for her. She pulled his prison-issue coat up to her chin, smelling him as if her nose were nestled to his neck and she fell asleep like this, wrapped up in him, warm.

Shell has at her fingertips all the information—the name, the address, the telephone number, the social security number, the bank account numbers, the security codes, the balances, the college funds, the deposit amounts, the direct deposit dates, the debts on homes, boats, cars, RVs, motorcycles, jet skis, ATVs, every toy ever purchased to help purge the weeks on weeks spent in *there* with *them*. She has all of this on hand. A quick keystroke is all it takes. Ampersand Hathaway, Lila. There it all is. She doesn't write it down, but she recognizes the address on the west end near the Ukrainian Club. She pulls it up several times before closing.

WHEN SHELL LEAVES AT four-thirty she forgets about Marty and gets in the car and pulls away. It isn't until she sees the cars speeding across the four-lane service road in front of the credit union that she remembers him and throws the car in reverse and drives recklessly back to the woods where she tied him up.

At first, she thinks she doesn't see him because he is sleeping deeper in the forest and has rooted down and found a soft cool spot. But when she gets out to look around, she sees his leash still tied to a tree; he slipped out of his collar and is gone.

As she drives through town looking for him, Shell sees old men sitting in the park reading the papers; she sees grocery carts that have fallen into the river and have gotten hung up on branches, plastic bags ripped and flapping like feathers from the trees along the river banks; she sees the prison, a fortress in the middle of the city where each day four hundred men work in shifts, unarmed and imprisoned by the lives they can afford because of it; she sees the guards turning their Super Duty trucks into the parking lot along the railroad tracks, a twelve-foot-tall metal statue of a guard carrying a bayonet on the turret of the prison, guarding the entrance—so ordinary and passable, like the doors of the DMV; but she doesn't see one person who looks helpful, not one person whom she can stop and ask, have you seen a little dog?

On Main Street, panic moves through her that is so forceful she has to pull the car to the side of the road. She can't catch her breath, so she opens her door and gets out and begins walking around the car trying to make her body release so she can fill her lungs with air. "Marty!" she yells out hoarsely. "Marty!" she tries to scream, but she bends over in defeat.

"Can I help you?" a woman asks her from behind.

Shell looks up and sees a woman standing on the steps of the Hardenberg Historical Museum. "Are you looking for something?" the woman asks.

"My dog," Shell says and begins to cry.

"I haven't seen a dog, but why don't you come in and I'll get you a glass of water. You look like you could use a hand. We can call the dogcatcher. The city probably has him. They usually do."

"I'm Cindy," she says, directing Shell to a small straight-backed chair in the foyer of the grand Victorian home that houses the museum.

"Thanks, Cindy," Shell says.

"Today's the last day," the woman says, pointing to the galleries on either side of them.

"Last day of what?"

"The exhibit. Haven't you heard about it? It's caused all kinds of problems in town. We've had record numbers come through this summer. I'm surprised there aren't more people here today, since it's the end. I'll call the dogcatcher; you take a look around. It will help you take your mind off things." Cindy hands her a program.

Shell takes it and looks out the propped-open door.

"Don't worry," Cindy says. "We'll find him."

Shell looks back at her. "Thank you."

Cindy sits at a small desk at the bottom of a beautiful carved oak staircase. She picks up the phone, and after she dials she gestures in the direction of the gallery to Shell's left. "Start over here," she says.

Shell walks into the first gallery and when she does she sees a case in the middle of the room that draws her over. In it is a piece of marble just like the one Ed has on his dresser that she likes to play with, rub its cool smooth surface against her cheek. The card next to it reads, "Demolition of the Death House commenced in 1958. Each Hardenberg Boy Scout was given a piece of marble from the death chamber floor." She touches her cheek and moves quickly away from the case.

On the wall to her left are cards with information. According to the cards, correctional officers drink, commit infidelity, abuse women and children, murder, and take their own lives at higher rates than everybody else. Shell can hear Ed and his guys: Sure, they'd say to this, but look what we keep you from. Here, however, was the evidence that despite their best efforts to keep it all locked up, they can't.

A small glass case in the middle of the room holds an intricate carving of an old man's face. It is a self-portrait of an unknown prisoner carved many years ago from a bar of soap. In the next case, there are examples of fine woodworking and oddities, a farm filled with animals made from small splinters of wood collected off the woodshop floor. And in the next a crèche made from papier-mâché. The faces cut out from magazines: the three wise men, Fidel Castro, Omar Sharif, and Yasser Arafat; Mother Mary, Benazir Bhutto; the baby Jesus, Brad Pitt.

"Shell," Cindy says coming around the corner. "I left a message. They're calling right back. They're checking with the kennel to see if any Bostons have come in. Would you like another glass of water?"

"No. Thank you," Shell says.

"OK. Well, don't hesitate to ask if you have any questions. I'd be happy to answer them for you while we wait."

Shell nods and continues to the next room. There is a cell, actual sized. Seven by seven by seven, the card reads. In it is a cot, a desk with a transparent typewriter, a half-sink, half-toilet, called a comby, according to the card, and above it a shelf with prisoner belongings stacked in a row. There are pieces of original art on the wall, and there are shoes old and worn, tucked under the cot, just waiting for someone. Shell can't help but feel that this cell is someone's home. As if someone is out for a few minutes and will be back any time now. It is tiny. The belongings are real. The cell is recreated exactly from the cell of a prisoner who is still living today just a few blocks away on the other side of the river.

Cindy returns. "Is that the real one?" Shell asks, standing in front of an electric chair.

"No," she says. "The first chair was destroyed in a fire; it's the oldest surviving chair. Did you know the chair was powered by the Hardenberg River?"

"That's creepy," Shell says and thinks of the crows nesting in the high branches in the trees along the river, and wonders what of these dead prisoners was left in that water, in those trees.

The next room is covered in photographs. She looks at the pictures of the men who toiled to build their own prison, and the women who were once housed there strolling the gardens in the central yard, families from town picnicking in the gardens of the old women's prison on the weekends. The pictures of the modern jail are far less appealing. There is not a tree to be found, just a concrete expanse, like an abandoned parking lot with men huddled along the edges.

In the next gallery, Shell sees an oak pedestal holding what looks like an ordinary telephone book. It is uncovered, and she can't resist opening the book and flipping through it. It isn't ancient. Perhaps twenty years old. For kicks, she looks up her own name, and there she is: Cavanaugh, S. 85 Alden Ave. Shell recalls her room at dusk on a summer evening, and remembers asking Ellen, "Should we tell her?" Gina was standing in the middle of the room. "Of course you should tell me," Gina said, sounding desperate. "We're the best of the best, right? Please tell me," she whispered.

"But you have to promise not to tell anyone, ever," Shell said.

Gina looked at Ellen, who giggled.

"I won't tell anyone. I promise," Gina said.

"OK," Shell said, leaning forward. "We've been talking to a prisoner," she whispered. "He's calling us tonight. We think. He calls on Saturday nights. We don't want to leave. In case he calls."

"You shouldn't do that, Shell. You know that," Gina said.

Shell turned away. Ellen shrugged. "What's the harm?" she asked in her diplomatic voice.

"You of all people know they're not all bad," Shell said.

Gina's eyes widened and the phone on the vanity behind her rang out clear and loud. The room filled with a prickly energy that made their skin feel like it might ignite—Shell can feel that energy now as she stands holding the phone book; she remembers bolting from the bed to the phone, the same princess phone, on the same wicker vanity that is in her room now, sitting in the vanity chair, checking herself in the mirror, then picking up the receiver: "Hello," she said in a sophisticated voice. The automated voice intoned through the phone into the dark room, a small wiry sound asking if Shell would accept a call from Hardenberg Correctional Facility from a prisoner named Darren. Shell could recite this call by heart; even now standing in the museum she remembers it vividly. The thin sounds of the call spun out of the phone, winding a web around them. Even Gina came closer to hear. Shell said, "Yes, I accept." There was a pause and they squeezed closer until all of them flanked the chair trying to hear the man's voice coming through the phone. "Hello?" he said. "Shell, my love, is it you?"

Gina pulled back. Shell watched herself in the mirror as someone called her his love. She straightened in the chair, her chest thrust forward, her chin lifted.

Ellen, their voice of reason, who had the calm face when things got hysterical, looked peaceful and laughed when he spoke.

Then a car's headlights flashed in the window, and Sid's car idled into the driveway. "Shit," Shell said. "Darren, I have to go."

"Can I call you later?" he asked and Gina said, "Give him my number. My mother's out of town. We can go there."

Shell knew even then that Gina was just trying to please Ellen and her. Gina never wanted to be a part of it. Shell is to blame for the whole thing: hiding out in Gina's house, Ronnie being sent to search the town for them, for him ending up dead.

"Shell, I'm sorry," Cindy says. "They don't have him. Not yet, anyway. They said to keep calling. Someone will turn him in. Nine times out of ten it works out."

Shell turns to her and stares at her blankly.

"Here. Take the number." Cindy hands her a piece of museum letterhead with the dogcatcher's number on it.

Shell reaches out for the paper and manages to say, "Thank you, Cindy. You've been too kind."

WHEN SHELL PULLS INTO the driveway, Ed is waiting there. His hands are on his hips and he looks up at the house, which is still tented and full of gas. The exterminators have come and gone. Dave and Pedro are not around. The chemicals trapped behind the tarps are killing off the infestation. It won't be safe for hours.

She is sick when she doesn't see Marty. She had hoped he'd find his way back on his own like in the movies where things always go right. But sitting in the driveway with her hand on the door handle she knows two things clearly: everything she thought she knew about her life was wrong; and she was not the good friend she always imagined herself to be. She deserves her life exactly as it is. She feels brittle.

Shell gets out of the car and walks to Ed. He doesn't look at her. He stands for a while without speaking, hands still on his hips. The air is remarkably cooler than it was that morning when she left. The cold front is moving in.

"Where you been?" he asks.

"Nowhere," she says and shivers. "Where you been?"

"None of your business," he says. "Where's Marty?"

"Gone," she says.

LAUGHLIN, L.

HE WASHES. HE HAS a good piece of soap from Georgy's cell and he is careful with it. He stands over the small sink, a small man with a slump to his shoulders and a tender set to his face. He is old now. It's official. When he washes, he begins with his hair. He puts his head under the faucet and lets the cold water wake his cells. When he encounters sensations that stimulate his nerves like this, he's aware of how his life is like a candle nearing the end of its wick. Sometimes life flickers out; sometimes life flickers on. This cold flickers him on. He scrubs his hair, but gently. The water drains from his scalp in rivulets, making white, baby-fine ribbons of hair that fall heavy into his eyes and soak his face. He runs his hands from his brow over his crown, sending water down his bare back. It drips down his backside and down his legs and pools on the floor. Then he scrubs his face, the places behind his ears. He uses his index fingers to clean inside his ears and he uses Georgy's soap to lather and scrub himself perfectly clean. His neck is next. He stretches to open the folds of skin that normally hang heavy with years, and he cleans in them. His sharp clavicles and shoulders, his armpits and ribs, the soft sags of his stomach, he attends to all of these. He reaches around to his back, hugging himself to make sure his spine, still strong, still holding him up like the trunk of a dead tree, is clean. He washes his backside, his underside. He stops for a moment when he touches his penis. He feels the low, slow stir of pleasure and it reminds him that life in this body has not been all bad. He cleans places he's taken for granted, the long slope of his right thigh, the outer edge of his hip, the top of his right knee, the bony cliff of his shin, the sagging meat of his calf. He cleans the skin on his ankle, his phalanges, the space between his toes. He repeats this same ritual on the left leg. Then he gently dries himself, starting at his hair. He rubs softly, and the soap releases its smell and in this way Georgy, the smell of him, mingles with Moses' smell and this rises up into his nose and he imagines he's breathing in the last of that boy. He loved him.

Moses dresses neatly. His pants and shirt are clean and freshly pressed. He tucks his shirt into his trousers flatly. His clothes hang. There's not much left of him to give the clothes shape. Don is worried about him these days. Losing Georgy has taken its toll and Don has tried to nourish him; Moses hasn't had much need for it. It was Don who convinced him to call Laughlin, L. Thought it would perk him up.

When he's dressed, he places Georgy's hat on his head. Today is for him. After the letter arrived from Laughlin, L. telling Georgy she'd be happy to come visit him, and she had a few things she'd like to discuss with him about the Lord, Moses gave in to Don's constant nags—he's been full of hope since *Gourmet* accepted his oxtails—and Moses called her. This visit would have thrilled Georgy.

Miller comes to get him. The whole block knows where he's going and there's a certain awe that he's pulled this off. Most have feigned illness to skip their day pressing plates just so they can watch him go. Walk the walk of a man who's got a girl from the outside coming to see him. They're excited about what might happen, so they're cheering. Moses walks out of his cell, and Miller frisks him. There is an energy in the block this morning. The sparrows are flying the upper air like trapeze artists. Men are clanging on the bars. Men are screaming and cackling and jumping. Moses doesn't look at them. He tries to ignore them. He just takes the stairs real carefully. There's nothing to this, he thinks to himself. He hopes. He takes a cautious step down, aware of all the small movements of his body. He's acquired a slow shuffle, the walk of a man who's lived his life in a small space.

IN THIRTY-SIX YEARS THE only free people he's seen are staff, like Lila and the guards, the nurses who cared for him at Hardenberg Memorial Hospital twenty-three years ago when he had his appendix removed, and the butcher who took it out of him, Dr. Gandhi something or other, so he's never seen this visiting room before. The green walls. The green tables. The low stools bolted to the floor that look like they are from an elementary school classroom. They're small. Other inmates wait like school kids, diminutive in their seats, sure not to step out of line for fear they'll lose the privilege of being here. The guards hover against the walls; their metal-colored uniforms have them looking like guns.

He sits on one of those silly stools and adjusts his shirt collar so it looks just so. One of the guards comes to him and says, "What do you think you're doing? Give me that."

Moses looks up at him, confused.

"The hat, old man," and the guy flicks the front of Georgy's Stetson so it falls back on Moses' small head. Moses grabs it and the guard takes it from him, walks it up to the guards' desk. He sits down next to an enormously fat guard Moses doesn't know, and throws the hat on the guy's fat head. They laugh. The fat one waves his arm like he's slinging a lasso and he bucks forward and back in his comically weak chair.

Without the hat, Moses is struck with a sinking exhaustion. The kind that sets in after over-excitement and nerves. He can feel himself becoming smaller. His mouth and eyes are dry. His throat full of broken glass. He sits and observes the room. His body stiff as a corpse. Only his eyes show life as they dart from visitor to visitor.

And the visitors shock the hell out of him. The only women dressed like ladies are old battle-axes who hobble in on canes. The rest of the women, and they are mostly women, look like hookers. Their dresses hardly covering their repulsively large asses, their nails long as beans, their hair twisted and curled and cemented into place. But then he's distracted by a girl who walks in alone. He recognizes her immediately. Knows her right away. It's clear to him even across the room who this is.

"You have to take a seat, lady," a guard says to her.

"Moses?" she asks.

The guard points her to the end of the room and takes her elbow and walks her to where he sits.

Moses can tell he's a much older man than she imagined. "You can touch, but don't give him anything. And keep your hands where I can see them," the guard says.

"I just have this," she says and holds up a Bible. The guard shrugs. He's seen this before.

Moses looks her up and down as she stands in front of him and then he looks away, shakes his head. "You couldn't even wear a dress?"

"What?" she asks, sitting down on the stool across from him.

"You have nice hair," he says and sucks at his teeth and taps his foot and looks off to the side like he'd rather be someplace else. "I didn't know you were a blonde," he says.

There's a young prisoner, a greasy hillbilly, at the next table staring at her. He licks his lips. An old guilty woman sits across from him and weeps. He looks at Laughlin, L. and sniffs the air.

"Don't pay any attention to him," Moses says. "Hey, what's your name?"

"Laura. Can you read?" she asks, opening the Bible up to a passage she has marked by a crocheted bookmark.

"You shouldn't bother with me."

"You're being ungrateful," she says and sits back in her chair, folding her arms across her chest.

Moses looks around the room with a twisted look on his face, as if he's in a conversation with someone else.

"What are you doing?" she asks.

Moses is restless. Jittery. He's batting things away from his face. He moves from side to side, crosses and uncrosses his legs. He looks like he doesn't even know where he is. "Let me smell your hair," he says.

"I will," she pauses for a moment, unsure of the bargain she's about to strike, "if you read with me," she says.

He stops his fidgeting. "Deal," he says. "But you have to read to me. My eyes are shit."

"Please don't cuss," she says and opens the book to a passage and begins to read. She has a beautiful voice and Moses, who doesn't care about the words or their promises, thinks how pleased Georgy would be that she came here to save him. That anyone would care about what became of him. It would have just been too much for that boy.

Laughlin, L. finishes the passage about mortal sin and says, "Let's pray." She takes his old hands in her warm young hands and Moses catches a whiff of her clean hair as a thick silky rope of it falls forward over her shoulder and over her breast. "Amen," she says.

"Amen," Moses says.

"Your hair," he reminds her.

"OK," she says and timidly leans forward and lets her hair fall down over her eyes.

At first he hovers at the edge, light as a bee.

Then he leans in closer, and a little closer, until he buries his face just above her ear and sniffs. He breathes in again, and this time it's so deep she pulls away. But he guides her gently back in. Her smell is like apples. Her hair touching his cheeks unlocks him. Each time he inhales her smell, it pulls some bit of an unknown sadness out of him. He leans his head on hers and she kindly doesn't pull away.

After a long moment, she pulls back, looks at him, a discrete wipe of her eyes. He is calm. "Your hair smells like apples," he says.

"Do you need anything?" she asks. "I could get you something and send it to you."

"I don't need anything," he says.

"My dog is in the car. I don't want him to wait too long."

"You can leave," he says.

"Do I have to wait until they tell me I can go or do I just leave?"

"I don't know," Moses says.

"Haven't you ever had a visitor before?"

"No," he says. "Never have."

"Oh," she says looking down. She sees a loose hair on the front of the t-shirt and she pulls it away. Moses reaches for it. "May I?" he asks.

"Huh?"

"The hair," he says.

"Oh. Sure," she shrugs.

He takes it and runs his fingers the length of the strand. Then he winds it around his finger delicately, as if it were gold or something that precious. He brings the finger to his cheek and gently rubs the fine hair along his skin.

"I'm going to leave now," she says.

"OK," Moses says, looking at the hair, trying to find its end.

SNOW

ON THE WAY TO the small ceremony for Jorge Padilla in the chapel of Souls Cemetery by Father Garcia, Catholic Chaplain of Hardenberg Correctional Facility, there is a small accident. The road to Souls is straight and starting to slick as the temperature drops and an icy rain begins falling. Ed drives like there is no danger even though the ice on the road pulls at the steering wheel, jerking it. "Can you believe this weather in September?" he asks.

Sid is staring out her window, "It's just awful."

Up ahead it looks like a thousand crows have landed in one small icy plot of corn stalks bent and toppled. "Jesus Christ, Sid, will you look at that?" She looks at the crows and back at him in amazement. The crows hop and flutter a few feet off the ground as they peck at corn kernels left over between the skeleton stalks bent like bony knees by the falling ice. And as if Ed gave a cue, they all take flight. And low, too. They soar around the car, nearly blocking the view of the road in front of them. Ed swerves to keep from hitting them and loses control of the car. They fly smoothly across the icy road in a dirty spray. If cars are coming, they can't know. No one in the car speaks. They can't hear anything, save the tires' icy skid like skates on a rink and the deep moan from the brake drums sounding low and sad.

Yet it is a peaceful, floating moment. One in which there is nothing they can do but hold on. And they do. Sid white-knuckled on the overhead door handle. Ed to the steering wheel still pretending to have some control. Gina holds the door and herself, her hand wrapped desperately around her middle, her head hanging, curling over on herself; she didn't survive two weeks hanging in Arthur's apartment to go like this, and she thinks of Jack Harding, how he and Veronica saved her and how grateful she is to have been saved.

Shell holds onto Marty, whom she won't let out of her sight since Dave found him at the duck pond and brought him safely home. And she holds onto her friend. The world flies by, spinning like a roulette wheel, the car the ball.

They end up facing the cemetery, as if nothing has happened. Before Ed starts back on driving, there is a moment when they all reach their hands out to touch one another. Lay their fingers on each other, Ed's hand on the girls' arms, Sid's on their cheeks, on Gina's belly, Shell's on her parents' aging shoulders, all of them touching as if to say, I'm so glad you're still here.

THE CHAPEL IS FREEZING. It is filled with the horrid odor of cheap perfume. Gina strides boyishly to her mother's side. Marie is dressed in a flouncy red thing and a thin, ratty rabbit hair coat with a hood. Gina leans down to her and gives her a hug. She whispers something to her mother. Her mother barks in her raspy smoker's voice, "Not possible. I'm too young to be a grandmother." She waves Gina away. But then a moment later walks over to her and inquisitively touches her daughter's flat stomach. The chaplain walks in and they become aware suddenly that there is an urn on the small altar, a candle already lit, and a bouquet of white lilies from Sid, Ed, and Shell.

The priest says his prayer to open the ceremony and speaks briefly of the good life of Jorge Padilla. Jorge took communion every day; Father Garcia had given it to him personally for the last ten years, and he had a powerful influence over each of the inmates who knew him during his long tenure at Hardenberg Correctional Facility, particularly his recently deceased friend and cellmate, Moses. Ed drops his head, closes his eyes and clasps his hands in front of himself for a moment. Shell sees this and sees in his profile his true face; he is a good man.

Marie dabs at her eyes and lets out a wail. Gina wraps her arm around her mother's shoulders. The priest invites anyone who might want to offer a personal sentiment to step forward. Ed separates himself just slightly from the small group of mourners. He turns toward them and takes out a piece of paper on which he's prepared a little something to say.

Ed unfolds the paper. "I…" he stops and clears his throat, reaches for a tissue, wipes his eyes, and blows his big nose then tries it again. "It doesn't make any sense," he says, "that the best man I ever knew I met inside the prison. But that's the way it is. Before Jorge died, he told me he didn't think he was able to be the father I was, but I regret to say that he was wrong. I don't know that living on the outside gave me any advantages. I still always felt like I couldn't protect my daughter from the way things go. And I'm sure if Jorge was in my shoes, he'd have done a much better job letting everyone know how much…" He falters again and has to stop to wipe his eyes. He coughs to cover up a sob, "… letting everyone in his life know how much they mean to him. My wife and my daughter are the world to me." He looks up at Shell and Sid. "I never tell you that. I should."

His paper shakes in his hands and he looks at it closely to find his spot. "Gina, I don't know if you can know how much the love you gave your dad affected the lives of so many people, men that most of the world had just given up on. Jorge used to get into trouble before you came along. But when you were born, he changed and that brought a lot of goodness into the hearts of some very bad men. Prisoners and guards. That's all I have to say. Jorge, you were a good man," he said, turning to address the urn. "And when people were around you, they were better people because of who you were. I promise to take care of Gina. I can only imagine how knowing you were going to have a grandchild could have been a blessing and a curse, so enjoy him…or her…wherever you are." Gina lets go of her mother and puts her long, skinny arms around Ed's neck. For the first time Shell's ever seen, she cries.

"Earth to earth," says the priest, "Ashes to ashes," he continues and they all turn and take each other's hands. "Dust to dust. In sure and certain hope of the Resurrection into eternal life," the Chaplain concludes.

Gina kisses her fingers and lays them on Jorge's urn one last time. Shell reaches her arm out to Gina, and Gina loops her arm in Shell's and lets her hold her up a little. Through the old leaded window of the chapel door, they see how the icy rain has turned finally to snow. "Snow always makes me think of Ellen," Gina says, squeezing Shell's arm. They look out the window of the chapel door. Together they see how the snow has mantled the trees, the gravestones, and the earth beautifully white.

THE WIND HAS SHIFTED. It was coming from the west, but now it comes from the north and it is seen in the speeding lower nimbus moving south. Most unusual. This pattern, the confusion in the upper air, the abnormality of it is seen in the tall grasses extending below the porch on which Ellen and Sakamoto sit. The grasses move in circles, as if the air were filled with invisible bodies running across their fringed tops, causing eddies and the most surprising evidence that things are all mixed up.

"You still have the dagger?" Sakamoto asks, handing Ellen a martini. They look out over the lawn, which leads to the forest, which leads to the rolling Green Mountains. It is dusk. They sit on lawn chairs on the high deck of an A-frame tucked into the side of the mountain. Each has a Hudson's Bay blanket on her lap. The arctic air is coming, unseasonable and quick. It is all wrong. Too early. There are still berries; there are still tiger lilies. The fields are still ripe with the color of the end of summer. Only the blush of the sumacs reveal what this early air is here to portend. Snow. And with this turning over of the air, with this churning of the atmosphere, there is an uncovering. Ellen is fighting it off by pulling the blanket up closer and tighter. But it doesn't help because what is being uncovered is in her and this is as harsh and as unexpected as the weather.

"Yes," Ellen says. She saw the silver dagger wrapped in its fine silk mahogany box in her underwear drawer when she frantically searched her room for the viewfinder the day she left Brooklyn and came to Vermont. Sakamoto had given it to her before her wedding. It was small and delicate with an ivory handle and she remembered standing in a sea of white flounce and tulle, her mother's wedding dress, while her mother-in-law taught her how to use it. Taught her exactly where to pierce her neck, how to hold the handle, the necessary angle of the blade and precisely the force she'd need to use to end her life quickly. Sakamoto said her mother had given her the dagger when she married Ichiro's father, Bill Collins; she'd taught her how to use it so that she could save her family from shame if things went wrong. Sakamoto told Ellen she'd chosen to share it with Ellen for a different reason. "It is a reminder to have fun, and not just in marriage, in life." Sakamoto was dressed in layered silks of different beautiful patterns and the ease of her dress matched her long undyed hair and her flowing and boundless personality. A potter, a professor of art history at a small, unremarkable liberal arts college in Vermont, and the widow of Bill Collins, she mixed herself a martini at four every afternoon and drank it alone with her dead husband, whether or not she had a lover.

This past month, she's shared the ritual with her daughter-in-law.

"I gave you that dagger so you wouldn't end up like this," she says and looks off into the distance. "I raised my son to be an artist," Sakamoto says as they look out at the field. "I don't know what went wrong." She holds out her drink and clinks glasses with Ellen, "Cheers, kid."

"There's nothing wrong with Ichiro," Ellen says.

"Oh, I know that. I just thought one day he'd have long hair like a hippie. My son would be beautiful with long hair."

Ellen smiles. "He would."

Sakamoto takes another sip of her drink and looks at Ellen. "I know who you are and you are good. You have brains, a heart as big as I've ever seen; you don't want to lose that. If you do, you'll lose yourself, kid. I love my son and I loved Bill, but marriage is marriage and it can do a number on a woman. My one regret with Bill is that we never watched porn together. Don't make that mistake." She sips her martini and looks off into an old life that she revisits this time each day.

209

Sakamoto hasn't asked Ellen many questions, except whose hideous car is that? and why are you dressed like it's the middle of winter? But that was it. Since that first day, Sakamoto has kept her fed, kept her in journals and medium-point blue pens, and has shared her cocktail hour with her. They usually drink silently, looking out over the mountains. The only sounds are the sounds of summer evenings. The calls of insects. Cracking dried branches on the forest floor as animals eat their fill of the late summer berries. During the day, Ellen walks on country roads and through fields. She threads gallon milk jugs with their tops cut off on a long thick men's leather belt and straps it around her waist and fills the jugs with the last of the season's yield. It is a prolific year and each day she gathers them with fear that this is it, but the small kitchen in Sakamoto's A-frame is overflowing with them, so they're being baked into muffins and pies, tossed generously onto salads.

The lawn is equally magical with chicory and asters, chocolate-brown dried stalks of some sort, goldenrod. The women wade through the tall grasses most days collecting all they can while the colors last. There is a sense that everything is about to end. The cold is here. Soon abundance will be over. Ellen is trying to make what she has done final. But she fears her compulsion to apologize to her mother, to beg her forgiveness, so she's gathered armfuls of flowers and sticks and leaves to cover the blazing ibis white car that sits behind Sakamoto's pottery studio and reminds Ellen of what she's done each time she sees it.

Ichiro is giving her breathing room, but she knows he is tormented. The house is small and she can hear the daily conversations Sakamoto has with him. "What have I told you? Patience, boy. You men always think everything is a result of something you did, so you think you have to fix everything. It's my fault. It's the way I raised you. Happens to the best of us. We tell you boys to be helpful and to fix things. Works well with plumbing, lousy with hearts. Sit tight, kid. Wait this out. I know it's hard." She always lowers her voice at the end of her conversations to mother him.

Sakamoto pops an olive into her mouth and tells Ellen, "He can wait. He will wait. He's a good boy. But you have to get your head screwed on straight before you can tell him anything honest. And he's been patient. He deserves honesty. Hopefully, for my son's sake, you'll find your way to him. I'd say back to him, but I don't think you were ever really with him. Were you?"

"I think so." Ellen doesn't like talking like this.

"Really?"

"When we first met. When we got married."

"On your wedding day your friends and I watched you become Claire right before our very eyes. Gina said it. She said, 'She looks just like Claire.' And she was right. You didn't marry my son that day, you married your mother."

"That's an awful thing to say," Ellen says and remembers that her mother has not called. There has been no search party. There has just been a quiet severing.

"Do you have passion for him?" Sakamoto asks. "He's your husband. You should. But you don't. I know because you're here with me when you should be with him. You can't have passion if you are not really living. And you have not been living. You have been role playing. The Worthingtons? That dinner club of yours? That's not enough for someone like you. Do you really like those people? It's a terrible thing to do to a kid, withhold love until they perform like a circus dog. Who you are is not who Claire wants you to be."

Ellen stares out at the birds floating higher and higher up into the thermals.

"Your friends know who you are. You should start there."

Ellen gets up and walks into the house.

Sakamoto yells after her. "You can't just keep running away!"

What Ellen hasn't realized—and she is seeing this clearly now as she stands in the back of the dark A-frame cottage looking out at the driveway that leads to the gravel road—is that it's not who Shell and Gina are that make them important to her; rather, it's the honest impulse that has always driven her to them that matters. The most courageous thing Ellen ever did is dare to have them as her friends. And the fact that she had lost this impulse, had forgotten to meet them, this was how she knew she'd lost herself. Sakamoto is right. With them she has the clearest version of her true self; with them she was entirely separate from her ambition to please Claire. This is the Ichiro problem, of course. She thinks of him and her stomach knots up. She wishes she knew if she chose him because she loved him or if she chose to be his wife to please Claire.

Her mother's car is covered in branches, buried in dead flowers and leaves, cloaked in night, its ostentatious whiteness finally muted by the country pitch. Snow begins to fall. Slowly at first. It looks like a fluke, but soon it picks up, dusting the detritus covering the car, filling in the view out the window. In this white canvas she thinks of bumping into Gina on Thirty-Fourth Street, new to New York and lost, turning in circles in the blinding blizzard, no landmarks to be seen, just the unexpected beacon of a friend, a cup of oolong in a warm tea house. She was happy then. Her apartment filled with found things. Real friends. Coney Island. She opens her palm and looks at the scar, red because she's cold. Reclaiming that woman isn't about a reunion. She needs to start simple. Find pure impulse and follow it. What is her desire right now? To step away from the window. To join her mother-in-law for another drink. To wait for what hunger comes next, find proper nourishment and feed it.

ACKNOWLEDGMENTS

FIRST, CLAUDIA ZULUAGA FOR taking my hand and bringing me here—you deserve a whole page; you are the beginning the middle and the end of this story. Victoria Redel and Mc McIlvoy for generosity. The late Carol Houk Smith for two hours on Treman porch that shaped the next five years. Robin Black for breaking my lifetime streak of not winning so much as a door prize. Victoria Barrett for her perfect pitch, vision and hard work, qualities that make her unstoppable. And Auburn, New York for giving itself to my imagination.

If the prison rings true, it's because of details that came by way of my Cayuga Community College colleagues. Theresa Misiaszek brought me inside, and Teresa Hoercher invited me to an evening with the church knitting group—thank you, ladies, for the crèche and the inside scoop. Also, Ted Conover's *Newjack* and Stuart O'Nan's *The Good Wife* were essential references.

This book benefitted from the generosity and wisdom of brilliant readers: Claudia Zuluaga, Michelle Wildgen, Rebecca Kinzie-Bastian, Avideh Bashirrad, Anneke McEvoy, Carla Panciera, Natalie Danford, Hope Chernov, and Kenneth Nichols. These friends slogged through drafts and aided my never-ending search for the elusive story. I am forever grateful to them.

This story is about friendship, a gift I'd know nothing of without these beautiful people: Anneke McEvoy, Elizabeth Ashby, Claudia

Zuluaga, Mike Lustig, Andrea Ace, Ivy Meeropol, Thomas Ambrose, Brenda Boboige, Rebecca Kinzie-Bastian, Carla Panciera, Carolyn Marten, Nicole Adsitt, Rae Howard, Jennifer Liddy, Yasmin Dalisay, Michelle Wildgen, Jeff Church, David Haggerty, Jeff Rosenthal, the Harts, the Clarkes, Team Looram, and Herminio Jacome.

This book is also about the unexpected shape a family can take. My beautiful family defies description. Gilda Brower, Bruce Yaw, Geraldine Germano-Yaw, Robert Brower, Patrick Brower, Erin Brower, the Brower Girls, the Germanos, the Marullos, the Ignelzis, the Andersons and the Lloyds, my Big Hill parents, the friends listed above who are also family, all know what I mean.

No one gave up more to this book than my husband, Douglas Lloyd. His gifts—love, time away to write, and an unwavering certainty that someday it would all come to this—have been mesmerizing. Thank you, Doug. Jed and Ella gave to this book their ninth month, when they still couldn't climb, and not a moment more. Their gift was putting my aspirations in the right place. Books are nothing compared to your pure love.

ABOUT THE AUTHOR

SARAH YAW WAS SIX months old when her parents moved from New Jersey to Central New York to live off the land. Eventually landing in Auburn, New York, she grew up a stone's throw from the country's oldest and most influential prison. Sarah received an MFA in fiction from Sarah Lawrence College; her work has appeared in *Salt Hill*. She is a tenured member of the faculty at Cayuga Community College, a certified Kripalu Yoga instructor, the mother of five-year-old twins, and is married to the photographer, Douglas Lloyd.

author photo by Douglas Lloyd